MW00572340

Also by
SARAH MORGENTHALER

MOOSE SPRINGS, ALASKA

The Tourist Attraction

Mistletoe and Mr. Right

Enjoy the View

The *Christmas* you *Found Me*

Sarah Morgenthaler

sourcebooks
casablanca

Copyright © 2024 by Sarah Morgenthaler
Cover and internal design © 2024 by Sourcebooks
Cover illustration by Sandra Chiu

Sourcebooks and the colophon are registered trademarks of Sourcebooks.

All rights reserved. No part of this book may be reproduced in any form or by
any electronic or mechanical means including information storage and retrieval
systems—except in the case of brief quotations embodied in critical articles or
reviews—without permission in writing from its publisher, Sourcebooks.

The characters and events portrayed in this book are fictitious or are used fictitiously. Any
similarity to real persons, living or dead, is purely coincidental and not intended by the author.

All brand names and product names used in this book are trademarks,
registered trademarks, or trade names of their respective holders. Sourcebooks
is not associated with any product or vendor in this book.

Published by Sourcebooks Casablanca, an imprint of Sourcebooks
P.O. Box 4410, Naperville, Illinois 60567-4410
(630) 961-3900
sourcebooks.com

Cataloging-in-Publication Data is on file with the Library of Congress.

Printed and bound in Canada.
MBP 10 9 8 7 6 5 4 3 2 1

For Kenney.
Thank you for the kind of love that lasts even after you're gone.
I'm going to love you forever, babe.

"If there ever comes a day when we can't be together,
keep me in your heart. I'll stay there forever."

—WINNIE THE POOH

This book contains references to the following subjects that might be difficult for certain readers: hospital scenes, terminal child illness, elderly dementia, post-partum depression, emotional abuse, threat of physical violence, illness, divorce, and grief. Thank you to my editor, my publisher Sourcebooks Casablanca, and the sensitivity readers at Tessera Editorial for helping me find a balance between tough topics and the story in my heart. Any mistakes or insensitivities are mine.

For anyone who has gone through or is currently going through any of the topics in this book, I want you to know I see you. I love you. And I'm so sorry this happened to you.

Chapter 1

WANTED: HUSBAND FOR HIRE

Temp to full-time position, based on satisfactory job performance.

Eligibility requirements: Ability to lift, push, or pull 50 pounds. Willingness to perform ranch work in extreme weather without whining. Experience with livestock a plus. Broad shoulders preferred.

Benefits include medical, dental, 401(k) matching.

Salary negotiable. *Current husbands need not apply.*

(Previous husbands of Sienna Naples
are ineligible for the position.)

THERE SHOULD BE A LIMIT TO HOW MUCH PERSONAL HORROR ONE should have to face first thing in the morning. It's only 9:30 a.m., and an ad cut out of today's local paper, featuring my recently changed marital status, stares at me from the passenger seat of my truck. It's just one in a growing pile I've found posted around town, accompanied by more than a few laughing faces.

And here I thought the most interesting part of my morning was waking up divorced today.

All week. Jess's text says they paid for the ad *all freaking week*, and it's online too. Our rural northern Idaho town of Caney Falls is finding this whole situation hysterical. Every place I go in town for supplies, I find another clipping. Tacked to the corkboard at the co-op where I buy horse grain. In the window of my usual gas station. At the local animal vet when I swing by for a refill on my dog's joint supplement. It's everywhere.

Leave it to my best friend to manage to make me laugh on a day when I'd normally be holed up, licking my wounds. The goofy ad is a reminder that they love and support me, even if it has resulted in my being jokingly propositioned all morning.

"All I want for Christmas is caffeine," I sing softly as I pull up to my favorite coffee shop, the Daily Grind, the suspension of my late-model Chevy truck squeaking from a bed loaded down with bags of horse and cattle feed. It's time for my next round of caffeine, since I've been up since 5:00 a.m. to get my work done today.

It's not like I was going to be able to sleep much last night anyway.

I'm trying really hard to feel the holiday spirit, despite knowing today is Divorce Finalization Day. The culmination of years of love, heartbreak, memories, and *so much effort* has now been labeled with a time of death: two weeks before Christmas.

Lucía, a teller at my local bank, brightens as we pass each other at the coffee shop entrance. "Thanks, Sienna," she says as I hold the door for her, the poor woman juggling two fully laden coffee carriers and a bag of pastries. "How's your day going so far?"

"More interesting than I wanted it to be," I reply ruefully.

She giggles as she hustles down the snow-lined sidewalk. I've been getting this all morning. Wide grins, snickers, a few waggled eyebrows.

"This is a regular Tuesday morning," I murmur to myself as I step inside, the rich scent of roasting coffee beans greeting me. "Nothing to see here. Move along."

I can handle a joke. Ranching next to the Frank Church Wilderness isn't for the faint of heart or the thin of skin. I'm a Naples, a family infamous for curly brunette hair, short statures, and digging our heels in.

It's etched into our DNA to fight hard, then fight even harder. Living on the edge of over two and half million acres of steep mountains, rushing rapids, and dangerous wildlife teaches you to be tough. Even the Salmon River winding through Caney Falls is known as the River of No Return. This is a bad place for people without some sort of significant backbone, and mine is iron strong. The issue isn't me. The issue is my ex-husband. Micah's just as tough as the rest of us, but having the whole town laughing at him isn't going to make his mood any better.

As of the twenty-day waiting period finalizing our divorce, I guess his moods aren't my problem anymore.

The chalkboard sign next to the tiny yellow coffee shop door reads CHOCOLATE, COFFEE, MEN: THE RICHER THE BETTER. Considering my already wealthy ex-husband is officially an even richer man as of today, I have to disagree. I like rich chocolate and coffee though, so I go to the woman leaning on the waist-high swinging door separating the Daily Grind's seating area from the barista station.

"Morning, Sanai," I greet the owner and barista. "Same as usual." Chocolate, espresso, caramel, almond milk. I've been known to splurge on a gingerbread latte a time or two when the weather gets cold. Sanai's been in town for about two years now, and her lattes have already become a requirement in most of our lives. Besides, if anyone can convince my nonexistent appetite to kick in today, it's Sanai and her breakfast sandwiches.

Sanai's embracing the holiday spirit better than I am. Her shoulder-length Havana twist braids sparkle with red and green gems, and she's wearing a cream-colored oversize sweater that makes me drool almost as much as the smell of coffee does. Christmas lights are strung around the ceiling, blinking with a holiday cheerfulness I'm desperately trying to find. The aroma of warm, fresh biscuits fills the air, mingling with the peppermint mocha the customer seated near us is sipping.

'Tis the freaking time of the year. I refuse to be a scrooge.

"Making a grain run?" Sanai asks, and I nod. "I was hoping you'd come in today."

Sanai and I have become friends, although she and Jess spend more time together than we do these days. I've been hiding out on the ranch too much—up to my eyeballs in work and nursing a broken heart—to be a very good friend to anyone lately.

"Jess has been here already, huh?"

The grin Sanai can't keep from her lips isn't a good sign, especially when she nods toward the job board beside my favorite table by the front window. Great. Just *perfect*.

I sling my coat over the back of the chair and rip down the ad before I settle in. As I wait for my coffee, I call up Jess. "*Caney Falls Daily* complaint department," I say in greeting.

"I was wondering how long it would take you."

Jess sounds far more cheerful than most people do in the morning. This is what being born and raised in a ranching town gets us: too many people used to waking up way too early to feed the cows. We're all half-useless after six at night, but we sure can keep a coffee shop busy before dawn.

"How many times have you been propositioned so far today?" Jess asks. "The paper has a running bet."

"Twice at the co-op," I reply, wrinkling my nose. "But I think they were just joking. You do realize you've made me the laughingstock of the entire town?"

"Actually, I've made Micah the laughingstock of the entire town. I've made you the newest hot commodity." I can hear the smugness in their voice. "You would not believe how many inquiries I've already had on the ad. I just emailed you a link to a folder with the raunchiest résumés. Open the pictures at your own risk."

I groan and lean back in my chair. "You know it would've been easier to write my name and number in a bathroom stall, right?"

"Yes, but this is much more fun. Hey, are you getting coffee today?"

"I'm about to be nose deep in a latte. Am I this predictable?"

"It's Tuesday, you always get coffee after grain on Tuesdays, and you're the most predictable human being on the planet."

I just chuckle because I've been hearing this from Jess my whole life.

"We have an actual applicant who wants to talk to you. I told him he should be able to catch you there today."

I groan. "I don't find it alarming at *all* you have an applicant for a totally fake ad that's only been up for a couple hours."

"Technically, the job posted online last night, just after midnight." They sound proud of themselves, which is never a good thing, not when Jess is in revenge mode. "Just meet with the guy. He sounds nice."

"If he's answering an ad for a husband, he sounds like a weirdo."

Jess laughs, a bright, cheerful sound, which matches the holiday music piping through the café's speakers. "You need to hire some help at the ranch, and in this economy, it's clear no one is going to be interested. Chalk it up to inventive advertising in a depressed labor market."

"I actually don't think that's what it means…"

"Trust me," they promise. "The labor market is depressed. Or at least experiencing some significant ennui. You think I love editing holiday pieces right now?"

"Just cancel the meeting, Jess." They don't know all the gritty details of my highly contested divorce settlement, so I don't blame them for assuming I can hire someone. I've been trying to keep from my friends how painful this divorce has been.

"You're no fun, you know that?" Jess sighs in playful dramatics, then snickers before hanging up.

Sanai brings me my coffee, and the heat of the mug warms my

winter-chilled hands. Settling deeper into my chair, I try and fail to resist opening the shared drive link Jess emailed me. I click on one photo and squeak, quickly closing it out.

Yep, there's definitely…interest…all right.

"Sienna?"

A quiet voice pulls my attention. I look up from my phone and realize there's a person standing near my table. I keep looking up and see his face, this stranger standing just far enough away he doesn't enter my personal space. He's tall, even for around these parts, and his dark-blue long-sleeved T-shirt stretches across his broad, muscled shoulders nicely. The shirt is loose at the waist though, and his face looks lean. His skin is the deep tan of a man who spends all day outside, even in winter, but what strikes me the most is for how strong he looks, he's *thin*.

"Hey, I'm Guy Maple. Are you Sienna? Someone from the Caney Falls newspaper said I might be able to meet you here. It's about the ad."

Oh no. *Oh no.* This isn't happening.

He doesn't quite meet my eyes, glancing at the window behind my shoulder as if he's regretting standing here. His isn't a natural leanness or the kind of thin that comes from using drugs. Guy looks like he's missed one or two meals a day for a while now, and what's left is muscle and sheer grit. His worn jeans are actually worn, not deliberately distressed, and his work boots are scuffed but clean.

I watch Guy shift back a little bit, as if he knows he's looming over me and he's uncomfortable about it. I realize I still haven't said anything.

"I'm Sienna," I slowly acknowledge, because as horrified as I am right now, this is real. Someone is actually answering the most mortifying personal ad I've ever been party to.

When I stand up, he looks physically relieved, although I don't have much more height standing than I do sitting. I'm five foot three with my boots on, and he's got almost a foot on me.

When we shake hands, it's firm, polite, and professional. No clamminess or hanging on too long. His hands are calloused, his nails neatly trimmed but scratched on the surface. When I look back up, pretty glacier-blue eyes glance at me and then away again.

"I'm actually here because of my daughter," Guy says in a quiet voice, as if feeling the need to explain himself. "She's had a tough go of it, and the medical bills…" He stops, pride causing the words to lodge in his throat. He looks like he'd rather be anywhere other than here.

"Do you want to sit down?" I ask Guy, because we're still standing there, and I realize this must be hard enough on him without being on display. We're talking privately, but in a coffee shop this size, eyes are on us.

"This isn't the good kind of sit, is it?" His mouth quirks up at the corner as he pulls out the chair across from me and sinks down into it. "To be honest, when I saw you here, the ad seemed too good to be true." As soon as I sit back down, Guy forges ahead, on the edge of babbling as his words tumble over each other. "In the ad, you said you needed a husband for hire. And you have medical insurance. We have medical insurance, but it's one of those high-deductible plans, which eats into what I try to set aside. And there are a lot of costs outside what insurance covers. Gas to get to the doctor appointments, missed work when she's having tough days, babysitters when I can get someone qualified—and the farther I travel looking for work, the less that happens. I work hard. Work's just getting harder to find."

"How old is your daughter?" I ask.

"Emma's four. She's in kidney failure. We've been on a transplant waiting list for a while now."

Abruptly, his eyes swing to me with a level of desperation I've never, not even on my worst day, felt. Suddenly I realize he's here ready to whore himself to me so his little girl can get a kidney transplant. The man is looking at me as if absolutely dead serious, and I have no idea what to say.

I have never in my entire life felt worse than I do right now.

"You're not from Caney Falls, are you?" I ask gently. Nobody who lives here could possibly have taken that ad seriously.

"No." He gives his head a small shake. "My daughter and I are originally from Bozeman, but we move around a lot for work." He's a Montana boy, which could explain why he's so tall.

"Do you have any family or friends in town?" I press. "Someone who can help?"

"We have family, but no one local. They've done what they could, when they could. I tried crowdsourced fundraising, but there's only so much people can give. Emma's doctors are all in Idaho Falls, so most of the time, it's just us."

Just us. Those two words resonate with me, although my "just us" all have hooves and tails and aren't in renal failure. So not the same, not even close.

Sanai comes by our table on her way to clean off another one, her eyes flickering between us curiously. "Hi. Is there anything I can get you?"

"I'm fine," Guy politely declines, then he looks at me and adds, "Unless I can buy you another coffee, Sienna?"

Guy doesn't have two pennies to his name, but he's here, in what's probably his nicest shirt, trying to do something for his daughter. There's no way this man isn't hungry. No one can walk into this place and not start drooling.

"You got lured here on false advertising," I tell him. "The least I can do is buy you breakfast."

Guy hesitates, then he caves and orders a plain coffee and a breakfast sandwich, the smallest, least expensive one on the menu.

"A basket of biscuits and huckleberry jam too, please," I add to the order, giving Sanai a pretty-please-just-go-along-with-it smile because she's looking at me curiously. Women are good at full conversations with just a few blinks. *Yes, I know. He's new. And yes, I'm feeding him. All this is totally Jess's fault.*

Totally, Sanai silently agrees.

Guy waits until she leaves before exhaling a quiet huff of breath. "So, false advertising. I take it you don't need a husband then?"

"I just finished getting rid of the last one," I admit, wrinkling my nose at the memory. "It was kind of a joke. There's a twenty-day waiting period before divorce finalizes in the state of Idaho, and we're officially on day twenty-one. My friend Jess works for the local paper and thought it would be funny to write the ad. I only learned they posted it this morning."

A flash of humor reaches his eyes. "And already you have a line at the door."

"It's the benefits package…" I joke, then my voice drifts off as I realize I might have embarrassed him. The benefits are exactly why he's here.

Guy's back to looking at his hands or behind my shoulder, and I don't know what to say.

"I wouldn't actually pay someone to marry me," I admit. "But for what it's worth, I appreciate how hard it must have been to show up here. Your daughter is a lucky girl to have a father who loves her so much."

Guy's smart enough to understand I'm trying to let him down easily, and he's either kind enough or desperate enough not to be a jerk about it. Instead, I see him mentally shift gears.

"Do you need any help out on your ranch? I'm a carpenter by trade, but I'm a quick learner. I work hard."

I believe him. At least I believe the hands in front of me, with all the little cuts and splits fingers get when someone spends a lot of time doing manual labor.

"I need the help, but most of my cash either whinnies, moos, or is tied up in land I won't sell." Certainly not after tearing my life apart to keep it that way. "I can't pay anyone until the next season of steers are sold, or offer insurance benefits."

"I understand." Guy's smile doesn't reach his eyes. "Well, it was worth a shot, right?"

"You miss all the shots you don't take." I hate how embarrassed he looks, so I ask, "Can I see a picture of Emma?"

Guy pulls a cell phone out of his back pocket and lays it on the table as he scrolls through his photos. He stops on a video of him and a little girl at a petting zoo and offers his phone to me so I can see better. The video is a little shaky, because he's obviously filming them himself, but his daughter is a cutie-pie, sitting on his shoulders with a beautiful grin on her face that matches the sweet smile on his own and goes straight to my heart. She's got his blue eyes and dark hair.

"The next one is my favorite." Guy indicates I can swipe to a second video, where his daughter is standing by a short fence, giggling as she feeds handfuls of hay to a pair of baby goats in pajamas.

Sanai returns with his breakfast sandwich and the biscuits, which I'm hoping will help us both choke down the awkwardness of this morning.

"Are you going to be in town long?" I ask.

"Not unless I can find work. I was hired on for a kitchen and bathroom remodel down the street, but my job was supposed to be for a month. The general contractor paused it two weeks early because everyone wants time off for Christmas."

Clearly, it's time off Guy can't afford. I doubt the homeowner is any happier with the contractor than Guy seems to be.

"I'm guessing taking the holidays off isn't an option for you?" I say gently.

He gives me a slight smile. "Not really. And I'm guessing you weren't expecting to hear a stranger's life story this morning."

"I've got a large latte and a biscuit in front of me." I lift my drink in silent encouragement for him to go on. The man needs a break, or maybe just five minutes of someone caring his life is falling apart.

Guy glances out the window again, then picks up his breakfast sandwich and sighs.

"It's this vicious cycle," he says in between bites, frustration filling his voice. "The insurance will cover the transplant, but you have to prove you can afford the anti-rejection drugs, and I can't show that kind of financial stability. I'm able to get work, but Em's in stage five kidney failure. I can't *not* take her when she needs dialysis, and I can't leave her alone when she's in the hospital. Emma gets too scared."

"That's awful."

Those two words feel so insignificant. If his situation feels awful to me, I can't fathom what Guy is experiencing. This isn't a sad story online or in the paper. This is his life. This is his daughter's life. He finishes the breakfast sandwich and wipes his mouth politely with his napkin. I nudge the basket of biscuits his way, and he caves. Guy has more restraint than most, and he only eats one, albeit slowly.

"Well, I need to get back to my daughter. Thank you for the breakfast, Sienna. It was nice to meet you." He almost manages to cover how disappointed he is, but I can see it in his eyes.

"Where is Emma now?"

"At the day care across the street. I don't like to leave her there very often. They're nice, but I'm always worried someone will give her something she can't eat or drink by accident."

I follow his gaze and suddenly understand why he's been checking out the window every few moments. I hear what he's saying and what he isn't. Childcare is incredibly expensive, even for just an hour or two.

"You could have brought her in," I tell him. "I would have bought you both breakfast."

"That's kind of you, but her diet is really strict." Guy hesitates, then says with quiet dignity, "My daughter's heard and faced a lot she shouldn't have had to deal with. I didn't want to bring her and have her hear…whatever this was going to be."

Like her father selling himself for a chance to save her life.

I've never felt so badly for a stranger as I do in this moment, so on impulse, I say, "I know a lot of people in town. I can ask around and see if anyone needs some help. Can I get your number?"

"Thanks, I really appreciate it. Anything will be great, but I'm better on my tools than most other work." Guy texts me his number, and I add him into my phone. He pauses and then he looks at me with too much kindness for someone with so much on his shoulders. "Sienna? I'm really sorry about your divorce. I hope you do something nice for yourself today. And I hope whoever your ex is, he's kicking himself for losing you."

Then he leaves, grabbing a worn, heavy tan Carhartt jacket from the hooks by the coffee shop door, hands stuffed in his pockets and head down as he hustles across the street. I watch him through the window, and the grim worry on his face smooths before he reaches the day care. He opens the door and disappears inside. A few minutes later, he walks back out to a white Dodge truck parked on the street with a small child in his arms. I can only see the back of her head and a sparkly rainbow unicorn horn sewn to the knit cap she's wearing, but the expression on his face as he looks down at her is so full of love, it makes my heart hurt.

I bet she's beaming right back at him. With a smile like Guy Maple's, it would be hard not to.

Chapter 2

I CAN'T STOP THINKING ABOUT GUY AND EMMA MAPLE. EVEN AS I arrive back home and find there's one very important speckled brown head missing from my cattle pen, they're still on my mind.

Cattle fencing lines one side of the two-mile-long drive from the main road to my family's cabin, existing both as a physical barrier for the herd and as a visual cue for when the snowdrifts get too deep to find the gravel road. Usually this time of year, I've taken a day to tie large red-and-green-plaid bows on the fencing, but my heart hasn't been in the decorating spirit this year.

Besides, knowing Jerkface—my bull—he'd probably try to eat them.

The cattle have spent the summer up in higher country, and I think Jerkface is resenting his loss of freedom more than most. Cattle are tough, and they can push hard against fencing, taking it down if they want to badly enough. This bull is special because he's a fence hopper. I've never actually caught him at it, but he's jumped my gate twice since I moved the herd down closer to the cabin, and the sucker is seven feet high.

I'd be impressed if it weren't such a massive pain to go find him again.

Today is mail delivery day, and while I have an actual mailbox on the main road, a lot of folks deep enough in the Frank Church Wilderness can only get their mail dropped by plane. I doubt Jerkface has gotten far, so I dial the tiny airport that services this area of the country. Most of their work is flying white-water rafters or hunting parties deeper into the wilderness, but with the wildfires we've been getting these last several years, they fly firefighters in and out a lot too.

Last summer was bad, with over 130,000 acres to the north of town burning for four months before anyone could successfully put it out. The problem with a place like this is you can't fight fires on steep mountains, not when the whole countryside is too thick with smoke to see where you're flying.

A lot of people lost livestock, including myself. Of the hundred-head herd Micah left on the ranch after we knew how the livestock would be split up, I'm down to sixty-one now. Sixty, since Jerkface decided to take a sightseeing trip.

I can't afford to lose my bull.

When no one at the airport answers my first call, I dial one of the regular delivery pilots directly. Jake answers his cell phone on the third ring, his voice muffled as if he's doing some sort of repair work in an enclosed space. Probably in one of the planes.

"Not a good time, Sienna," he says by way of greeting. The gruff, "don't bother me when I'm working" tone is normal around these parts, but the fact that Jake did pick up means something to me. When you're part of a very public breakup in a small town, people don't just treat your failed marriage as fodder for the gossip mill. They also tend to choose sides. Micah's got a lot of weight in this town, and he likes to talk. Me? Not so much. I retreated to my ranch, nursing my broken heart in silence and in as much privacy as possible, but I can feel the eyes on me and the quiet when I go into a room in town.

Another reason the ad in the paper made me smile despite being embarrassed is that Jess is firmly Team Sienna, and they're not afraid to let everyone know it.

"It's not a great time for me either," I joke tiredly. "Jerkface took another flying leap today while I was in town. I don't suppose you had eyes on my bull during your morning flight?"

"Sorry, Sienna, I didn't notice any strays, but I wasn't really looking. You know how it gets."

I do know. Everyone has a lot on their plates, and one big cow butt is going to look like another.

"Hold on, let me radio it out. Charley's making a run right now. He might have seen something."

Considering Jake and Charley are two of Micah's closest friends, I appreciate that they are trying to help me. We might have known each other all our lives, but divorce has a way of forcing people to choose sides. Micah's not been quiet about how mad he is over our divorce settlement.

Jake hangs up without saying goodbye, but a couple minutes later, he calls me back. "Sienna, Charley asked if it's the monster one with the speckled face."

"That's him." Monster is an understatement. Jerkface is big enough, even I give him some side-eye. He isn't the best product of years of my and Micah's careful stock breeding programs, but the bull is incredibly important to my little ranch. He's not mean per se—at least not more than any other bull—but he's a fast sucker for how big he is, and I'm always extra careful around him.

"Charley made an extra loop over your place and spotted him down by the river. South of the bend just past the big rockslide from last year."

"Thanks, Jake." I exhale a sigh of relief. "Tell Charley he's a lifesaver."

It's the truth, in more ways than one. A sweet guy I've known since grade school, Charley's the first to volunteer when someone needs evacuating or the firefighters need a ride over the mountains. He's the last out there still looking if someone is hurt or lost in the woods. He's always been quiet and a little shy, but he's one of the bravest, most kindhearted people I know.

"Uh, Charley wants me to ask you if the ad is serious? Jess made a run past the hangar today and posted it to the board."

I groan into my hand. "No, but he'll be on my good list if he throws it in the trash."

Jake chuckles, a rare sound from the crabby pilot. "Charley's had it bad for you since freshman year. You'll have to tell him yourself because I'm not breaking my buddy's heart. We've got too much to get done today."

Charley's heart will have to wait, even if I'm sure Jake's just teasing me. My already busy day just got a lot busier. If I grab my truck and stock trailer and drive across the river, it wouldn't be far to my bull's last known location. Unfortunately, that would put me on the wrong side of the water, and there's no way I'm taking a horse or my bull through the partially frozen Salmon River two weeks before Christmas. It's just far too cold. I'm going to need some help.

My twelve-year-old golden retriever Barley agrees to rouse himself and accompany me outside today, but he takes two steps in the cold and turns his once-red head to give me a look that speaks volumes.

"You didn't complain this much when you were a puppy," I remind him as we head across the property to the barn. "You're too young to be this crotchety."

Barley abandons me for a bale of hay, but he knows what it means when I pull out a worn, tan Carhartt dog jacket for him. Barley stays on the hay as I grab a saddle and head to the horse pen, but despite staring at me relentlessly with his disappointed eyes, his tail thumps once in acknowledgment. I know he's ready to work.

Compared to how full the horse pen used to be, it feels very scarce now. Instead of a small herd of horses, I've only got one mare, two donkeys, and one very moody mule, the latter of which is trying his best to remain unnoticed as he lips at the remaining bits of this morning's hay. Unlike Barley, Legs is refusing to make eye contact. He shuffles a little behind the closest donkey, as if I could possibly avoid seeing the seventeen-hand-tall mule. His extra-long ears flick backward, and he turns again, keeping his rear end pointed my way.

"That's too big and handsome of a butt for me not to notice you, buddy."

Legs's ears turn at the sound of my voice before he remembers himself and goes back in hiding mode.

"Let me guess, you don't want to ride the fences today and would rather hang out with the ladies?"

Typical guy, ignoring the hand that feeds him for the pretty sorrel in the corner.

As mules go, Legs is particularly ugly. He's also smarter than is technically safe, and I have to keep an eye out when I ride him. Just because a mule of his caliber can walk a razor-edge cliffside trail without a single misstep doesn't mean he doesn't find it fun to drop me like a sack of flour if I'm not paying attention.

I think it's why I like him so much. I prefer people not to go easy on me, and my mule? He is definitely people.

"I hate to not disappoint you for once," I tell Legs, patting his shoulder as I move past him. "But I need Lulu on this one."

Unlike Legs, Lulu doesn't complain as I saddle her up, standing with the docile acceptance that makes her breed such good work horses. Lulu's a sweetheart of a Quarter Horse, and I appreciate the shorter stretch for my legs as I swing up on her back.

Barley watches me disconsolately from the barn door, and when I whistle twice, he sighs and rises to his paws.

The river gurgles beneath its crust of ice as I ride along the shore, Barley following at a slow pace. I hate having to ask him to come out here today; the old retriever has paid his dues and should be in retirement.

Like too many things in my life, he's been dusted off and asked to give a little more. A good cattle dog takes a long time to train, and even though his breed isn't as commonly used as the shepherds and border collies that work these herds, Barley was one of the best.

I can't get the bull in by myself, and since Micah got the rest of the working dogs in the divorce, today I need Barley. I'll make it up to him tonight with an extra treat and some serious belly-rubbing time. But for now, we have to make the best of what we've got.

Guy and Emma Maple flash through my mind unbidden as I follow the river south, scanning the landscape. Starting over has been tough, but there are worse things than a bull who likes to pretend he's an Olympic show jumper. Like being desperate enough to reply to a fake marriage ad. Like being four years old and having stage five chronic kidney disease with dialysis not working well.

I don't even know exactly what it means, other than Guy's little girl needs a transplant to live.

I give Lulu her head and let her pick her way along the snowy ground, weaving in and out of thick brush, thicker snowbanks, and tall evergreens. When people think about Idaho, they think about potatoes, but what most people don't realize is how much of my home state is wilderness. Take a picture of my backyard, and you'll see nothing but snow-covered mountains, steep wooded hills, and the Salmon River.

This river is like a marriage. Sometimes it's beautiful, glittering in the sunshine as it rushes past, filling your ears with the low, reassuring cadence of water. But one wrong step and you're in it deep, frozen and drowning, with no one to grab your hand as you reach for help.

I love this river, but I loved my ex-husband too.

The Naples Ranch butts up to the Frank Church Wilderness about thirty minutes outside town. The farther north and west you go, the rougher and tougher this country gets. The land isn't ours, even though there's a sign hanging over the driveway for the last several generations with the Naples name on it. This is Nez Perce/Nimiipuu land, cruelly stolen from them by white settlers, then passed back and forth for several decades until my great-grandmother won it in a card game.

She used to say, even back then, this wasn't ours to own; we were just caretakers of it for a little while. There've been a lot of times over the years when it would have been easy to split it up and sell it, but we Naples are a strong-willed lot. In a world of half-acre tract homes, the Naples Ranch is still a thousand acres of wilderness, with just enough cleared for our cabin, our barn, and a paddock to work the horses or sort the herd of cattle we keep.

It used to upset my ex-husband so much that we could sell some of the acreage and just...didn't. He used to refer to it as being married to an heiress with a bucket over her head, determined to eat cheeseburgers instead of filet mignon.

Micah never got it. You don't sell what doesn't belong to you in the first place.

Considering the fact that the property isn't within the Frank Church Wilderness, the State of Idaho disagrees. It took nine years of marriage for Micah to decide he was done with us but another year of arguing with lawyers to realize I was going to drain our joint bank account digging my heels in, fighting for the ranch to stay in one piece. Honestly, it would have broken my heart, but I would have even signed over my half of the property rights if it had been written he couldn't parcel up the property. Micah caved, but I sure paid for it. If I wanted the ranch? Whole and unharmed? No problem. Then he was going to take every single thing we'd built together.

He got it all. Down to the antique silver in my great-grandmother's kitchen hutch. I signed away my rights to any of the inheritance from his family, all the local businesses we'd started together, all the investments we'd made, and nearly every penny in our shared bank accounts. I got to keep Legs, Lulu, the donkeys, and a small herd of cattle to start over again. It was almost...almost...enough to cover the difference between what Micah's theoretical half of the ranch was valued at if he'd been allowed to butcher it into chunks. So now he's got what he needs, and I have the peace of mind knowing I'm not the Naples who let everyone else in my family down.

Barley lets out a soft woof, pulling me from my thoughts. I follow his sight line toward the stand of trees a hundred or so yards ahead of us, and there he is: the jerk face himself.

The massive brown bull turns and lows, a loud, miserable sound. As if it's my fault he's out here alone without a round bale of hay in front of him.

"Don't complain to me," I say to Jerkface. "You're the one who decided to be a pain in the butt today."

Barley lowers his head, focusing on the bull before us. Lulu's ears perk up, and I keep the reins loose in my hand. We're a motley crew, but we know how to do our jobs. Mine is to not get in Lulu's or Barley's ways. Barley's not as fast as he used to be, and this bull might make cute little calves, but he's a problem on a good day. With some exceptions, bulls don't tend to like being told where to go or what to do.

He snorts, breath condensing in the cold winter air. When he wheels and starts to dart around me, Lulu drops into a lower stance, cutting off his path, then swinging sideways to do it again as the bull tries to dart around our other side.

A cutting horse like Lulu comes around once in a blue moon, and I need her a lot more for the babies she's going to make than to get this guy back in the corral. But man, is she beautiful when she works. Like a crouching cat, liquid smooth as she swings back and forth, frustrating the bull and holding it in place until he spins the way we want him to move.

We trot after him, with Barley barking and nipping at Jerkface's heels to keep him going toward the ranch.

I don't like to move my cattle very quickly. The process sometimes stresses them out, but this bull is young enough to be full of extra energy. Between Barley and Lulu, we keep him headed back toward the homestead, but the deep snow is tough on Barley, and even though it's her job, I cringe every time Lulu cuts back and forth on this kind of ground.

"Safe and sound," I mutter to the animals I love, even Jerkface. "Let's all just get home safe and sound."

Finally, we get my bull into the corral, and I side pass Lulu over to the gate to close it as fast as possible. Barley pants longer than he should, and I wait for him to catch his breath before riding to the barn. Working dogs are complex creatures. I don't want to hurt his feelings by leaving him when we always used to return together, with Barley a few steps ahead of me.

When he's ready, Barley pads off toward the barn, and I follow. "Good boy," I tell him as I dismount, bending down to scratch behind his graying ears before tending to Lulu.

I still have a truck bed of grain to unload and everyone to feed. By the time I'm done, the sun has slipped behind the mountains, leaving a soft glow on the snow. Chilled and tired from the day, I let Barley into the cabin in front of me.

The house is too quiet. I've learned to appreciate the soft snores of my dog, the lowing of the cattle outside, or the occasional whinny or bray. Even the soft crackle of the fireplace in the living room. If it weren't for the animals in my life, I would be surrounded by nothing but silence.

I haven't even bothered to try to decorate for Christmas. There doesn't seem to be any point.

I try not to hate it. This is the life I fought to keep, and it's mine now. Me. The cabin. The coffee maker. This is as good as it's going to get. I don't miss my marriage. I miss the man I thought I married, and I miss the life I hoped we were going to have together.

I miss when this cabin was more than my house; it was my family's home.

Micah used to feel like this place was too small for the three of us when Dad was here. Even when it was just the two of us, he found it confining. But my whole life, these hand-hewn log walls were full. Full of my mother's laughter and my father playing his guitar in the evenings. I'm still not used to the silence from his garage-size workshop, where I heard metal thumping on metal or a muttered curse of annoyance every single day of my life.

I've never lived anywhere but this cabin. I was my parents' rainbow baby, after a lot of years of trying and almost giving up on having children. There are a lot of benefits to having mature parents, but there's one fairly rough negative: watching them get older. We lost Mom to breast cancer before I hit high school, and I didn't want to leave Dad alone, even after Micah and I got married. Micah always tried to be understanding, although the worse Dad's dementia got, the harder it was on everyone.

Dad is the one who decided he wasn't going to stay, choosing to sign over the property to both of us and sell the bulk of his cattle to cover the cost of a long-term care facility. He didn't want to be a burden on us, and considering how far his illness has progressed recently, it was a brave decision by a brave man to protect his family.

Thinking about medical expenses makes me think about Guy and Emma Maple again. I fix myself a cup of coffee and start to do some research. Guy's social media presence is sparse but there. His pictures are private, but the fundraising posts to cover medical expenses and posts thanking friends and family for the well wishes for Emma go back three years.

The whole situation is gut-wrenching. If the child is four, she's been sick three-quarters of her life.

I look up chronic kidney disease on the internet, my heart sinking with every sentence I read. I wish I could give Guy a job, and I think about who might be hiring right now. The man was just so stressed, so desperate, and I'm starting to understand why. If Emma's dialysis isn't working as well anymore, then getting a new kidney is her only option. Without it, Emma has a death sentence.

"That poor little girl," I murmur, shaking my head. "That poor *family*." And right at Christmastime too.

Something pops into my head, but it's absurd. Sheer, unadulterated absurdity. If I didn't know I had decaf coffee in my hands, I would say I'd had too many glasses of wine.

"It's ridiculous, right?" I ask Barley, earning a single eye opening before lazily closing again.

Except…it's logical ridiculousness if someone looked at the entire situation with dispassionate eyes. I sit there, my brain rolling around all the reasons why this is a bad idea. Then it keeps coming back to how Guy stood there today, desperate for anything to help his daughter.

I think about how, for the first time in a long time, I honestly have no one whose opinion matters to me. How I have nothing to lose.

"Screw it," I mutter, and I reach for my phone. I scroll to Guy's contact, and when the option for a video call shows on my screen, I lean my phone against my desk and hit the button. This is the kind of conversation you have face-to-face.

The call rings several times, and I almost chicken out and end it, then Guy's face pops up on the screen. He gives me a quick smile of greeting. "Sienna? Hey."

The man is just as handsome as he was this morning, although he's a bit wild-eyed. I suppose I would be too if I were him. He probably thinks I'm calling him about work.

"Hey, sorry to surprise you. This isn't a work call thing. It's another… thing."

He almost manages to cover being disappointed. "If it's a coffee shop thing, I'm going to say yes. That was the best breakfast I've had in years."

Oh. Ooooooh. He thinks I'm calling to ask him out on a date. Sorry, I'm jumping a few steps here.

"Daddy, who is it?" a child's voice asks cheerfully in the background.

"It's a new friend I made today, Em. Her name is Sienna." Guy turns his head from the phone, and I don't hear what Emma says next, but I do catch Guy's murmurs. "Not now, baby. I'm not sure why she's calling."

Yep, I'm in a full-blown panic attack here. I know why I'm calling, but I'm not *sure* about it at all.

"Emma says hi," Guy tells me in a fond voice. "I told her earlier that you were very nice, and now she wants to meet you. So, what can I do for you, Sienna?"

"Well, okay. This is a little awkward. Is it possible for you to go somewhere Emma can't hear?"

Guy's expression is puzzled, but he nods. "Yeah, gimme a sec." To his credit, he covers the camera on his phone with his thumb so I don't have to see a dizzying pattern of wall and floor as he goes to a more private place. I hear the soft shut of a door, and when he removes his finger, it looks like he's outside a brick building. Maybe it's a motel room.

"I've got to warn you that I'm not really into this kind of thing." He's trying to be kind, whatever he means, but firm too. "Especially not with my daughter in the other room."

Suddenly I understand, and I spit my coffee onto my phone. "Oh *no*! Oh no, not that. I'm not… Noooo."

I frantically wipe the coffee spit off the screen, revealing a chuckling Guy. He flashes me a knee-melting smile. "I'm open to getting to know each other though," he says, and if I didn't know better, I'd think he was flirting with me.

I sputter and try to recompose myself. "Okay, why I called was not about…that. It *is* about getting to know each other though. I mean, it would kind of be a given, I suppose."

Blue eyes blink at me, and his head tilts slightly. He clearly has no idea what I'm talking about.

"I don't have work for you, but I've been thinking about you and Emma a lot today. And I was thinking I do have really good insurance. Part of my divorce settlement included me being able to stay on our company's plan, either single or remarried, so I can't get kicked off the insurance no matter what." One of the few things I didn't lose in the divorce. My eyes drop as I stare at the coffee in between my hands. "If we *did* get married, it would cover you both."

The silence between us is deafening. I don't have to look at the phone to know he's staring at me like I've sprouted a second head. I mean, pretty much no one marries someone they just met, unless Vegas and copious amounts of alcohol are involved. Or it's a love-at-first-sight kind of romance—not that I believe those exist anymore.

"I remembered you said you need to show financial stability to keep Emma on the transplant list, right? I'm land poor: I have a lot of physical property without any actual cash to my name. I'll never sell the ranch, but all the bank—" I pause and add dryly, "And my ex-husband see is over a thousand acres of possible liquifiable assets. It should be more than enough to cover what you said the transplant board needed to see."

Guy inhales a tight breath. "Sienna, are you saying you want to get married?"

"I'm saying I want Emma to get a kidney." I glance back at the phone. "This would kind of be like a…marriage of convenience thing, I guess?"

"What would you want out of it?" Guy asks me quietly, staring at the phone so intensely it makes my heart start racing. "This is a big deal you're talking about."

"I guess…it's been a bad year. And it's almost Christmas. I wouldn't have to actually pay for the anti-rejection medication, correct? Just show we have the financial stability to cover them when she gets the kidney."

Guy closes his eyes, and I see him take a deep, steadying breath. "No, I would pay for everything. I'll sign whatever you'd need me to sign so you don't worry."

"I would want you to sign a prenup. I fought too hard for this ranch to stay whole, and I can't risk it now. And I guess…that's it. I don't need anything from you. I just want to help." My words sound so flimsy, so inadequate, and I wonder if he thinks I'm lying to him. "We don't even have to see each other beyond the paperwork. Maybe we could get coffee sometimes and you can tell me how she's doing."

"You just want coffee?"

Guy's holding the phone in his hands, and I have his complete, utter attention. I don't know if I've ever had that kind of attention from someone, the way he's looking at me.

"Maybe breakfast with the coffee?" I joke awkwardly. "Umm, yeah. That's all."

There's another long moment of silence, and then Guy says in a whisper, "If you're willing to do this for us, I promise I'll be a good husband to you, Sienna. I won't lie to you, I won't cheat on you, and I'll do my best never to hurt you." Guy's voice catches, then he clears his throat. "I can't promise I'll love you, but when I give my word, I mean it. I'll work hard, and I'll always have your back. And when you want out, I'll do that too. Whatever you need."

"Same deal for both of us, okay? If you want out, then we'll call it," I tell him. "You don't know me. Two weeks in, you could end up hating my guts and regretting this."

"I highly doubt it," Guy tells me quietly. "And you don't know me either, but I know I'll do anything to keep my daughter on the transplant list."

"Even meet me at the courthouse tomorrow? Nine thirty?" I met the man at 9:30 this morning. Might as well make it a full twenty-four hours before getting married to him.

A flicker of the muscles in his jaw is the only thing telling me this hits him hard. Guy blinks rapidly, turning his face away to look at the brick wall next to him. I have the feeling Emma is on the other side of the wall. Then he says in an even quieter voice, "We both will."

I end the call and sit back in my chair, my heart pounding in my chest.

"It isn't real," I tell Barley, who's snoring softly and no longer listening. "It isn't a real marriage."

This is a marriage of convenience. A way to help someone take care of his dying child. This isn't love. If I've learned anything the hard way, marriage for love might exist, but not for me. But doing a good thing? I can still have that.

Assuming I'm brave enough…and reckless enough…to take the leap.

Chapter 3

"Making good choices," I singsong under my breath as I drive toward the courthouse. It's 9:23 in the morning, meaning I have a whole seven more minutes to run screaming the other way.

My hands grip down too hard on the steering wheel. Right now, I have no clue if what I'm doing is the right thing or if I'm suffering from the kind of postdivorce reckless impulsivity that makes for good movies and very bad actual life choices. A manila folder rests on the passenger seat of my truck, my purse parked on top of it so if I slam on the brakes, my birth certificate and the freshly printed prenup from my very worried lawyer won't go flying. The courthouse has everything we need, including a notary for the prenup.

There isn't a waiting period in Idaho. Once we have the marriage license, we can get married today. No state requirement to take a step back and think this one over. No witnesses needed, which is a relief. I doubt anyone I know would agree to this wild plan of mine, let alone sign as a witness.

Well, Jess would. They would probably find it highly entertaining, even if somewhat alarming.

I've kept the prenup simple. Everything Guy brings into the marriage is his. Everything I bring into the marriage is mine. After the marriage, there's an equal distribution of any combined assets, which won't exist.

I've learned my lesson about combined assets. Honestly, it's possible I won't see him more than once or twice after this until it's time to get a divorce.

My knuckles pale on the steering wheel. I guess I hadn't thought about the idea of being a two-time divorcée.

"That's future Sienna's problem," I mutter to myself, glancing at the clock. It's 9:25 a.m., meaning I now have five minutes to get there on time. "Focus on the present. You're getting married today."

Oh man. I'm getting married today. I glance down at my clothing, wondering if I'm overdressed or underdressed. No one ever told me what to wear to a not-fake-but-kind-of-fake wedding. Slacks and a nice sweater seem right. For a few horrifying moments, I imagine myself getting out of the truck in a massive white wedding dress, walking up to a stranger, bouquet in hand, then I shudder.

I park my truck across the street from the courthouse, wondering if I hallucinated all this as I cross the street and head up the steps. Maybe this is just a prank, to see if I'd fall for it? Maybe this is real, but Guy changed his mind, like a rational human being about to marry a complete stranger might?

Or maybe he's standing outside the courthouse doors, holding a little girl with a massive, sparkly rainbow bow on her headband. She's wearing a Christmas-red dress with equally sparkly rainbow-colored boots and a fluffy child's jacket. Emma's hair is wispy thin but a deep brunette color. Her eyes are the same ice blue as her father's, and the combination is striking.

She might be the most beautiful child I've ever seen.

Guy has her wrapped up in a second, larger jacket, the same heavy Carhartt he was wearing yesterday. Suddenly I feel guilty for driving five miles under the speed limit all the way to the courthouse. They're waiting outside for me, and I wonder how long they've been here. Clearly Guy doesn't want his daughter to get too cold.

The Christmas You Found Me 31

"Good morning," I say, because it seems like a logical greeting. Good morning, what are we actually doing? Good morning, we've both lost our minds. Except seeing his daughter's shy look as she presses her cheek against Guy's shirt, maybe I haven't lost my mind at all.

"Hey," he says, looking as anxious as I feel. He starts to move toward me, then hesitates. Do we hug? Do we shake hands? I want to laugh at how incredibly awkward this is, but it'll probably come out sounding a bit hysterical.

Was Guy this tall yesterday? He's wearing a tie around the neck of his collared shirt, and his boots look like another round of scrubbing happened after our breakfast date yesterday. His eyes crinkle at the corners when he offers me a tentative smile, softening the harsher angles of his jaw. I want to feed him. It's a bizarre compulsion that's hit me twice now. If the Department of Ill-Advised Impulsivity and Borderline Insurance Fraud ask, I think he's handsome and I want to feed him.

"Emma, this is Sienna. She's a new friend of mine."

"Hi, Emma." Focusing on his daughter is easier than looking at Guy. I smile at her and earn a shy smile in return, then she turns her whole face into Guy's shoulder. "I like your boots," I add.

"They're her favorite. We weren't sure what to wear today." He clears his throat. "You look nice."

"Daddy," Emma says, tugging his sleeve. "Don't forget."

He looks down at her and then murmurs, "Oh yeah. We brought these for you."

Guy digs into the bag looped over his shoulder and gives something to his daughter. When he takes a closer step toward me, Emma hands me a small bouquet of white roses. I have wedding flowers.

"They're beautiful," I say, because two people are looking at me with nervous uncertainty. Wishing I had brought something other than paperwork to give them, I take one of the prettiest roses and hand it back to Emma. Then I break off a second rose two inches beneath the bud and tuck it into Guy's shirt pocket. "There," I decide. "Now we're all ready."

Emma's smile is brighter and no longer as shy, instantly warming my heart. A marriage for love sure didn't do a thing but cause me a whole lot of misery. Yesterday morning, I'd have sworn I'd never say "I do" again, unless the question was if I wanted another cupcake. But marrying a man to help this little girl? The queasiness in my stomach doesn't settle so much as just stops getting worse by the moment.

"I guess we just go inside?" I say, because I suppose this is it. There's a clerk with a form or something in there.

Guy sets Emma down on the concrete and follows me up the steps. "Wait, Sienna."

Yes, please stop us from making this mistake. My internalized nesting button has lodged into the On setting, and I can't stop myself from making bad choices.

"Are you taking my last name, or am I taking yours?" he asks.

Oh yeah, because married people do that sometimes, and they usually know before reaching the courthouse. I have no idea, so I stare up at him, blinking rapidly as if it'll make my brain function better. "Ummm... Do you want to hyphenate?"

I get the feeling my indecision amuses him. "You want to be Sienna Naples-Maple?"

"Hmm, good point. You could be Guy Maple-Naples."

We start laughing because this is ludicrous, but it's happening. The people near us are looking at us like we've lost our minds, and even Emma giggles. I turn to her, kneeling down to her level.

"Emma, what do you think? Should we be Naples or Maple?" Let the cutie-pie in the sequined bow decide this one.

She giggles again, giving me a toothy grin. "Maple."

The Maples we will be. And isn't this going to make my ex-husband completely lose his mind if he ever finds out, considering I refused to take Micah's last name?

Writing a different last name on the marriage license is easier knowing Emma's keeping hers. I finish and twist the form toward Guy. He hesitates as he looks at the marriage license, then glances at me. I see it in his eyes, the momentary panic, as if he, too, is struggling with what we're about to do. Then his gaze goes to Emma, sitting on the chair next to us, and Guy's expression softens. I can't read what it means, but unlike mine, his hand doesn't tremble when he signs his name. Then we both reach for our wallets to pay the thirty-dollar fee for the wedding.

"I don't mind covering it," Guy promises, even as I nudge my card toward the clerk.

"Want to split it fifty-fifty? Might as well go into this thing as equals," I joke, cringing internally at myself.

Guy just nods in understanding, seeming unbothered with the clerk's annoyance at running two cards.

My last wedding was an overly excessive event. My father had grumbled more than once, and I secretly agreed with him. But Micah liked bigger, better, and brighter, so we had a massive wedding at his family's luxurious mountain lodge home with me stuffed into a fluffy white dress and my father walking me down the aisle.

Standing in front of a court officiant in a dark wood-paneled office with unidentifiable stains on the threadbare green carpet is a far cry from the wedding of anyone's dreams.

If I want out of this, now is the time. Grab my nonexistent veil and run for the hills. But there's no one outside with a boom box held over their head, blasting love songs. No one knows or cares I'm here except the man next to me and the little girl in the corner. Fighting kidney failure for three years of her four-year life. The wrongness of her situation overrides the wrongness of marrying a stranger.

They start the ceremony and ask if we want to say our own vows. I shake my head because I have no idea what to say. I'm unaware I'm shivering slightly until Guy takes my hands. I can feel the roughness of the calluses there. Men who do physical labor for a living have hands like these, and it gives me a momentary relief, my poor brain desperate for something familiar to latch on to. Everything else about him is different, but these hands I understand.

I wonder what it's like on his side of this. I wonder if his heart is pounding in his chest so hard it's making it hard to hear out of his ears too.

Guy's eyes gaze down at me intensely.

"Sienna, I know we just met, and all this is a lot. We don't know each other, and I'm not expecting anything here. But I promise I'll be a good husband to you. I'll stand at your side, and I'll have your back. I'll be your friend and your partner. Whatever you need from me, I'm here. I'll be loyal to you, and I'll be good to you, from the moment I wake up until I go to sleep and all the minutes in between."

It's nice. And in his own way, Guy's vows are a whole lot more honest than my last exchange of vows had been. I wish I could think of something to say back other than "I'll feed you." I think he deserves better than my wordless presence or my trembling fingers gripping too hard on his own.

I really didn't expect this reaction from myself. Yeah, I'm pretty much scared to death.

The officiant continues in a calm if not particularly emotionally invested voice. "Guy Maple, do you take this woman to be your lawfully wedded wife? To have and to hold, for better or for worse, in sickness and in health, 'til death do you part?"

Until his daughter's life...or death...do we part.

He squeezes my hands gently, holding my eyes. Then his quiet voice says, "I do."

"Sienna Naples, do you take this man to be your lawfully wedded husband? To have and to hold, for better or for worse, in sickness and in health, 'til death do you part?"

I freeze. I absolutely freeze. Whatever words I think I'm going to say stick in my throat. I just got divorced, and it was awful. It was *so* awful, and I haven't even begun to process what went wrong and why. Yet here I am, saying these words all over again. I haven't even stopped bleeding from the wound that is my divorce, let alone had time to heal and deal with the scars.

Then Guy's hand is gently cupping my jaw, his body close to mine as he leans down and whispers in my ear. "It's okay. If you can't do this, it'll be okay."

Guy knows I'm scared, and he's giving me an out. He's giving me a chance to pick myself when I don't remember a time in my life when I got to put myself first. I can go home. I can be done with this. Life won't be any easier, but it won't have to be harder.

It won't have to be like theirs.

I look over at Emma, and she's holding on to the white flower I gave her like it means something special to her. This little girl is dying, and her father is emotionally bleeding out on his feet. I'm a Naples, now a Maple, and it's time for me to be as brave as everyone else in this room.

Guy's hand is still touching my face when I look up into his eyes. "I do."

Chapter 4

THEY PRONOUNCE US THE MAPLE FAMILY AND SEND US OFF INTO OUR new lives together.

"What happens now?" I ask as we head down the steps of the courthouse.

At my side, Guy exhales a soft laugh. He's walking closer to me than when we entered the building, and it occurs to me how much he stayed out of my personal space up until this point. I would still have to stretch to brush my fingers against his shoulder, but he's within arm's reach now.

"I actually have no clue," he says. "I kind of didn't think past this part."

"We'd usually be headed for our honeymoon, but I'm fairly certain I'm going to be headed home to clean some horse stalls."

Guy stops and picks up Emma before we start across the street to the parking lot. "We could get something to eat. Or just go home? I've never been married before, so I'm just winging it here."

We pause a few feet away from my truck, two strangers with only a piece of paper and a mission between us and not a single thing else.

"Where do you live?" I ask, uncomfortably aware of how little I know about these two people. I'd never even asked him if he'd been married before—not that it would have mattered, I guess.

"We've been at the extended stay on the other side of town." Guy's expression shifts to one of slight embarrassment.

I know the motel, the most budget-conscious place to stay in town. The price is low and for good reasons. There are very few places in town that aren't safe, but…it's not great. Even the firefighters in the summers would rather sleep on the ground in a tent when the town is crowded than sleep in our extended stay.

My brain is resisting all of this, but my heart is making a serious case for not driving away, knowing Guy and Emma are headed back to their motel. I wouldn't even ask Barley to sleep there, and he likes to roll in cow pies. I officially have a stepdaughter now, and even if I have zero idea of what to do with the handsome man in front of me, I know there's one thing almost every small child loves: horses.

Okay. Well, in for a penny, in for a pound, I guess.

"Do you need help packing your stuff?" When Guy tips his head at my question, I quirk a half smile. "Did I forget to add that room and board are typically provided in all 'husband for hire' employment?"

And just like last night on the phone, I have one hundred percent of Guy's attention. I didn't even realize how halfheartedly Micah used to listen to me until now, because I'm not sure Guy's even aware of people walking past us, he's so focused on me. Guy moves closer, and I have to tilt my head back to keep holding his eyes. As if realizing what he's doing, he shifts backward again.

"You don't have to support me, Sienna," he says quietly. "I know this is all moving really fast, and it's okay if you need time to get to know us."

I lean against my truck, glancing at the bits of old hay and corn kernels that like to gather beneath the exposed ball hitch in the center of the bed. Not looking directly at him makes this easier.

"No time like the present," I say like this isn't a big deal. Yep, I add in silent disbelief at my own spontaneity. I move random people into my house *all* the time. I definitely *don't* have a stack of neatly organized to-do lists on my phone. I don't have a work planner, a life planner, or a backup in-case-I-get-wild-and-do-something-spontaneous planner.

I finally have something to stick in that one.

I'm guessing Guy doesn't have a life planner, because he closes his eyes and rocks back a little on his feet. Then he exhales and nods. "Okay, let's go move into your place."

He sounds bemused, as if he's not sure any of this is really happening.

Oh, trust me, buddy. This is happening.

Guy's truck is an older model white Dodge with an extended cab and a long bed, the kind of plain fleet truck contractors drive. It looks a little beat-up, and I wonder if he managed to get it cheap off a jobsite. He catches my eyes flickering over it, and I don't want him to think I'm judging him by his vehicle. I'm the first person to appreciate a good work truck that's seen better days. I just need to make sure it will manage to get to my place without getting stuck.

"Do you have four-wheel drive?" I ask, resting my hand on the side of the bed and giving the truck a pat. When he shakes his head, I bite my lower lip.

"I suppose I should have asked you where you lived," Guy admits. "Or should we technically consider it a jobsite?"

We share a quick grin, and I appreciate that he at least has a sense of humor about all this. I tell him where the ranch is, explaining I'm about a half hour from town, depending on weather and traffic.

Emma has been quiet, playing with the rose I shared with her, but she must know what a jobsite is, because she looks at me curiously. "Daddy, is Sen-na your new boss?"

"There's way too much to unpack in that question, baby." Guy gives Emma an amused look as he adjusts her on his hip. "No, Sienna is my wife. We just got married, remember?"

"I'm a new friend," I tell Emma. "I hope we can be friends too."

I earn a pretty smile from her but otherwise no answer. The novelty of the courthouse wedding has worn off, so Emma goes back to playing with her flower.

"So *are* you my new boss?" Guy asks me out of the corner of his mouth, and for a moment, his eyes brighten with humor. I bet in a different, kinder world, those eyes would sparkle a lot. Then Emma wiggles and says she's cold, and Guy immediately shifts into protective father mode, getting her into the truck with the heater turned on and wrapping an extra blanket around her. By the time he's done, he turns back to me with the stressed, haunted look I'm only now realizing is his normal.

Life has done a number on this family. Focusing on that makes it easier to follow him across town, to help him move from his place into mine.

I suppose I'm being fairly productive today. Chores, check. Get married, check. Acquire new roommates, in progress.

He parks and I get out, overly aware I've got a very recognizable truck and I'm outside the sleaziest motel in town. I keep waiting to get a text message from someone demanding to know what I'm doing as I follow Guy and Emma inside the room, but my phone stays silent.

I haven't been inside this motel since the after-party of my junior prom. It was rough then, and other than slapping a new coat of streaky beige paint on the damaged walls and ripping out the old, stained carpets, everything is the same. Down to the rusty doorknobs, beaten-up mini fridges, and light fixtures from the eighties. I don't want to know if the bathrooms have been updated, but I'm guessing that's a no too.

Emma's toys are spread out on one of the two beds, but everything else is apparently tucked away in drawers or placed on the dresser in an attempt at tidiness. A Minnesota Vikings coffee mug, a child's dinnerware set, and a Nalgene water bottle dry on a kitchen towel atop the mini fridge. A half-empty bottle of blue dish soap is neatly tucked next to a damp sponge beside the microwave.

Someone put a lot of effort into decorating the two-foot-tall artificial Christmas tree next to the television. Each little branch is covered with construction-paper stars, reindeer clothespins, and popsicle-stick snowman ornaments. A strand of dollar-store twinkle lights runs the length of the TV stand, and two Christmas stockings hang off the edge, secured by clear adhesive tabs.

They've tried to make it a home, even though they've only been here a couple of weeks. Not Guy's fault the place has a faint musty smell or the bed comforters are almost as stained as the courthouse's carpeting.

"Daddy, I don't want my jacket," Emma says as she climbs onto the toy-covered bed.

"You'll get too cold without it, Em," he tells her, but when she insists, he helps her out of the jacket and into the llamacorn hoodie I'd seen her in yesterday. Even from where I'm hovering just inside the open doorway, I notice a large bump under the skin of her left inner forearm.

Guy's paying closer attention to me than I realize because he says, "That's her fistula. It's where they give her dialysis."

"Oh. Okay."

I wish I had something better to say, but Guy already starts hustling around the room, packing up his daughter's things with the efficiency of a man who's done this too many times. Emma settles in to play on an inexpensive and well-loved purple child's tablet, as if her daddy moving her out of hotel rooms without warning is nothing new.

"What's your family going to think when you tell them you married a stranger?" I ask, trying to cut the tension between us.

"It's just me and my sister, and she's overseas right now." Guy exhales a tight laugh. "She'll probably think I've lost my mind, but Hayden will understand once I explain the situation."

There's a door connected to the adjoining room, and ripping out the old carpets has left a half-inch gap between the new thinner flooring and the bottom of the door. As I stand there, awkwardly intruding into Guy's and Emma's personal space, I watch the shadow of the next-door occupant moving around from beneath the adjoining door, listening to their feet thump. What would be annoying in the daytime would feel very different at night, and I'm not surprised Emma's bed is the one deeper in the room, away from where a prying eye might be able to look under and see.

"I usually stuff a towel there." Guy must have followed my line of sight, and the expression on his face is tight. "Housekeeping came in this morning while we were gone. They always take it."

"I hate to break it to you, but housekeeping doesn't show up often at the ranch."

Actually, I'm fairly tidy, even if I'm not the kind of person who loves a good deep cleaning, but I get the feeling my vacuuming habits aren't a deal-breaker.

"All we need is a roof and four walls," Guy promises. "Technically a roof and some lumber, because I can slap a few walls up if necessary. Perk of the trade."

"I might even go full luxury and provide some insulation," I joke, cringing at the sound of my own voice. At least he gives me a quick smile in acknowledgment of my attempt at defusing the tension.

His movements are quick and a little jerky as he starts to pack away things in worn reusable grocery bags, pulling color-coded plastic food containers out of the fridge and stuffing them together with a lunchbox-size ice pack from the miniature freezer. I wonder how this would feel in reverse, if I was in Guy's shoes, making these decisions for my child, packing all my belongings up to go to the unknown house of a stranger.

I'd probably be scared sick with stress.

"Is there anything I can do to help?" I ask, shifting on my feet and unsure where to stand. Moving deeper into the motel room feels like an invasion of their privacy. He's grabbing toothbrushes, toothpaste, and deodorant from the bathroom, personal objects with labels that aren't the same as the ones in my bathroom. My brain quietly screeches in horror, not at the objects themselves but at the fact that this is even happening. I'm married again. A stranger and his daughter are moving in…right now. This very minute. I tell myself to hush. *Be braver than this, Sienna.* The world isn't ending because the man uses Sensodyne instead of Crest.

Guy glances at me as he packs his daughter's clothes into a small, beat-up carry-on suitcase with gold and pink lettering on it, spelling out her name. "Are you as completely freaked out as I am?" he asks.

"Yep. How am I doing at covering it?" We share another quick smile, albeit tighter this time.

"You're a shade paler than you were at the courthouse and about three shades paler than at coffee yesterday." He starts to zip Emma's suitcase, pauses as he flexes his fingers, and then Guy exhales a breath. "I can't keep my hands from shaking."

I cross the room and meet him at Emma's bed. His hands didn't falter when he signed the marriage license, but they're trembling now. Guy's strong enough he's liable to accidentally break the worn zipper on her suitcase. I don't know why I do it, but I take his hand in mine.

We need to just pause and take a beat, to breathe and let our brains catch up.

Guy's hand is much larger than mine, and I squeeze his fingers reassuringly.

"I know this is all moving fast, but we *chose* to do this," I remind Guy before tilting my head toward Emma. "For *very* good reasons. We already did the hard part this morning, and the rest of it is just logistics. If that very good reason doesn't feel settled at the ranch or you don't like it there, then we can reevaluate. I promise the ranch is a decent enough place, but it doesn't have to be forever. It doesn't even have to be tonight if you change your mind."

Guy takes a deep breath, then he nods, exhaling slowly. "One day at a time?"

"One day, one hour… I'm kind of winging it here."

"You and me both," Guy murmurs. "Okay, it would probably look weird if we weren't living together, since we're married now."

"Probably." I start to let go of his hand, but my pinkie catches on his index finger. Guy looks down, then turns his hand so our fingers line up, my slender one against his larger, rougher one. My ring finger still holds the pale, smoother circle of skin where my wedding ring used to be.

For a moment, it's all I can do not to cry. I've never felt as divorced as I am right now, fingertip to fingertip with someone else. I've had nowhere near enough time to move on before suddenly finding myself in this situation.

"When I prayed for a miracle, I didn't realize it would come in such a small package," Guy says quietly.

I'm no one's miracle, least of all these two people's. I'm a full bottle of cheap red wine every Friday night in a bubbleless bathtub. I'm a great credit score with no one to buy anything for, a drained bank account even if I had wanted to buy it, and a brutal awareness of the impermanency of the people in our lives. I'm a stuffed daily planner with nothing but the plastic spiral binding surviving after I finished burning my life to the ground.

I look over at Emma and think it doesn't really matter who I am right now. I'll deal with the fallout of my life later, after she gets her kidney. After these two get their own lives back.

"Miracles always come in small packages," I say, tilting my head toward Guy's daughter. For a moment, we stand there, and I realize we're both smiling at Emma. Then I blush and let go of Guy's hand. "Come on. Let's go home."

Chapter 5

I HELP GUY CARRY HIS AND EMMA'S THINGS TO HIS TRUCK AND WAIT while he checks out early.

They must move around a lot, because it barely took him twenty minutes to get all their possessions packed up and us back on the road, headed toward the ranch. The pair seem like old pros at this.

I keep checking in my rearview mirror to make sure they're behind me as I follow the winding river out of town. Yep, it's them, including the little Christmas tree Guy had put on the front passenger seat, properly seat-belted in per Emma's insistence. A string of tinsel catches the morning sunlight and reflects back at me, sparkling with the holiday spirit. Mentally, I add it to the list of unexpected things in my life as of the last twenty-four hours. Scraggly new Christmas tree? Check.

I keep my hands tightly at ten and two, making sure to stay perfectly within the lines and never more than a single mile over the speed limit. As if my brain—stuffed full of undeniable logic—has decided of all the things happening right now, not driving perfectly is the one that will bring judgment my way.

"Text Jess," I tell my phone as I drive. "Hey, I did something today. You know the man from the coffee shop? The one you wanted me to hire? I sort of married him, and he and his daughter are moving in right now. Call me back when you can."

A moment later, my phone chirps with a text message. I tell the car to read the message as I slow down for a particularly tight switchback. "WHAT? In a meeting, can't leave. ARE YOU KIDDING ME?"

The voice dryly dictates Jess's message to me, failing to express their reaction to a sufficient degree. I definitely need a distraction right now, and since Jess is busy, I turn my satellite radio to the news. There's a promising new medication to treat Alzheimer's, but I change the station to some holiday music instead. Four years ago, I would have been hanging on to every word, desperate for something that could have made a difference in my father's health. These medications have come too late for the man sitting in a recliner at the long-term care facility back in town. Dad is too far progressed in his disease for new treatments to do more than slow his mental decline. Nothing will bring him back to who he once was.

Today I turn the music up a little louder to drown out my thoughts.

We're almost to the turnoff for the ranch when Jess's number pops up on my dashboard. "Talk to me, Goose," I say in lieu of a greeting.

Jess doesn't even say hello before launching in. "Okay, on the off chance you are not pulling a retribution prank on me, I called my contact at the police department, and they ran a background check on him. Guy Maple, no priors, no speeding tickets in the last five years. Only listed family is a sister and his daughter. If he's murdering people and hiding them in the woods, he's really good at it."

"That's wonderful," I say, aware my sarcasm is barely covering my panic. "Because we're pulling up to my wooded ranch as we speak."

"Seriously?"

"Yep. The cutie-pie in the llamacorn hoodie is in the back seat of the truck behind me."

There's a long pause, followed by a low whistle. "That must have been one seriously good coffee date. I can't believe I actually tried to cancel your meeting with him. Wait, why were you at the extended stay?

Sanai just texted me that you were spotted over there. Oh, well of *course* you were at the extended stay."

I can practically hear their eyebrows waggling.

"It's not what you think." I roll my eyes. "I didn't hop out of his bed and run straight to the courthouse."

"Such a shame." Jess sighs with playful dramatics. "Here I was living vicariously through you, and you refuse to be tawdry for Christmas."

"Sadly, I'm still myself. And I was helping them move out of the extended stay."

There's another silence as Jess processes the new information. "Maybe not tawdry, but you're definitely not acting like yourself. You've absolutely lost your marbles, Naples."

There's a pause, then I mumble, "It's technically Maple now."

"You changed your name? Oh man, Micah is going to flip. This is getting better and better." Jess eagerly continues on, their mind going a mile a minute. "Aren't you at least going to have a reception? A honeymoon?"

"No? I mean, it's weird, right?" I wonder if between the two of us, we're only capable of bad ideas. I can't imagine anything more awkward than admitting to the people we know, the people who have been gossiping about me for the last year, that I just *hired* a husband.

This time, Jess's sigh is genuine, and they sound disappointed. "Was there at least a cake?"

"There were flowers," I say. "And a prenup saying upon the event of a divorce, Guy gets what he brought into the marriage."

"Which is a big fat question mark. What if he has massive debts? Or a horrible credit score? Or what if he's secretly a CIA agent and he's using you as cover for a covert operation?"

"Then he'd probably have access to better healthcare," I quip.

"Sienna, let's be real here. Why did you actually marry this man?"

I don't tell them why, because...well...the real reason isn't right.

That a good man would have to go to these kinds of lengths to take care of his daughter is all kinds of wrong, and if I tell them, Jess will look at him with pity.

I don't know Guy from Adam, but I know one thing: the man I married deserves better than pity.

"It's complicated," I hedge.

"We're rain checking this conversation because my editor is walking in, and I have to go. Don't get murdered."

"Trust me, I'm trying my best." I end the call as I turn off the main road and cross over the river on a rickety steel bridge, reaching the property line of my family's ranch.

Two heavy cedar logs rest upright on either side of the drive, with a header spanning the width of the gravel. A raw-edge cedar placard dangles from two pieces of chain link below the header, the words NAPLES RANCH burned into the sign in large, clear letters. Even in my distraction this morning, I still remembered to close the gate behind me, so I pause and get out to open it, grabbing the mail from the mailbox and pulling my truck forward. I wave Guy and Emma through, then I close the gate behind me.

There are too many animals on the property to leave it open, even if the nagging voice in the back of my mind reminds me I'm closing myself in with strangers.

It's a good thing Guy drives a truck, because I'm not sure a car could reach the ranch in the winter. Unlike some of the properties deeper in the Frank Church Wilderness, my place is accessible all year long, assuming I spend plenty of time with a snowplow extension on my tractor and keep my truck in four-wheel drive. The layer of heavy gravel gets washed away easily, so it's not a great trek on the best of days. Not a lot of people need chains for their tires to get out of their driveways to a main road, but it's a small, if inconvenient, price to pay for living somewhere this beautiful, this remote, and this free. Ever since I was a child, I've always felt like the ranch was a safe place from the eyes of the world, where I could just be me.

I'm hoping, for a little while, it gets to be a safe place for Emma too.

Two miles is a long driveway for most people. Out here, it's not so abnormal. I go slow, keeping an eye on the truck behind me to make sure they don't slide off the ice pack. Then the drive turns a curve, and the ranch comes into view.

I slow down even more, giving them a chance to take it in. With the snow-covered rocky-faced mountains rising in the background, the dark firs against a blanket of white, and the wisp of smoke coming from the chimney of the two-story log cabin resting in front of the wilderness backdrop, it's a beautiful sight. I pull up to the cabin, parking my truck nose into the split-rail fencing that separates the cabin's front yard and the drive. Lulu and Legs are nibbling at the remains of their breakfast hay by the pen's fence, and behind them, my cattle mill around in the larger cattle pen. Guy parks next to me, so I get out and walk around the front of my truck to meet him. Cattle lowing fills the air, and the earthy scent of livestock mingles with the fresh, crisp mountain air coming down through the river valley.

Guy's gazing around the property, his daughter in his arms. I can't tell what he thinks; his expression is oddly blank. Emma's eyes are wide, and she tugs on his shirtsleeve.

"Daddy, see the horses?"

"Yeah, baby, I see them." He gives her a smile, then turns the look my way, albeit a shyer version. "When you said you had a ranch, I guess I was thinking more work and less—"

Guy gestures to the property, and I have to admit, I can understand.

"Trust me, there's plenty of work," I promise ruefully, but I pause and look around, soaking in the view.

It's even better in summer, because I love being able to see the grass on the ground, but there's something special about the Frank Church Wilderness in winter. Locals spend a lot of time thinking about the logistics of living here, the mud and the snow and the washouts and mudslides. The fires in the summer and the rough river rapids that make transportation upriver so tricky. When was the last time I stood in my driveway and simply inhaled the brisk scent of snow mixing with evergreens?

For a moment, I wish I'd put more effort into decorating for the holidays like I used to before my dad got sick. I haven't bothered to pull the five-foot-wide wreath out of storage and hang it over the entrance of the horse barn. I haven't strung Christmas lights on the porch or hung my mother's favorite reindeer-and-sleigh wind chimes.

From the front porch, Barley manages to rouse himself from his normal ennui and gives a halfhearted woof.

"Daddy, a doggie!"

"He's really good with kids," I promise when Guy glances at me before setting her down. "It's me he's ambivalent toward."

When I whistle for Barley, he comes over, wagging his bushy gray-red tail as he heads straight for Emma, putting his nose in her stomach. She dissolves into giggles, wrapping her arms around his neck. He politely lets Guy pet him, then turns his attention back to Emma, ignoring me completely.

"I see what you mean," he murmurs.

"You'd think I hadn't fed him the last ten years. And I should have asked if either of you have allergies," I say, adding one more thing to the list of what never occurred to me until too late.

"Emma has an allergy to peaches. Not bad, but it leaves her lips red."

"What about you?" I ask.

This time, the smile he passes my way is stronger. "I'm allergic to the bad vending machine food back at the motel."

"Are you hungry?"

Of course he is. One look at this man and I'm hungry. Well…not like that. Mostly not like that. A little like that, but I'm not supposed to be thinking thoughts like this.

"Emma had her lunch on the drive over." Which isn't quite the same thing as "yes, we both ate."

We grab the first of their bags out of his truck, then Guy follows me up the steps of the cabin.

A low whistle escapes him as we enter, and I pause, trying to see what he sees. I've lived here my whole life, so I'm used to the place. What started as a one-room homestead has been added on to over the years with hard work and attention to detail, with my parents' and grandparents' personal touches. The end result is a two-story log cabin with age-marred but gleaming hardwood floors, hand-hewn log walls, and a river rock fireplace that was my mother's pride and joy.

"This is beautiful craftsmanship," Guy says, looking at the fireplace with appreciation.

"Yeah, it almost ended my parent's marriage. Mom insisted on hand picking every stone and each being placed just right. Dad disappeared into the high country for a month after it was done." I smile fondly at the memory, patting a hand on the six-foot-wide live-edge cedar mantle.

Emma starts to take off, but Guy is fast, catching her in a muscled arm. "Gotta take your shoes off first, baby," he says to his daughter.

"It's fine," I tell Emma. "I don't always take my shoes off, so I might be a bad example."

"Your house, your rules," Guy says, standing there looking a little lost.

"Sen-na, why is your Christmas tree empty?" Emma suddenly asks, pointing a finger at the tree I stuck in the corner of the living room last week with nothing but a string of lights and a lopsided star. She's right. It's empty, even though I never thought of it that way.

"I just haven't finished decorating it yet," I say, because it's easier than explaining the full truth. Opening a box of decorations by myself was too much, wine didn't help, and it was easier to have the lights and the star than it was to have a long, one-sided conversation with myself about loneliness during the holidays.

Guy doesn't seem to know what to do with himself. I'm not much help because I have no idea what to do with him either. Emma's easier, the child happily exploring as I give them both a tour.

A nice large kitchen is the newest addition, open to the much more modest original living space, with a large kitchen island and picture windows overlooking the mountainous landscape. The cabin has two bedrooms upstairs, a master with its own small bathroom and a guest room across the hall next to a second bathroom.

There's a third tiny room on the main floor just off the living room that was part of the original cabin and is now my office. Between the desk, the filing cabinets, and too many boxes of my parents' things I haven't had the heart to deal with yet, it's stuffed to the brim. I'm barely able to squeeze in there to work, and turning it into a makeshift third bedroom isn't going to happen anytime soon. So I take them up to the second bedroom, showing them where the second bath is.

"I was thinking Emma could have this guest room across from my room?" I phrase it as a question. "When the second story was added, we put a wood-burning stove in the master bedroom to help heat the upstairs. Most of our power is from the solar panels outside, so it helps to have the extra warmth in winter."

Guy gives the room an appreciative look. It's not huge, but there's enough room for the full-size guest bed, a dresser, and plenty of floor space to play on.

"This will be great," he says. "It's been a long time since Em's had a room of her own."

Our eyes meet, and I'm pretty sure we're both thinking the same uncomfortable thing. Where's Guy going to sleep?

"Umm, the office downstairs could fit a sofa bed eventually," I tell him. "But I need to bulldoze my way through a few things first. Are you okay with the couch for now?"

I mean, we are married and there's a perfectly big queen-size bed across the hall in the master bedroom, but my brain is blanking out at the mere thought. Nope. No beautiful strangers in my bed the second day I know them, married to them or not.

"Anywhere is fine," Guy promises, and he sounds like he means it.

I get the feeling I could ask him to sleep in the barn and he'd probably accept. Emma seems delighted to have her own room, and Barley pushes in between us all, his fluffy tail wagging as he jumps up on Emma's bed. I shoo him off, but he ignores me, which makes Emma giggle. She's got a graying red nose on her leg and massive puppy dog eyes gazing up at her imploringly.

"He likes you, Emma. Barley doesn't bother to come upstairs for me," I tell them, because it's nice to see her smiling. Then I frown at the light layer of dust in the room. "This room hasn't been used in years, and I didn't even consider freshening the bedding. I kind of didn't think any of this through."

"You and me both," Guy murmurs. "I can take care of it if you show me where the laundry is."

His hands keep flexing as he helps me strip the guest bedding, and I show him how to use the laundry in the mudroom off the porch. We load all their food into my fridge, and even though Emma wants to go outside and see the horses, it's nap time. I guess nap time is nonnegotiable, even when horses and new homes are involved. Guy gets Emma settled down on the couch while I switch the sheets over to the dryer.

He joins me, looking like he doesn't know where to stand or if it's crowding me if he tries to help. The awkwardness level is cranked up to a thousand, and I'm not sure whether to laugh or cry, but here we are: two absolute strangers now married and doing laundry.

"Are you okay, Sienna?" Guy asks quietly. "You're pale again."

"And you're shaky again."

We share a quick smile, and he leans back against the wall, stuffing his hands into his pockets, shoulders relaxing in a little slump. "It's been an interesting day. A really good one, but...interesting."

He's not wrong. I look up at Guy, and I wonder if all Montana boys are this tall or if I've just found the tallest one and stuffed him into my laundry room. He's watching me as if I'm the only one in the room, which technically I am. It's enough to make me want to take a step back and reevaluate. But a Naples doesn't back down, especially when the stakes are high. I lift my chin a little higher and meet Guy's eyes, ignoring the fact that they really are the prettiest color of blue.

"Okay, first things first," I say. "What do I need to know about Emma?"

———————

Apparently, there's a *lot* to know about Emma.

The sheer amount of information in front of me is overwhelming. At least Guy has it all organized neatly in a lavender binder with glittery tabs, puffy paint rainbows, and smiley-face flower stickers all over it. The label reads "Emma's Awesome Binder," and I wonder if that's for Guy as much as it is for Emma.

We're sitting at the dining room table, speaking quietly so we don't disturb Emma's nap.

"I've got this arranged by her daily routine in the front," Guy tells me. "I keep track of when she wakes up, how she slept, and how she feels. We do a blood pressure check first thing in the morning and before bedtime when she's feeling good, sometimes at noon if she's feeling bad.

I track everything she eats and drinks, down to the last ounce. If there's anything that helps, anything I can do, it's worth doing." He hesitates, then adds, "She's only allowed a very limited amount of water. Don't be surprised if she doesn't go to the bathroom more than once a day. Sometimes even less. Her kidneys don't work, so she can't flush out liquids and filter waste."

"That makes sense," I say, trying to keep my face impassive so I don't show any emotion that might upset him. I can't help my dad get better, I couldn't help my marriage, but I can pay attention and help Guy and Emma any way they ask. I've already decided to get checked if I'm a donor match for her.

It never occurred to me the little girl was too sick to even pee.

Guy flips a few pages to the "Dietary" tab. "These are what she's allowed to eat, how much, and how often. And here's the medication she has to take every time she eats." He indicates one of several pill bottles on the table in front of us. "Emma needs binders so her body doesn't hold too much phosphorus. I prep her food in color-coded plastic containers, so she knows to have the yellow containers for breakfast, the blue for lunch, and she can have two of the little pink ones for snacks."

"This is a pretty strict diet," I murmur, running a finger down the page of allowed foods. "Does she ever have a hard time with it?"

"The no-dairy one is rough," he admits. "The no chocolate too. She's had ice cream a few times, and she loves it, so it can be a fight when she sees other kids with ice cream. I make fruit-and-ice smoothies she likes, but they have to be milk- and yogurt-free, and no melons or bananas. Most of the time, Emma understands she's special, and it means some treats aren't for her."

"But sometimes she struggles with it?" I glance over my shoulder at the little girl snoozing on the couch.

"Don't we all?" Guy's voice sounds different, and I glance at him, and his jaw is tensed as he looks at Emma, blinking hard. Without thinking, I rest my hand on his, and those blue eyes shift to my fingers. After a brief moment, he rolls his hand just a little so his thumb lightly brushes mine, a silent acceptance of my offer of comfort.

A part of me desperately wants to shove a whole pot roast down this man's throat. But that part has been running roughshod over the rest of me today, so I clear my throat awkwardly and pull back my hand. Instead, I thumb through the book. "So, umm, diet, check. Routine, check. This is the list of Emma's doctors?"

"Yeah. The most important one is her nephrologist, Dr. Sanghvi, and her pediatrician in Idaho Falls. She also has a hematologist and a dietician. She sometimes sees a physical therapist and an occupational therapist to help with some of her pain and her development issues. Not having functional kidneys is brutal on the body, especially when you're supposed to be growing."

It's so much, I can barely retain everything he's saying. The child taking a nap on the couch has more doctor appointments in a month than I've had for years.

Guy's voice drops to nearly a whisper. "I know she's frail, but she's been through so much. Emma's strong. I know she can beat this. She just needs more time."

Unable to stop myself, I reach over and squeeze his hand again. Guy closes his eyes, takes a deep breath, then seems to refocus.

"Umm, that's pretty much it. We have a social worker who tries to help make some of the financial difficulties easier, but she's done as much as she can. Then there's the pediatric dialysis center in Caney Falls. The rest of this is for the transplant list." This time, Guy clears his throat, sounding apologetic. "I hate to ask, but I already emailed my contact with the donation center, and they sent the paperwork for us to fill out."

"The paperwork proving we can afford Emma's anti-rejection medicine?"

"There's no we in this, Sienna," Guy promises. "You won't have to pay any of it. I'll sign whatever you want me to sign so you have legal reassurances, but I won't stick you with the bill."

I nod and say, "Let's look at those forms. No reason why we can't send them in today."

To Guy's credit, he doesn't make any comments about the assets I list on the paperwork. Between the two of us, our liquid cash is meager at best, but adding in the property value of the ranch more than makes up for it. Then he makes a call to whoever has been handling Emma's case. Clearly someone in the office is looking out for Emma, because the approval comes through within an hour.

It's like a physical weight has been lifted off Guy's broad shoulders. He excuses himself and steps out on the porch, and I know I need to give him some privacy. Still, when he returns with red-rimmed eyes and whispers a choked "Thank you, Sienna," I almost tear up too.

A Naples doesn't cry, but for once, I'm tempted to make an exception.

Chapter 6

THERE'S A STRANGE MAN DOWNSTAIRS UNDRESSING IN MY LIVING room.

Everyone has technically gone to bed, so it seems likely varying stages of undress are occurring downstairs. Which means it's not ideal timing to go get a drink of water, but my throat has decided to become the Sahara Desert just to mess with me.

Did I lose the humidifier in the divorce? *Of course* I did.

I'm aware the day has been a lot for my unexpected houseguests, and after introducing them to the cattle, Guy threw himself into helping with chores like a man desperate to prove his worth. Considering I've been managing on my own for the last year, having an extra set of hands was almost as surreal as my updated living situation. Helping Emma get her room made up with her toys and their little Christmas tree was fun, but we literally bumped into each other as we tried to navigate around the kitchen making dinner together.

I'm not sure whether to laugh or cry from the sheer awkwardness. I think maybe this was a really big mistake. Not that I'd take it back, not in an instant, if this helps Emma. But the rest of it is so uncomfortable. Barley doesn't have my problem, because he already made himself at home, curled up next to Emma's bed so she could pet him while Guy read her a bedtime Christmas story.

We're playing house, for all intents and purposes. I'm no better than another motel for them, even if I like to think the property is prettier. And now Guy Maple is married to me and probably in his underwear on my couch. This is…not ideal. I'm not cool and collected. This whole situation has definitely damaged my calm.

I don't want to bother him, but I'm one of those people who gets thirsty overnight, and it feels ridiculous to drink water out of my cupped palm in the bathroom just to avoid going downstairs. This is my house. Just because there's a man downstairs on the couch doesn't mean it stopped being my house. And if he's in his underwear, then I will just deal with it, because I'm an adult, and adults wear underwear.

Usually.

My mind starts to stray as I slip down the stairs, wondering if maybe I've got it all wrong and maybe he doesn't wear underwear and maybe there's a *naked* man on my couch. I keep one eye closed just in case, but nope. There's no one on the couch, because Guy's in the kitchen, in a faded pair of red flannel pajama pants and a T-shirt, on the floor doing push-ups.

One-armed push-ups. Like, the kind people do in movies and TV shows, not the kind that happens in my perfectly innocent kitchen. I've never even seen one of those in real life, and there he goes, driving my poor eyes to distraction as he does ten on one arm, then switches to the other. He's come by those muscles honestly, it appears. And boy, does he have a lot of them. They all seem to be deciding to flex at the same time.

Sweat beads on his forehead despite the evening chill, and I'm pretty sure it's dripping onto my kitchen floor. For a moment, I stand there, finding myself oddly jealous of my floorboards.

With a grunt of exertion, Guy finishes the last push-up and then rolls to his feet before turning and seeing me. We have a lovely, shared moment of us both standing there, our eyes resembling deer caught in headlights. Only he's caught being absurdly sexy and I'm caught watching him.

"Umm, hey," I say, raising my fingers in a painfully awkward mini wave. *Yes, Sienna. That will cover being a voyeur. Well done.*

"Sorry, did I wake you?" Guy looks embarrassed. "I wasn't sure how much sound would carry upstairs. I was trying to be quiet."

"You were," I reply as I move into the kitchen. "I just wanted to get a drink."

The sink is too close to where he's standing, so I head around to the fridge instead. I try to act like it's no big deal to pour some milk into my favorite mug while wearing pajamas, when *all that* is happening on the other side of the island.

"I usually try to get in a quick workout before I sleep." Guy gives me a shy smile, running a hand through his short dark hair, oblivious to how the action makes his arm muscles flex one more time.

Don't say it. Don't say it, Sienna.

"So… I guess I don't have to ask if you even lift, bro?"

He flashes me the kind of grin I should not be seeing at this time of night in my kitchen, when no one is around to stuff my libido back in my pocket but me.

"I used to," Guy admits. "But the more we traveled, the easier it was to just switch to body-weight stuff."

"Ah."

The wise *ah*, as if I know what body-weight stuff is. I can deduce… there was a lot of body-weight stuff just happening on my floor a few minutes ago.

"If this is a bad place, I can go outside," Guy offers.

I shake my head and give him a smile, because the uncomfortable look on his face is back, and I like a relaxed Guy a whole lot better. "It'd make a great Christmas card, but I doubt you'd enjoy push-ups in the snow."

Oh no, did I say that out loud? So this is what it feels like when your entire body cringes. The man actually blushes, but his eyes sparkle, and he looks amused instead of horrified at my joke. I clear my throat.

"Do you lift?"

I wish I could tell him yes, because I see him trying to find some common ground. We don't know what to say to each other when Emma isn't in the room, and that's making this even harder. At least he doesn't add the "bro."

Okay, so we'll talk…lifting. "Outside bales of hay and big mule hooves? Not really. I don't think I've tried to do push-ups since high school. I ran cross-country though."

"You don't seem like the running type," Guy says, his eyes crinkling as he gazes down at me.

"I wasn't fast," I start to say, then realize what he means. He's giving me a compliment. "Oh. Yeah, it's kind of a family thing. We're a stubborn lot. We'd rather dig our heels in, but technically, we can jog if needed."

He looks sweaty, so I pour him a glass of water and hand it to him. Guy's fingers are large, and it's a tall, narrow glass. His fingers brush mine as he takes it with a murmured thanks. I try really hard not to let it affect me, but in the last forty-eight hours, his touch has been the closest to any actual human connection I've had since Micah and I separated.

Suddenly wishing I could take his hand and squeeze it, I retreat to the sink.

"Exercise helps me handle what's going on with Emma," Guy admits. "No matter what else is happening, I can control my own body and my own mind. I can stay healthy and strong for her."

"What do you do for *you*?" I don't know why I ask, but the words just pop out.

Blue eyes linger on me for a moment, then he glances down at the glass in his hands. "I don't know," Guy says quietly. "No one's asked me about me in a long time. I don't think I actually do anything that's not centered around Emma." He hesitates, then his face brightens. "I like rock climbing, but I can't remember the last time I went."

"Good thing we've got lots of rocks." I glance toward the window. If the man wants to climb, he could have married into worse. Half the ranch is on the side of a mountain.

"Hey, I got a call tonight after you went upstairs," Guy brings up. "From one of the guys on the job I just had. The town needs an extra set of hands for the Christmas village they're building in town, and the foreman said he'd let me bring Emma. Unless you need me to stay and help around here tomorrow? I know the ad was a joke, but there's a lot of work here, and I'm happy to help."

"You're allowed to take Emma to the jobsites?" I ask curiously before I realize what he's not saying. He probably takes Emma because he can't afford to leave her in day care.

"When I can," Guy says softly. "It doesn't always work out easily, but Em and I are a team."

"Do you want to leave her here?" I venture, not sure if I'm overstepping my bounds. "There's nothing I'm doing tomorrow I can't do while keeping an eye on her."

Guy shifts uncertainly, glancing up the stairs where his daughter is sleeping in her new room with Barley, who's made it clear he's her dog now, not mine. "Yeah?"

"Only if you're comfortable with it. You don't know me any more than I know you. Leaving her with me is probably a scary thought."

"Leaving her with *anyone* is a scary thought." He sucks in a tight breath. "But my daughter deserves more than dirty hotels and watching videos in the back seat of my truck all day. Are you sure? Her schedule can be a lot."

I move closer to him, leaning on the other side of the kitchen island.

"I mean... We're married now. It would be good to get to know Emma a little better. And it gets quiet around here, so it would be nice to have the company." I try not to make it sound as pathetic as it feels. If I'm being honest with myself, I'm the loneliest I've ever been in my life—not that Guy needs to know.

"I'll ask her in the morning if she wants to stay here or go with me. But knowing my daughter, she'll pick staying here." Guy's voice catches a little, then he blinks rapidly before nodding. "Thank you, Sienna."

"Don't thank me too much. Remember, you're a man about to spend his wedding night on the couch." I tease him, because it's easier than saying what I'm really thinking. *Eat something. Eat everything in this house, and I'll go find more.*

"I'm going to sleep tonight knowing Emma is going to stay on the transplant list," he says in a tone I usually reserve for melted chocolate. "You have no idea how hard I prayed for that. Then God answered me. I'm the happiest man in the world right now."

When he reaches across the island and gently squeezes my hand, I'm tempted to believe him.

Chapter 7

THE LUNCH BOX ON THE KITCHEN COUNTER STARES AT ME. I STARE back at it.

We've been doing this the last couple minutes as the unfamiliar sound of a man getting ready for work filters through the house. Across the kitchen island from me, Emma wriggles in her seat, ignoring the breakfast in front of her.

"Sen-na, what are you doing?" she asks.

"I'm trying to decide if I should pack your daddy a lunch, since he starts his first day of work today." I don't want to overstep here, and I don't want him to think I'm weird. It's just that he's also been hustling around all morning, helping me with chores despite having places to be, and making sure I have everything I could possibly need for a day with Emma alone.

If nothing else, the man is focused.

"Baby, eat your breakfast for Sienna, okay?" Guy says as he comes into the kitchen, pulling a long-sleeve button-up work shirt over the shirt he's already wearing. On a morning this cold, I'm glad he's layering.

"I'm not hungry." As she gets out of her seat, Guy kneels down next to her so they are on the same level. He takes her hand when she starts to head toward Barley.

"Emma, you know how important it is for you to stay nice and strong. Sienna said you can spend the day here with her and Barley, which is going to be a lot more fun than going to work with me. But part of the deal is you have to eat for her and do what she says. Okay?"

She sighs as if greatly put upon, then gets back on her seat. Guy smooths a hand over her hair, dropping a kiss to the top of his daughter's head.

"You sure you don't mind?" he asks quietly, and I shake my head.

"Nope. We're all about having a girls' day over here."

Guy seems unsettled, although it might also have something to do with starting at a new jobsite this morning. We've been up since five, which is normal for me, so he can be at work by seven. I see him stuff an off-brand protein bar into his lunch box along with a thermos of coffee. As he finishes gulping down what was left in his morning mug, I have a feeling those bulk, discount protein bars are part of the reason the man has next to no extra meat on his bones.

He pauses as if mentally calculating something, then adds a second bar into the lunch box. Two protein bars aren't enough to keep a man his size going when working construction in the winter. He'll be burning calories left and right. Guy's been on a very tight budget for a while now, and I wonder how many times he didn't add a second bar even though he needed it.

"I'll be back to say goodbye," he tells us, including me and my almost empty breakfast plate in his quick scan of the room. "I'm going to get the truck started."

I finished my breakfast a few minutes ago, and I've been mostly staying out of Guy's way. He's the single parent in the room, and he's the one who knows what needs to be done before he goes. There's a few more bites of scrambled egg warming on the stove, and he finishes them off before heading outside. Even though I had him park his truck overnight in the detached garage, midwinter in Idaho is rough on an engine if it doesn't get a chance to warm up. As he hustles across the drive toward the garage, I think about how he checked my breakfast plate too, as if making sure we both had enough before he took more. I don't even think he realizes he's doing it.

As my new kind-of-fake husband, there are going to be a lot of changes in Guy Maple's life. Having to take care of me is not one of them.

The lunch box on the counter continues to stare at me. Okay, I just can't. My brain will not allow me to watch him leave with two of the worst-looking protein bars I have ever seen and not at least put up some kind of a fight. I've got about five minutes before he takes off, so I slap together a ham and cheese sandwich, think about it, then make a second. I'm taking a risk here, because maybe he just loves these rock-hard, off-brand protein bars. Maybe he'll be ticked I interfered.

Then I think about the fact that he has eaten everything I've put in front of him and opt for forgiveness instead of permission.

"Can you make them into snowmen?" Emma asks suddenly. "Daddy makes my sandwiches into snowmen."

"Why, yes, I can. Want to help me?"

The thing about sandwich cutouts is they leave a lot of waste trimmings and make the sandwich a lot smaller, so I sneak in a third. Guy's going to have a three-snowperson family in his lunch. All he'll be missing is a snowdog and a snowmule. I stick the sandwich trimmings into a plastic container and back in the fridge, then I stuff a baggie of carrot sticks and some cookies in the lunch box. Then I steal the protein bars back out. The lunch box is heavy enough with the thermos of coffee and the bottle of water he packed that I don't know if he'll notice the extra weight.

I hold up my finger to my lips and wink at Emma. She giggles as she watches me quickly hide the loaf of bread and return to my place at the island, drinking my coffee.

Guy hustles back in, then sighs as he sees his daughter hasn't eaten anything more yet. "Emma, baby, please finish your breakfast."

"Don't worry. We'll do something fun after she's done."

"What are we doing?" Emma perks up.

"I'll tell you after breakfast." I wink at her again as I offer Guy his heavy Carhartt jacket.

"I was going to leave it here for her," he tells me, sounding worried.

"When we go outside, I'll put my spare work jacket over hers. It's the same kind, and it'll fit her better."

Guy gives me an appreciative nod, then he shrugs his jacket on. He gives his daughter a hug and a kiss on the top of her head but hesitates when he looks at me. I tell Barley to stay, and I head to the door with a tall Montana boy at my heels.

I don't know why I walk Guy out to his truck, except I just sort of... want to.

The snow crunches beneath our feet as we head to the workshop on the other side of the drive. The sliding door is open, and the truck lights are turned down low so they don't blind us. A soft rumble of a truck engine on this concrete floor is familiar to me in a way that hits hard. The feeling of walking next to someone in the morning hits deeper.

Guy pauses at the front of the truck, then turns to me. "I'll be back by four thirty probably," he says. "But if you need anything, I'll have my phone on me."

"I'll text if I run into any questions or problems."

"And her meals—"

"I'll log them and what she drinks. And not a drop more today than the water bottle you have in the fridge. And I won't forget the binders when she eats. I'll log that she had her medication too."

"She has a lot of stomach issues. Don't be surprised if it's a fight to get her to eat, but she needs the energy. And if she starts to look puffy..."

"I'll call you right away."

He hesitates, glancing at the house again, and I'm not offended.

Emma's a very sick little girl, and it only makes sense that it's hard for him to leave her with me, a virtual stranger. I've kept my hands tucked into my pockets because I didn't wear a jacket out here. I'm used to the cold, but I'm less used to worried fathers hovering at their truck doors. I step closer and offer him my chilled fingers, squeezing gently as I soften my voice.

"Guy, I promise if Emma so much as sneezes wrong, I'm going to panic and drive to the jobsite. Trust me, the last thing you need to worry about is me not calling you if there's something you need to know. I'll follow your directions to the letter and text you immediately if anything unexpected comes up. I promise to keep you so informed, it'll be annoying every time my face pops up on your phone."

A sweet smile shifts his features from worried father to far-too-handsome pretend-husband-man-fellow. "I'm not sure that's possible. By the way, you look really nice this morning, Sienna."

Confused, I look down at what I'm wearing. Work jeans, check, tennis shoes that will later be changed for muck boots, double check. Boring brown extra-warm sweatshirt. Check check check.

Warm fingertips brush my cheek, asking silently for me to look back upward.

"You really don't see it, do you?" Guy's expression has softened, and I'm trying really hard not to read too much into it when he smiles again. His arm goes around my waist in the briefest of hugs, and then he steps away. "Have a good day, Sienna."

I'm sure I just imagine it when he gives me a little wink.

———

"You said we're doing something fun," Emma reminds me after she's finished enough of her breakfast that I can feel comfortable calling it good.

"We are going to make Christmas stockings for the animals."

I don't know why that pops up in my mind, but I used to love decorating stockings for the animals when I was little. It seems like the kind of thing she might enjoy. Plus, if I get a decorating station set up in the barn, I can clean stalls, scrub water buckets, and work on fixing the barn roof while keeping an eye on Emma.

"For all of them?" she asks, and I nod.

"Yep, for all of them. But let's just make one for all the cows. They don't mind sharing."

I log how much she ate and drank in her rainbow sparkle–colored tablet, then I take a picture of the info on the off chance I didn't do something right. Text of the day number one: sending Guy a screenshot of her breakfast. Then I take a picture of Emma making a silly face from behind her chair, and I send that too. Guy's probably in town by now, but I get an immediate reply of a heart on the first picture, and then a picture comes in of him parked in town, still in his truck and making a silly face just like Emma's, only from behind his coffee tumbler. She giggles when I show her the pic.

Thank goodness for Emma's art supplies, because if it were just my stuff, we'd be making Christmas stockings out of my old socks and a dried-out Sharpie. Emma's got everything we need, including enough felt to make a barn full of Christmas stockings.

After I make a sock-shaped cardboard pattern, she helps me trace the pattern onto the felt with my Sharpie. Emma makes a big production of asking Barley what decorations the horse, mule, and donkeys prefer while I cut the socks out for her. I stifle my giggle when she tells me the cattle don't like Christmas, not even Jerkface, so she doesn't want to make them a stocking. Clearly they aren't as fun as the other animals right now, but I'm guessing she'll change her mind after she sees her first cute little calf in springtime.

When she's done decorating the stockings, I'll superglue them at the seams, but there's a lot of work waiting for me today. I get Emma dressed in her warmest-looking clothes, and the three of us and our art supplies head off to the barn.

I'm not ashamed to admit that hanging out with Emma is the most fun I've had in a really long time.

I nab the portable heater from the garage and take it over to the barn with us. Portable heaters in barns are dangerous, because all it takes is forgetting to turn one off just once, and you have a barn fire. My animals have thick, warm winter coats, and I've got a stack of horse blankets if it drops too cold. Before Emma, I never used a portable heater in my barn except for the absolute coldest days, but I have a feeling I'll be using it a lot more. If she likes spending the day with me, I'm going to need to think of better ways to make the barn more Emma-friendly.

I lay down an unused horse blanket on a few bales of hay in the barn, making a comfortable workstation for Emma. The heater goes on top of an overturned bucket so it's at a good height for her and far away enough from the hay so I won't be watching it every other second to make sure it didn't get knocked over into the haystack.

Barley sticks to Emma like glue, following her around anytime she moves and sitting beside her on the hay bale, so close she's leaning on him half the time. Barley watches her with liquid brown eyes as she throws herself into decorating with the kind of enthusiasm I haven't felt in a long time.

"Sen-na?" The sound of my name pulls my attention over to where Emma is decorating Legs's stocking. "How will Santa know where to find us?"

She doesn't sound worried, but she's such a carbon copy of her father. There's this tiny expression change that gives her away. It's in the way they tighten their mouths, although easier to see with Guy and his stronger jaw.

"Did your daddy send in a change of address form to the post office when you and he moved here?"

Emma tilts her head, thinking about it. "I'll ask him later."

That works.

"Or *you* could ask him now," she adds.

I smile despite myself, then sneak a glance over at the little girl. She giggles when she sees me looking, and I playfully sigh and pull out my phone. I can already tell Emma's got my number. Telling her no is going to be beyond hard, and especially when it's Santa related.

I dictate a text message to Guy so she knows what I'm saying. "Emma wants to know if you put in a change of address at the post office so Santa can find you."

I wait, and then three little dots begin to move on my phone, indicating he's texting me back. I show her my phone and read Guy's reply out loud to her.

"He says, 'Oops. Tell Em I'll swing by after work and fast-track it so Santa doesn't get mad at me.'"

At her expression of alarm, I ruffle the knitted hat on her head, and I dictate a second text. "No worries. Just send me your previous info, and I'll do it over lunch."

There's more than enough work around the barn where I can keep an eye on Emma, so I switch to replacing a board Legs kicked and split in his stall. Emma is deep in her decorating, and I move on to digging out the hard-packed snow around the stall runout doors connecting the barn stalls to the horse pen. I had barely been able to slide them open after the animals had their morning grain. Legs wanders over to see what I'm doing, and Emma giggles when she sees the tall mule lipping at the collar of my jacket.

"Sen-na, why doesn't Legs live inside with us like Barley?"

I pause, then look at him. "Legs? Why don't you live inside with us?"

I love how Emma laughs when Legs snorts and wanders away. I swear the mule knew exactly what he was doing when he started shaking his head as if horrified at the very idea.

About an hour later, I get another text from Guy. It's a picture of his lunch box, opened to the stack of sandwiches.

When a good day gets better, he sends, including a smiley heart emoji and a drooling emoji.

The man emoji'd me. Twice. Oh dear, things seem to be getting serious.

"Sen-na, did Daddy say something funny?"

"Hmm? Oh, he just thanked us for the lunch. Why?"

"'Cause you're smiling."

Hmm, maybe I am. After Emma finishes with the stockings, I tell her we'll glue them tonight inside the house, where the glue will set up better.

I'm not used to coming back inside during the brightest, warmest hours of the day, but Emma's lunchtime is at noon, and I dutifully give her the lunch Guy has ready for her in the fridge.

She picks at her lunch just like she did for breakfast, and this time, she doesn't eat as much. A text to Guy gives me a thumbs-up that she's eaten enough, and I record it just as promised. Emma looks tired, and Guy has it written down on the "Emma Sheet" that twelve thirty to two is her nap time. She promises me she always naps with her headphones on and her show on her tablet when her daddy is working, so I go along with it. If it's not what Guy wants, he can talk to Emma tonight.

I'm very aware I'm not a permanent presence in her life, and the last thing I want to do is overstep.

Emma wants me to watch the show she's picked—a cute holiday cartoon with Rudolph and a little kid Santa—so I settle in against her headboard and listen through my own earbuds while Barley stares at me coldly for taking his place. Since she's out within a couple minutes, I give up my seat to the dog and sneak out of the room. Which means I have an hour and a half to stop and think about this situation I'm in right now.

The blanket Guy used to sleep on the couch is neatly folded, with his pillow smoothed and lying on top of it. I don't know if he's just a very tidy person or if it's the same courtesy one would have when staying as a guest in someone's house. I had noticed his suitcase tucked in the corner of Emma's room, just as neatly set out of the way.

For such a big cabin, there's zero actual space for him.

The stacks of plastic storage tubs in my office are just…overwhelming, but I finally have a reason to try to clear them out some. My parents' things are in these tubs, and back when Dad was more himself, he told me to go through them, keep what I want, and get rid of the rest.

I'm not ready, not anywhere close, but I can work on moving the tubs up the stairs and over to my room. I work quietly, hoping Emma's headphones keep her from waking up. It's hard work, especially trying to tiptoe on squeaky wooden stairs, but I make a solid enough dent in the project to feel like at some point, Guy will have a bit of privacy.

I flop down in my office chair, so lost in thought about my new roommates, I nearly jump out of my skin when the landline phone rings loudly right next to me.

It's still set at a higher volume ring from back when my dad was here and had a hard time hearing the phone. I grab it without checking the caller ID, wincing because I'm afraid the noise may have just woken up Emma.

"This is Sienna," I say, craning my head to see through the study door, just in case little feet appear at the top of the staircase.

"We need to talk."

And that's why you always check the caller ID. I grimace, feeling the tension in the back of my neck ratchet up.

"Hello to you too, Micah."

There's something about the people you've known your entire life. The people who've known you their entire lives. There's no hiding from them, not in a town this size. There's no pretending everything is fine. And when you spent all of high school, all of college, and another ten years of marriage with a person, even if you hate it, they know you. You know them.

And you can tell when they are furious.

"Our insurance company sent over something to me."

Ahh, yep. Since Micah is the insurance plan administrator now instead of me, I suppose the insurance company would send over notice of my change in status. Well, I suppose it's one way for him to find out.

"I'm assuming this is some kind of mistake."

"It's not a mistake, Micah," I tell him, closing my eyes to brace myself.

The moment of silence from the other side of the phone is like the calm before the storm. No matter how he reacts, I will not engage. What I choose to do with my life is my business. I don't owe him any explanations.

"You got married the day after our divorce finalized?"

"Sen-na?" a sleepy voice says from the study doorway. She looks confused and a little uncertain, and she hasn't had as much of a nap as Guy said she needed. "I'm thirsty."

"Okay, baby, I'm coming. Micah, I'm sorry, but I can't talk right now. Goodbye."

I can't fight with Micah and double-check Emma is getting a safe amount of liquid at the same time. He starts to say something else, but I hang up the phone.

I text Guy to confirm the amount of water Emma is allowed, and he replies back immediately, so I don't have to be stressed about an upset, thirsty Emma. Barley presses his nose against my hand as I put Emma back in bed to finish her nap, and I realize the fury in Micah's voice still has me a little shaken. So this time I finish watching Emma's show even after she falls asleep, and when she's napped long enough, I put a smile on my face and focus on my afternoon with her. Emma knowing she has a safe, comfortable place to live is more important than my ex rattling me.

Still. Too many conversations like today have happened with Micah, and I wish I had never taken the call. Some triggers are just more hardwired than others.

I keep a close eye for signs Emma's too cold or getting weary, but she seems to be happy as a clam to stay with me as I work. Maybe it's from growing up being on jobsites with her father, but she's very good at picking a place to play and not leaving the spot.

She especially likes riding on the ATV with me when I go to check on the cattle.

I'm going to need to ride the fence line soon and check for any downed poles or loose wire, but there's a big difference between hanging out with me on an ATV and riding horseback up and down the mountains in winter. That task is just going to have to wait for the weekend when Guy's off work.

There's absolutely no doubt in my mind if I said I couldn't watch Emma that he'd take her to work without blinking twice. But the truth is I like having company. Unlike Legs and Barley, when I talk to Emma, she talks right back.

My phone chirps at me as we get back to the barn.

"'Leaving the site, need anything from town?'" I read out loud because Emma had seen her father's photo pop up on my screen.

It's been a really long time since someone asked me that. It's been even longer since I felt a little thrill of anticipation that comes with someone being on their way home.

"Take it down a notch, Naples," I murmur to myself.

"Sen-na, aren't you a Maple now, like us?" Emma asks me.

Clearly, one can't get anything by these sharp ears, not even a mutter at my own very confused libido. "Yep, that's right."

I reply to his text with a no thank you, hesitate, then add a smiley face. I can't remember the last time I smiley faced a man, but it probably stopped around the time I stopped shaving my legs before a Friday night because my television streaming service and carton of ice cream couldn't have cared less how hairy I was.

We are starting the evening feeding when the sound of a vehicle coming up the drive makes Barley's head come up. He doesn't bark the way he usually does, and I glance out the barn door to see Guy's truck.

"You don't know him yet. You do realize this, right?"

Barley thumps his tail once to acknowledge my comment, but then he turns his head back to Emma, muzzle on his paws and staring up at her with big brown eyes.

"I think Barley loves you, Emma."

"Aww. I love him. *So* much." When she hugs him around the fluffy neck, Barley starts licking her neck and ear, which only causes Emma to dissolve into giggles.

"Is this where the party is?" I hear Guy say as he pokes his head into the barn.

This is a lot dirtier version of the man who left this morning, and whatever he was doing in between emojis, it must have been hard. But Guy seems full of energy as he goes straight for his daughter.

"There's my girl." Guy sweeps her up into a huge hug. "I missed you today, baby."

She doesn't return the sentiment apparently, because Emma launches into a babbling account of all the things we've done today, what she liked, what she thought was silly, and what she liked despite it being silly.

"It looks like I missed out on all the fun," Guy says with a chuckle. "Hey, Sienna. Thanks for watching Em today."

"She was great company." I smile at him in greeting, and there's this awkward moment when I'm not sure if I should hug him or not. If he was just a friend, I'd hug him, or if we were dating, I'd hug him. But this whole married-with-zero-chance-to-get-to-know-each-other situation has kind of warped the normal rules. Still, I don't want Guy to feel like I don't care he came back.

"I put some coffee on when you texted you were on your way," I say instead, because nothing says "sorry I have no social skills" like caffeine.

"That sounds great. Want a cup?"

"No, thanks. I don't drink caffeine after noon." Trust me, I want to, but sleep comes hard enough as it is these days.

"Coffee first, then put me to work," he tells me, and I almost take him up on it. But after a first day at a new job, the last thing I'd want to do is jump headfirst into more hard labor.

"We're almost done if you want to grab a shower."

Guy hesitates, then he nods and leans over, ruffling Barley's ears before giving my dog a pat.

When he leaves, Emma gives me an interesting look. "Daddy looks at you funny."

"Maybe your daddy thinks I'm funny-looking," I tell her, making a silly face. Emma squeals with childish laughter, and yes, it's a little high-pitched, but I love hearing her laugh. We chase each other around the barn until finally Legs kicks his stall door in protest.

"Oops, guess we better get to work. Old man grumpy pants over there isn't happy with us." He probably just knocked loose the new board I put up, but I don't mind.

And as I start to feed the horses, I have to admit that maybe, just maybe, I look at Guy funny too.

Chapter 8

THERE'S A MAN COOKING DINNER IN MY KITCHEN. AND HERE I thought one-armed push-ups were the sexiest thing that could happen in there.

His dark hair is still damp, and there's moisture beading along the side of his neck as the scent of an unfamiliar shampoo mixes with the aroma of something equally unfamiliar grilling in a pan. He's changed into sweatpants and a T-shirt, and I can't help admiring how good the shirt looks stretching across his muscled shoulders.

The man is still too thin though. I should have stuck one more extra snowman into his lunch. I can't help sneaking in closer to the stove, sniffing curiously. Whatever it is he's cooking, it smells good. I'm not sneaky enough, because he catches me watching.

"Hey," Guy says, giving me a shy smile. "You were still working, so I got started on dinner. I hope you don't mind?"

"Feeding me is always a good thing," I promise him. "What are you making?"

Guy tilts the pan my way, looking proud. "These are Emma's favorite kind of veggie burgers. She has to be careful what protein sources she eats, but these are good. I make a bunch of them at a time so we have leftovers. They're easy to cook up on a hot plate when we're traveling."

So now I know what some of the containers in my fridge are. I was too busy today to go poking my nose around in them, despite being curious.

Guy suddenly stills, looking down at his pan and the browning burgers. "And it's just occurring to me you're a cattle farmer." He squeezes his eyes closed as if mentally berating himself, and his voice shifts to a more stressed-sounding version of himself. "Okay, I can make you something else."

I join him by the stovetop and pat his arm to reassure him. The happy, relaxed man I saw in the barn is gone, and I don't want that for him. Not because Guy was just trying to make Emma a healthy dinner.

"Don't worry. Since I'm the daughter and former daughter-in-law of multigenerational cattle farmers and the former co-owner of one of the largest cattle farms in the state of Idaho, people *think* I've never actually eaten a veggie burger." I give him a quick smile. "And they'd be wrong. These look delicious."

And if it's awful, I'll choke it down, and he'll never be the wiser.

"Anything I can do to help?" I ask. The look he gives me is hard to read, but then he shakes his head with a bemused smile.

I settle into a seat at the kitchen island, watching a stranger try to find his way around my cooking utensils. There's a salt grinder near the stove, and I notice he doesn't touch it. Instead, he sprinkles seasoning from a small Tupperware container onto the burgers. Everything he's making is homemade and, from the look of it, as healthy as humanly possible.

Guy's doing what he can to keep his daughter safe and healthy.

"How was Emma today?" Guy asks as if reading my mind, his voice dropping with seriousness.

I think about the day, about what she said and did, filtering through the lists he'd given me about her condition.

"She wanted to drink more than you said she could, and she didn't like the restriction, but it wasn't an issue. And like yesterday, her appetite isn't much. I logged her lunch and snack in the tablet like you showed me."

"Thank you."

"You already knew, didn't you?"

Guy gives me a quick smile over his shoulder. "I have access to the food log from my phone, and it pinged me anytime you entered something. If it happens again, it's okay to give her a few ice chips or one of the mouth swabs in her bag. She likes the lemon ones more than the mint-flavored."

His smile triggers a memory of a conversation earlier with his daughter. "Emma thinks you look at me funny," I joke.

"I do look at you funny." Guy laughs and lowers the heat before turning and resting his arms on the island catty-corner from me. "A gorgeous woman sent me to work with snowman cutout sandwiches and Oreos, took care of my daughter all day, and made Emma laugh in a way I haven't heard in forever. And when I came home, there was coffee waiting for me. If I'm looking at you funny, it's because I'm trying to figure out if I'm hallucinating all this."

I don't expect the gorgeous comment, and my face heats up.

"I'm currently hallucinating a dinner that doesn't involve me doing anything," I reply, leaning over in my seat and giving his waist an impulsive hug.

When Guy realizes what I'm doing and wraps his muscled arm around my shoulders, squeezing gently, I realize I've made a critical error here. The man gives an excellent hug, and I've been working with a severe deficit.

You're leaning too long, my brain tells me, but it takes a moment for me to force myself to pull away. My face must be beet red now because my cheeks feel hot. As soon as I drop my arm, he moves away.

"Sorry," I mumble, because clearly, I can't be trusted to not plaster myself all over him.

"I'm not. It was a great way to end a great day." Guy opens the lid on a pot of brown rice, and a rich scent hits my nose, making my mouth water. He scoops out a little bite of it, offering me the spoon. "Here, tell me if you want this hotter. I went with mild seasonings because I wasn't sure if you liked spicy."

"What about Emma?" I have my list of rules, and avoiding spicy foods is in there.

"I set aside her rice before I seasoned it." Guy waggles the spoon at me, so I accept the bite of rice.

I definitely miss the sodium, but the subtle flavors of garlic, onion, and curry are delicious. True, if I were alone, I'd drop a slab of butter on my rice and grind up the saltshaker for a while, but these two don't just choose to eat healthy. They *need* to eat healthy. Already, my brain is starting to make the mental switch.

"Yum," I decide. "And go as hot as you want. I'm not afraid."

He dips into a second small Tupperware of seasoning, and soon the scent of heated chili pepper makes Barley sneeze in the living room.

While Emma tries to teach Barley how to use a tissue, Guy portions out the veggie burgers on scoops of rice, and I set the table. We sit down to eat together, and the whole situation is…surreal. We're a picture of domestic bliss, except for the tiny little part where it's all a lie. A complete and utter lie. It hits me hard all of a sudden, how this was supposed to be what Micah and I should have had, only a real version. Not the version where I've never even been on a date with the man across from me, unless you count meeting at the Daily Grind.

"What was the job like?" I ask, trying to distract myself.

"Good." Guy sounds pleased. "We got a lot done, so the foreman was happy."

I try desperately to think of something else to say, but nothing comes. An old song plays in my mind, the lyrics messing with me. *This is not my beautiful house. This is not my beautiful wife.*

This is not my beautiful life, my brain adds of its own accord.

I don't regret helping them, but it's different when Guy's in the room. The fun, relaxed day with Emma was easier. Having Guy sitting within arm's reach feels entirely different, almost as if the air between us is charged. I'm overly aware of his presence, of the sound of his voice, of his low laughter when Emma says something he thinks is funny. His hands are particularly distracting, especially connected to the muscled forearms resting on my dining table.

The same hands I recognized as familiar yesterday suddenly seem very large, very male, and very new.

"Can we, Sen-na?" Emma asks, pulling me from where I was watching Guy's hands.

Blinking, I try to focus on Emma and recall what she just said.

"I doubt Sienna wants to make a whole new set of stockings, Em." Guy saves me from my inattention. "One for each animal is just fine."

"But Legs is big. He should have two."

"She makes a fair point. But Dunkin and Paddlewhack are small. Should they only get half a stocking?"

Emma giggles and shakes her head.

Guy's eyebrow raises. "Dunkin and Paddlewhack?"

"The *donkeys*, Daddy." Emma gives him a look that says he's embarrassing her.

Guy grins at me. "Oh, the donkeys. Sorry, I'm still learning everyone's names."

Emma launches into a description of all the animals, and I'm impressed by how much she's retained just from being here for a short time. It's a lot of information, and despite Guy giving his daughter his complete attention, he's looking a little lost.

"Don't worry, I didn't name the cows. Just the bull," I murmur to him.

We agree the donkeys aren't losing any stockings, and only Legs is getting a second one. Guy logs Emma's food and liquid with a few quick taps of his fingers, much more quickly than I did today. There are so many tiny things happening around me, and they're all new.

This is not my beautiful life.

"Daddy, are you going to stress-ercise?"

"Not until after everyone goes to bed."

"Why?"

Guy glances at me, but I don't know why any more than Emma does. "I don't want to get in Sienna's way, sweetie. Her routine and our routines are different. We're kind of taking over the house, and she deserves some peace from our noise."

"I don't mind the push-ups."

Why did I say that? Why didn't I just say I don't mind the exercise?

I clear my throat, adding, "This is your home too. Whatever makes you two happy. We'll get our routines blended."

He's smart, and I can see him watching me out of the corner of his eye. I have a feeling Guy knows I'm unsettled, but I don't think he's going to ask me about it in front of Emma.

We finish eating, and even though my mouth enjoyed the meal, my stomach is resisting the sudden change of food and spices. A little walk will probably do me good, and I need to take a beat and try to recenter.

"I need to go double-check the cattle gate," I tell him. "Leave the dishes for me, okay? You cooked, so I'll clean."

Checking the gate isn't a lie, although I already checked it earlier today. I know because I have my list on my phone, and there's a little mark next to "Evening chores, check the gate." I just need to step away for a minute because good intentions aside, this is a lot. A lot of new. A lot of noise and brightness and laughter and changes and too-nice hugs.

I haven't eaten dinner with someone else for over four months.

When I return to the house, I end up lingering on the porch, and I'm sitting on top of the wooden rail when my phone chirps. I glance down at the number calling and feel a rush of relief at the much-needed normalcy. Sometimes it feels like in a world of texting, Jess and I are the only ones who still like to talk on the phone.

"Hey, good timing," I tell them. Somehow Jess always seems to know when to call.

"I was promised details, and so far, all I have are pictures of a cutie-pie making stockings in the barn," they say by way of greeting. "Please tell me you're in Aruba right now."

"Nope, I'm sitting on the railing, listening to the moos. The moon is pretty tonight, isn't it?"

"Spill, woman. I refuse to hit dating apps during cuffing season, so I'm living vicariously through you."

"Cuffing season?"

"People who would rather be single but who lock it down with someone over the holidays so they won't be alone. I mean, most don't go so far as to marry them, but…"

I exhale a small laugh. "I think I went beyond a cuff and did a full ball and chain on this," I joke as I watch Jerkface lumber toward the water trough.

Maybe something in my tone gives me away because they wait a moment for me to continue, and when I don't, Jess asks, "Are you okay?"

"Yep."

Nope. Nope nope nope.

"If you weren't okay, would you tell me?"

My heart warms at their gentle prodding. "Don't worry. Guy's nice. I think I'm just still getting used to having male energy around the house again. He's a good cook though."

"The fact that he cooked is raising my opinion of him already. How about the stepdaughter?"

A sigh escapes me. "Emma's perfect. Adorable. Brilliant and so much better to talk to than Barley."

"A sack of potatoes is better to talk to than Barley. Let's have dinner soon because I want to meet them. Oh hey, I've got to go. My date's about to arrive."

"I thought you weren't participating in cuffing season," I remind them.

"And *I* thought you were going be in Aruba right now."

I can practically hear Jess waggling their eyebrows, so I end the call with a laugh and a "Be safe."

Dating is scary for all of us, and I don't know what I would do without them.

Jess and I have spent a lot of holidays together. I'm lost in memories of running around the yard with them and Charley as a child, throwing snowballs and making snow ponies in the front lawn, when I hear the squeak of the door opening behind me. I look over my shoulder, my hands tightening on the railing for balance.

Guy gives me a tentative smile as he sticks his head out. "Are you up for some company?"

"My porch is your porch," I say, patting the railing in invitation.

He props the door open a bit so we can still hear Emma call, and he meets me at the rail. "I wasn't sure if 'check the gate' meant check the gate, leave me alone, or follow me and let's flirt with each other under the moonlight. Since I'm hoping for the last one, I brought a cookie to break the ice."

I blink and then find myself laughing despite myself.

"Feeding me treats is a really good opener," I promise, accepting the small bakery box he offers me. I know he's joking about flirting, but when I look inside the box, I see a frosted sugar cookie shaped like a snowflake and dusted with blue and silver sugar crystals. "This might be the best pickup line I've ever gotten."

"I wanted a snowman to continue the trend, but this was prettier." He must have picked it up after work, because it's from the best place in town and definitely *not* renal-diet friendly. "Is Emma still awake?" The cookie looks delicious, and I don't want to eat it in front of her.

"Yep. She doesn't want to take a bath before bed until she asks you a super-important question, which she wouldn't share with me." Guy sounds amused. "Now she's watching *Rudolph* with Barley."

"The cute cartoon one she had on earlier or the creepy puppet one with the terrifying snow monster?"

"Terrifying snow monster and island of misfit toys."

I shudder. "That one stayed with me, but hey, more power to Emma if she likes it. Well, supersecret important questions take precedence." I start to move, but Guy signals for me to stay.

"She's happy on the couch, and I can see her through the window," Guy promises. "She can wait a minute."

"Is that how this works?" I ask him, earning a second, softer laugh.

"No, I pretty much come when called. If you manage to tell her no, teach me the trick of it. Em's had me wrapped around her little finger since she was born." He leans against the post next to me, looking out at the edges of the cleared part of the ranch. "Do you have to worry about bears out here?"

"Sometimes we get them and some wolves too, although they tend to stay higher in the range. More often than not, it's a coyote causing trouble, going after the calves or colts. They're why I have Dunkin and Paddlewhack."

"The donkeys?"

"Yep. Dunkin and Paddlewhack, like all donkeys worth their salt, absolutely hate coyotes and will run them off the herds. I pair them with the cattle each season. Seriously cuts down on losses. Paddlewhack especially loves his calves, so try not to get him riled up."

I wink at Guy to let him know I'm teasing…mostly.

"Why did you name him Paddlewhack?"

"Because if I ever tried to get him to work, I'd probably have to whack his butt with a boat paddle," I joke. "Not that I ever would. Besides, guarding babies is what he's the best at, so I leave him be, and he keeps them safe for me. It's a good relationship, built on mutual understanding of each other's limitations. I suck at running down coyotes, but I only have two feet."

"You like animals a lot more than people, don't you?"

"Depends on the people." I lean over and nudge his shoulder with my elbow. "The donkeys never make me dinner."

Guy gives me a kind look. "Never in my entire adult life has anyone but a drive-through window made me lunch. I think I stared at my lunch for a full minute before I realized it was actually mine."

"What you're saying is we're the pretend-married version of Dunkin and Paddlewhack?"

"I can think of worse things to be." Guy grins down at me. "Relationship goals, right?" He pauses, then adds, "Do you want some time out here alone? Emma can ask her supersecret question after a bath, despite what she's convinced herself."

"No, I'm good." And I am, despite being overwhelmed. Probably because after a lot of years of not having someone care enough to check on me, I appreciate he's out here.

Suddenly he blinks, then turns to look through the windows to where Emma is still sitting with Barley. "I grew up near Yellowstone," Guy tells me. "There were always bears wandering in and out of town, so I'm used to double-checking for wildlife when I'm outside. But I never even thought to ask you if there were weapons in the house."

"You mean you forgot something in between a wedding, moving, and starting a new job in a twenty-four-hour span?" I gently tease.

"Admittedly, it's a pretty big oversight."

I nod. "True. For what it's worth, almost all the guns were Micah's, and he took them with him. I only keep a rifle locked up in the gun safe in my closet in case an accident happens and I have to put one of my animals down. I don't like guns, so I don't keep it on me when I'm riding or working. I carry bear spray and an air horn instead. Both do a plenty-good job at keeping wildlife at bay. The code for the safe is my mom's birthday, if you ever need it. I'll write it down for you."

Guy nods, accepting what I say as truth. Which is a whole lot nicer than the constant arguments I'd had with Micah because I don't like guns. I eat my cookie, watching the way the moonlight gleams on the snow-covered mountains around us.

"What about your parents? Are they in Montana? You said you have a sister overseas, but you've never mentioned them."

"My sister and I grew up in foster care."

I blink at his unexpected answer. "That must have been difficult."

"It was, but we were lucky. We only got shuffled around a couple homes before we were placed together with really nice foster parents. They kept us together and made sure we knew we were loved. They take in a lot of kids, so they have their hands full, but we still keep in touch on birthdays and holidays. They can't leave Montana very often, but my foster parents were some of the first to get tested when Emma got sick. They're good people."

"What's your sister like?" I don't know why I'm asking so many questions, but it's easier to focus on him and Emma right now than on my own feelings.

Guy chuckles. "Hayden was wild growing up. Well, we both were, but she has this no-holds-barred approach to life I was always envious of. She's a year older than me, and she left right before I found out about Emma's illness." His face grows more serious. "Hayden was tested too when Emma got sick, but she wasn't a match for Em. We both tried to find our birth parents, but the records were sealed. It's better to have a kidney from someone her same size, but it was worth a shot."

"Is it hard not knowing what happened to them?"

"It used to bother me a lot, but after Emma got sick, a lot of things didn't matter as much anymore." He's quiet for a while, then says, "Are you okay, Sienna? Did I do something to upset you? I feel like we ran you out of your house."

The fact that he didn't say "did we upset you" makes me respect him even more. I almost tell him the same thing I told Jess, but then I hesitate and reconsider.

"No, you both were fun tonight," I reassure him, and as I say the words, I know they're true. "I don't know why I started feeling overwhelmed in there. I've lived my whole life in this house, on this property, and you both have a lot more change happening than I do."

"You have two people in your home, eating your food, stealing your shower and your dog," he reminds me. "If you weren't feeling overwhelmed, I'd ask to have some of what you're having."

I break my cookie in half and offer him part.

Guy chuckles but shakes his head. "You watched my daughter all day. You earned that cookie."

"Emma's welcome with me anytime. I like having someone to talk to. It gets lonely out here."

His muscled arms cross on the railing next to my leg, not too close but close enough I feel a silent comradery in his company.

"Hey, Sienna? If this gets to be too much, I'll understand. Just because you're helping us out for now doesn't mean you have to help us forever. You made my daughter happy today, which means a whole lot more to me than you realize."

"She made me happy too."

Guy's quiet for a moment before whispering softly, "Emma is the best thing to ever happen to me."

He doesn't say out loud that he's losing her. He doesn't have to. It lies between us, a truth that brought two strangers together. There's a reason why it's okay tonight was overwhelming. The reason has a supersecret question and a father who's beside himself trying to fix something he just can't make better.

For a moment, just a moment, I want to lean over and rest against his shoulder. Instead, I hand him half of the cookie, and in the quiet of the winter moonlight, we share it together.

Chapter 9

A FOOT OF SNOW DROPS IN THE COLD OF THE NIGHT, AND IT'S STILL falling when my alarm beeps softly, telling me it's time to get up.

Guy hasn't been here long enough to realize the lane into the property will be unpassable, and showing up late for work on the second day of a new job isn't the best look. I dress as quietly as I can, tiptoeing down the darkened stairs and avoiding the boards where I know they creak. The living room is chilly this early in the morning, and the man-size lump on the couch has both blankets piled up on top of him. If he's been getting cold at night, he hasn't mentioned it.

Something tells me that cold or not, Guy will never mention it.

He's just so *different* from my ex. Micah worked hard, but he never had a problem telling me or anyone else what he was thinking. If he'd spent a cold night on the couch, Micah would have been grumbling and blustery about it to anyone within earshot. I wonder if Guy isn't a complainer or if things have been so hard, he doesn't even register an uncomfortable night on the couch. Either way, I need to make sure to add extra wood to the fireplace woodstove, because Emma and I might be toasty warm upstairs, but clearly Guy isn't.

The real cold hits me as I step into the mudroom, my sock-covered feet protesting the icy concrete. I pull on a pair of coveralls, thick fleece-lined work gloves, and my warmest hat before stuffing my feet into my work boots. Then I glance at the thermometer hanging outside the window and grimace at six degrees Fahrenheit. A single-digit morning is never a great way to start the day, and I add a heavy winter jacket on top of my coveralls.

In this getup, I always feel like a kid in too-thick winter clothing, straight out of *A Christmas Story*. I head to an old, repurposed, and somewhat dilapidated wooden cattle shed tucked behind the cattle pen; it's now my tool shed. My great-grandparents built this with their own hands, and restoring the shed to its former glory is on my never-ending list of things I'd love to get done someday.

"Someday but not today," I murmur as I fiddle with my dad's old tractor. "Come on, baby. Be nice to me this morning." I sweet-talk it until Monster rumbles to life. The thing is so beat up, Micah didn't want the tractor added to the list of assets. Or maybe even a painful divorce wasn't enough to make him take my dad's pride and joy away from me. The metal seat is cold enough to feel through the clothing I'm wearing, so I stick an old blanket beneath me before I drive it out of the shed.

As I pass by the house, I see a light in the kitchen, and I frown because Guy shouldn't be up yet. Waking up Micah always made him crabby… No. I'm not going to keep thinking about my ex. I'm not going to assume Guy's going to react the same ways as Micah did. And if he does, well, then his butt can clear the road of snow next time.

I hate that I'm fighting with fictional versions of two husbands in my head. Not only is this unhealthy and will leave me stressed and anxious, it isn't even fair.

"Focus on what's in front of you," I tell myself for the hundredth time this month, a mantra that helps…until it's late at night and there's nothing else in front of me to focus on except a book I don't want to read and a tub in need of scrubbing.

Clearing the entire lane of snow isn't necessary as long as there's room for one vehicle to get in and out. But I'm already here, so I scrape the drive to the main road and back, then make a sweep past the barn and the garage. I feed the horses and use Monster to dump a new round bale of hay into the cattle pen. All the water trough and water bucket heaters are working, and I leave Lulu, the donkeys, and Legs inside their stalls. With wind like today, the windchill must be in the negatives, so they get to spend the day snug in the barn where it's warmer.

The cattle don't have the same kind of barn the horses do, but they're sheltered under their lean-tos. Cattle are tough, and as long as they're fed, dry, and out of the wind, they can handle the cold better than the rest of us can. Despite my clothing, I'm chilled through, and the cabin feels wonderfully warm when I finish my chores and go inside.

Guy's built up the fire, bless the man.

There's a bowl of oatmeal with fresh berries waiting for me on the kitchen island, covered with a paper towel so it doesn't get cold. Guy's waiting for me too, dressed for work and finishing his own breakfast.

"Thanks for making it warmer in here," I tell him as I head to the sink to wash my hands. The warm water stings my icy fingers, so I turn the temperature colder.

"Sure. I figured you'd be an ice cube about now. You didn't have to do that, by the way."

"Unless you wanted to take the ATV into town, it's a little necessary." I shrug, turning off the water. "It's just a part of rural living. We don't get as much snow as you Montana boys, but it adds up."

"This Montana boy would have done it for you," Guy says sweetly. "Anything you need around here, Sienna, just let me know. This whole husband-for-hire gig has been the easiest job I've taken."

"Yes, but the benefits are crap," I joke as I dry off my hands and add lotion to them.

"Not from where I'm standing," he murmurs as he gets up.

Did he just flirt with me? Probably not. He's probably just being appreciative of having a place other than the extended stay in town. My stomach growls, and I gratefully take my bowl of oatmeal. "Mmm, this smells good. I'm starting to get spoiled with all the cooking."

"Says the woman who's been out since four plowing the drive."

Guy gazes down at me, and those eyes are far too blue for this early in the morning. I'm not supposed to be lost in my fake-but-not-fake husband's eyes before dawn, or at any time really, and we're standing too close. I start to move right as he tries to give me space by stepping the same way. We bump arms, which shouldn't be a big deal, except those are really nice arms.

I exhale a small laugh. "I forgot I like dancing."

"Me too."

Sticking my face in a bowl of oatmeal is easier than meeting his warm gaze. A few bites in, I see him start to pack his lunch, so I get up and pull out a loaf of bread, moving the box of off-brand protein bars out of his reach.

"Nope, I can't do it. These look awful."

"They're not that bad." Guy flashes me a grin. "I bought them, so I need to eat them."

"If you want to feast on them when I'm out with Jess, go for it. But people know me in this town, and I have a reputation to maintain."

"Jess?" His tone is accepting, but I know a silent question when I don't hear one.

"Jess is my best friend. They and I have been thick as thieves since grade school. They want to meet you and Emma."

Guy smiles. "Sure, if they're important to you, I'd love to meet them."

The fact that he uses Jess's preferred pronouns is definitely important to me, and I find myself wanting to hug him. Instead, I pack his lunch, repeatedly stealing out the protein bar Guy keeps teasingly putting back in. Then I look around because someone has been missing from our morning. "Where's Emma? Doesn't she want breakfast?"

"She's still in bed for a little longer. Em's having a slow morning," he tells me. "I think she's tired from being out in the cold yesterday."

"Oh no." I freeze. I'd had so much fun with her yesterday, we'd all decided for her to try staying with me again today. Did I mess up letting her play in the barn for so long?

Guy must have read my mind because he puts a hand on my shoulder, squeezing it. "You're doing great, Sienna, she just gets tired. It's part of this. Some days are better than others."

"We can stay in today," I tell him. "Keep it low-key."

"Emma's a tough cookie, and there have been a lot of times we were on jobsites when she was having a tired day. Just keep her warm and make a bed in the truck if you need to go work outside. She'll be good for you."

I nod, thinking about what we can do together since we'll be inside all day. Then I hand him his lunch, stealing the protein bar out one more time. "Over my dead body, mister. You're not eating chalk when Emma and I have leftover veggie burgers."

"Yes, ma'am," he says, eyes dancing with humor. "Thanks, Sienna."

"Yep. Umm... Have a good day?"

"You too."

I can tell we're both in a "maybe hug" zone because he's lingering outside my personal space, and I keep edging into his.

"Don't judge me," I finally say, caving and wrapping my arms around his waist.

Guy's low, warm laugh is the best part of an already nice morning. Even better are the arms he gently wraps around my upper back, snugging me in close. "Safe space," he promises. "I'm a judgment-free zone."

"I keep forgetting how tall you are," I tell his rib cage. "Okay, go. Be all construction-y."

He grins at me and heads out the door. For a bitterly cold day, the man certainly has a spring in his step.

The feeling isn't mutual, because when I go into Emma's room to wake her at the time Guy wanted, I have to coax her into getting up and dressed. Emma is definitely having a tired day. Despite Guy's assurances, I'm not sure today counts as being "good" for me. She absolutely refuses to eat breakfast, and she pitches a complete fit when I can't give her more water. She doesn't want ice chips or a mouth swab. All suggestions of fun things we can do are met with a shrill no, and when she wants to play outside, she doesn't take being told it's too cold very well. More than once, Barley and I glance at each other, wondering where the sweet child of yesterday has disappeared to.

Every time Barley walks up to her, she marches away, until I tell him to go lie down on his orthopedic cushion in the corner. Then I join Emma on the bottom stair step, where she's glaring down at her toys and knocking them together with a little extra force. "Emma? You don't seem very happy today. Do you want to talk about it?"

"No."

That's fair. When I'm having a crap day, I rarely want to talk about it either.

"Is there something you would like to do? We could watch a Christmas movie."

"No. When's Daddy coming home?"

"He just left for work, sweetie. He's not going to be back until this evening."

At which point I learn this is the wrong thing to say. She doesn't start to cry; Emma full on *bawls*. No matter how I try to soothe her, it doesn't work, and Barley—who never breaks a command when he's asked to do something—breaks one now. He scoots over on the floor on his belly, whining and trying to get her to let him snuggle her. But Emma doesn't want either of us, that's clear.

I send a text to Guy, asking if he's free for a call, because I don't want to alarm him thinking it's an emergency by calling unexpectedly. I don't even have to wait for a reply text, because within two minutes, his name pops up on my phone on a video call.

"Everything okay?" Guy's face takes up the bulk of the screen, but I can see the jobsite and the other workers behind him. Whatever he's been doing this morning, he's already covered in sawdust, and he's wearing the hard hat usually tucked in his truck's back seat. Guy's cheeks and nose are ruddy from the cold.

"I think Emma needs to see your face," I hedge, feeling guilty because he's clearly busy, and I know how construction sites are run. If you're wearing a hard hat or there's heavy equipment moving, OSHA rules are clear. No phones. He's liable to get chewed out by the foreman for talking on the phone on-site instead of stepping away.

"She's having a tough day," I add, "but we'll keep it quick."

"I'll drag up on this job right now if I have to," Guy tells me in a firm voice. He pulls off his hard hat and moves so his back is against the white boxy office trailer I'd just seen in the background. "Emma comes first."

"She really wants to play outside, but it's so cold." I let Guy know the issue before handing over the phone to Emma.

"Yeah, it's too cold. Hey there, baby girl." Guy's face brightens as he sees her. "Are you having fun with Sienna?"

"*No.* I want to be with you."

"Emma, we're going to have a real talk right now, okay? You can be at work with me, which will mean staying in the truck the rest of the day, or you can spend the day with Sienna, where Barley is and all your toys and movies are. It'll be a lot more fun, and if you choose to be with me, there's no changing your mind."

Emma hits her toys together again but with less force. "What if you came back here instead?" she tries.

"I wish I could, but I've got to work. That's what parents do."

She starts crying and doesn't answer him, despite Guy making a comforting noise over the phone.

"Sienna, can I talk to you privately for a minute?"

"Of course." I head up the stairs and take the phone into my bedroom, then into the bathroom, where Emma can't hear. A sudden smile flashes across his face. "What?"

"Nothing. I just never took you as the type to have an inappropriately graphic rubber ducky shower curtain."

"That's the beauty of being divorced. You're not subjected to the whims of someone else." I try to stay serious, then I find myself grinning too. "Okay, I'd had way too much wine that night and it seemed funny. Once it arrived in the mail, it would have signified failure to send it back."

"Onward and upward?"

"Always."

"Sienna, you've been absolutely amazing from the first moment I met you. But Emma's a lot some days. You don't have to shoulder this. She used to be better at handling disappointments, but the sicker she gets, the harder it is on her." The expression on his face tightens. "I can come home. The foreman here is a nice guy, and I think he'll understand."

I hesitate, weighing what Emma needs but also what he and I need. The animals have been fed, and technically, I'm good until tonight's feeding. Unless something unexpected happens, I can catch up this weekend on any work I miss today.

"Is there a way she can get what she wants but not be an Emma popsicle?" I ask.

"Unless you can suddenly make outside not have a windchill of negative ten, I think we're stuck."

Well, now that he mentions it...

"I have an idea. If worse comes to worst, I'll drive her into the site so she can see you, but let me see if I can make the windchill disappear for a while."

"You're a Christmas miracle, Sienna." Guy flashes me a sexy smile, and he's obviously joking, but for a moment, he holds my eyes a little longer than necessary. "You call me if you need anything, okay? You two come first."

His words linger as I head back down the stairs, where Emma has her head resting on top of Barley's, her little arms around his neck. He probably just misspoke when he included me, but Emma absolutely comes first for Guy and for me too. Until this little girl gets her kidney, she's priority number one.

I take her hand and smile down at her. "Come on, sugar. You and I are going ice-skating."

———

Sometimes I wake up crying.

Even after good days, when I get to indoor ice-skate in circles with a giggling child in my arms, listening to her tell me about all her favorite things. And good nights, when I spend the evening with help finishing my chores—a blessing if there ever was one for an overworked rancher—and I learn a low-salt diet can be delicious in the hands of a man who likes to cook. When I don't feel like just an extra body in the room when we read Emma a bedtime Christmas story but maybe a real friend to them. Even though I go to bed wondering exactly what kind of muscly things are happening in my kitchen and fall asleep with a little smile on my face…it doesn't change the fact that sometimes I just wake up sobbing.

This happens to me more than I'd like to admit, and even in the silence and the darkness of my empty bedroom, it's humiliating. Sometimes it's because of Micah, sometimes my dad. Even though it's been years, sometimes the tears on my face are because of my mom. I usually don't remember my dreams, so I never know exactly what triggers the grief, I just wake up in it, utterly overwhelmed.

"Sienna?"

A soft tap at my door makes me sit up, rapidly scrubbing at the tears on my face. Guy's voice is husky with sleep, unsurprising since it's three in the morning.

"Are you okay?"

"I'm good. I just had a bad dream. Sorry I woke you."

"You didn't. I was checking on Emma," Guy says quietly through the door. He hesitates and then asks again, "Are you sure you're okay?"

"Yeah, gimme a sec."

One more swipe at my eyes and I get up, glancing down at my pajamas to make sure I'm actually wearing them tonight. Guy's leaning against the doorframe when I open the door, and for once, he doesn't step backward to give me more room. Instead, he gazes down at me, brow furrowed. His eyes sweep my face and then drop down to the wet spots on my tank top where I dried off my face.

"Bad dream, huh?" he says softly. "I get those too."

"You have to be up for work in two hours," I remind him. I tilt my head because I suddenly have a feeling. "You weren't just checking on Emma, were you?"

"We're married, Sienna. I'm not going to walk past the room if you're crying."

"Didn't you know?" I tell him wryly. "I'm a Naples. We don't cry."

Guy nods acquiescence, then he offers me his hand. When I take it, he hooks his index finger around my pinkie and gives it a little tug.

"For what it's worth, Maples do cry," he says quietly. "We don't make a habit of judging each other for it, and we accept it for what it is. Life is rough sometimes."

"The typical Naples will hop on a horse and work themselves to exhaustion instead of processing any pesky things like emotions." My joke sounds hollow to my own ears. I clear my throat, eyes flickering across the hall to Emma's room. "And we definitely don't complain about it to people with a lot worse on their plates."

"Believe it or not, Sienna, our hard days don't have to be mutually exclusive."

I blink, then suddenly I laugh. "If someone had told Micah that, I might still be married."

He looks like he wants to hug me, and I want the hug. If I stopped lying to myself, the wet spots on my shirt and I might admit I *need* the hug. Still, I can't do it. There are only a couple inches between us, but I can't cross the distance and let this man comfort me.

"Emma's okay?"

"She's dead to the world, using your dog as a teddy bear." Guy chuckles despite the tiredness on his face. He squeezes my fingers before dropping his hand and stepping back. "I suppose I better try to do the same."

Losing the sheer presence of him makes the air around me feel empty, as if my personal bubble is regretting returning to its normal state of emptiness.

"Hey, Guy? Thanks."

"Anytime. Oh, you should know, Barley woke me up to come check on you. He likes you more than you think." He starts toward the stairs, then Guy pauses at the top, turning and suddenly giving me a knee-melting smile. "We all do. Good night, Sienna."

As he heads back down to the crappy couch I've got him sleeping on, I decide I'm going to figure out how to be tougher, or at least quieter. Guy needs more than just sufficient food to get through what he and Emma are dealing with. He needs sleep. He needs a *break*. And he definitely shouldn't have to take care of me. That was never in the ad's job description.

Still, as I curl back up in my big, empty bed, I can't help but think that in another place and time, in a world that didn't rest so heavily on his broad shoulders, maybe accepting a moment of comfort wouldn't be such a bad thing.

Chapter 10

Sometimes I wish I drove an economy car instead of this truck. Yes, I need it for the ranch, but parking downtown can be a pain. Especially where I'm headed.

Even though it's Saturday and Guy has the weekend off, he and Emma were up and out the door first thing this morning. There's a medical center in town that offers pediatric dialysis, which was one of the reasons why Guy looked for work in this area. Up until meeting them, I didn't even know it was more difficult to find pediatric dialysis than adult dialysis treatments. I've learned they go three times a week, and it takes between three and four hours to get through the treatment. I can't imagine how rough it must be asking Emma to sit still so long while her blood is being cleaned.

Guy didn't ask me to go, and I didn't offer, unsure if this was the sort of thing they would rather have privacy for. Instead, I decide to knock some things off my increasingly neglected to-do list, and when it reaches mid-morning, I go get a coffee at Sanai's. It's been a few days since I've been here, and the latte in my hands feels decadent. It's also full of all the things Emma can't have, and I feel guilty as I drink my liquid courage. I linger, chatting with Sanai for longer than I'd planned, before finally taking a deep breath.

It's December 15—only a week and a half until Christmas—and I'm going to see my dad.

The parking lot at my father's long-term care facility is cramped, so

I leave my truck in the grocery store lot next door and trek across the snowy divider. The brief walk gives me a moment to collect myself and mentally prepare for what's coming next.

A couple of years ago, when my dad first moved into the facility, he made me promise not to come visit when he started to get too bad. I get it, I really do. I just miss him, and life has been…complicated…lately. I'm a person of my word, but he's not going to know I broke my promise.

Jeff Naples won't even know I'm his daughter.

After I sign in, one of the nursing assistants tells me where to find my father. He's in a chair in the corner of the activity hall, watching an old Western next to one of the facility's Christmas trees. We never watched much television while I was growing up. There was never a whole lot of free time when the ranch was at its prime, but Dad did like his Westerns.

I pause in the entry of the activity hall, breathing through my mouth because there's something about the smell of this place that makes me sad. It's a good facility. Lots of them aren't, and I'm grateful the people here care as much as they do. But my father hated being inside, and I wonder if there's a part of him buried deep down that remembers the scent of a storm on the wind or a crisp, fresh snowfall.

My dad was never a tall man, and my momma sure didn't add to the height in the family. But Jeff Naples was always strong. I used to think he was as big as a mountain, as tough as the Salmon River, and could do no wrong.

I still think these things. I also think time has a way of wearing down mountains and slowing rivers. Dying or not, in my eyes, my daddy will never be able to do wrong.

I settle down on a chair next to him, making sure to face him so he can see me. Small things sometimes make it easier for him.

"Hello, Mr. Naples."

When Dad ignores me, I know it's not one of the good days. He's only recognized me twice this year, but on better days, he'll talk to me. Today I just sit next to him, listening to the show and fiddling with my coffee cup. He's not really here, but he's still *here*. The same part of my heart mourning the first is determined to cling to the second.

"My daughter's married," Dad suddenly says. "Married a rancher from the next town over. Good man, treats her well. Still waiting on those grandkids though."

My eyes well up with tears. I wanted to give him grandchildren, more than anything. Sometimes life isn't what we planned.

"I bet she's really happy," I say, earning myself a very familiar snort.

"Naw, my girl's only happy on a horse, riding up and down these hills like she hasn't got a neck to break."

Which was true when I was ten. Well, it's probably still true now, but Legs keeps my neck nice and safe. "She must love you a whole lot," I tell him, because I love seeing this tough, old-man smile.

"She's a good girl."

"You're a good dad."

I shouldn't say it, but the words slip out. I know it's a mistake because I see the confusion in his eyes. His body language changes, and he frowns, staring hard at the television, like I'm no longer there. I want to hug him, but he won't understand why.

"Mr. Naples? Will your wife mind too much if I hold your hand?"

When he doesn't answer, I take his fingers in mine. The age spots have been there for a long time, but the weakness of his grip is new enough I'm still not used to it. I want to hold his hand harder, just so he can't let go, but I keep my fingers loose. This version of Jeff Naples doesn't know me.

"Sienna."

My head snaps up, but he's not looking at me.

"My girl's name is Sienna. You look a lot like her."

"I've been told she looked a lot like her mother."

"That's better than looking like me," he says, and when he moves his arm away, I fold my hands in my lap. He angles his body from me, a sign he's done talking to me or simply done with the stranger in the room. It's time for me to leave, or he'll start to grow agitated. Alzheimer's is a cruel disease, and it's stripped him of everything that made him my father. But he's still a man who deserves peace before he goes.

If it means leaving him alone on a bad day, then that's what I need to do.

I will not cry in front of him. I will not cry in this room or in this building. It's a promise I made to myself years ago. He'd be so angry if he knew I was still visiting him, but it's almost Christmas. I just *can't*. I have to see him, even if it breaks my heart.

"I know I promised, Daddy, but I love you," I whisper. Then I tell the same lie I've been telling him for a long time now. "Don't worry, okay? I'm really happy."

I press a kiss to his age-spotted forehead, then leave, keeping my head down as I hurry to my truck. *Don't cry until you get to the truck, Sienna. The lump in your throat? Hold it in.*

I'm almost there when I notice something different about the Chevy's windshield. A copy of Jess's husband-for-hire ad is tucked under my windshield wiper, rolled around a very cold red rose. I unfold the paper and see the ad has been crossed out with a purple Sharpie, the same one Emma and I were drawing with last night.

"Job vacancy filled," I read aloud. There's also a doodle of a sandwich with a smiley face and a Santa hat. I can't help but laugh, breathing in the scent of the rose as I get in my truck. The lump in my throat is still there, but it's softened to manageable levels.

Maybe I'm happier than I realize.

Hammond's Feed and Supply sits on the corner a block down from my father's long-term care facility. As I drive past, I glance at the side lot where the employees park. A certain truck I no longer co-own isn't there, so I make a U-turn and head back.

We opened the store a couple of years ago due to convenience more than anything else. Micah and I were both tired of having to drive an hour to the nearest big-box tractor supply store, and we were a lot closer to town than some of the people in the Frank Church Wilderness. The need was there in the community, and we already had the cattle business set up. Expanding to include the store wasn't terribly difficult, although it never turned much of a profit.

I don't miss the extra hours we spent keeping up with the bookkeeping and employee shortages, but I do miss being able to buy my horse and cattle feed at wholesale prices. Now I only come in here when it's absolutely necessary, but this place has everything a rancher needs when they come to town, which was the point.

My new family has a lot of cow crap in their lives. They need some muck boots.

As I walk toward the store, I see a familiar figure in a cowboy hat coming out, a heavy bag of horse grain balanced on one shoulder and a second arm full of salt blocks. It's strange sometimes, remembering what someone looked like as a child and then knowing them as an adult too. I can't remember a time in my or Jess's life when Charley, a pleasantly handsome man with a constant five-o'clock shadow of scruff, wasn't there in the background. Steadfast, reliable, and too shy to do much more than touch his cowboy hat and murmur "Ma'am."

Charley is like these mountains. Quiet. Steady. There.

"Is all that for Boop?" I ask him in lieu of greeting.

Our local cowboy pilot and locator of lost bulls gives me a shy smile. "They've got a sale on the apple salt blocks he likes," Charley says.

And in Charley's world, whatever Boop wants, Boop gets.

Boop is Charley's miniature horse. A two-year-old, dapple-gray stud colt with a black mark on the end of his nose, Boop barely comes to Charley's hip. He's also convinced that Charley is his mom. Charley rescued the mini as a foal during last summer's wildfires, when a lot of stock were lost, injured, or abandoned. Picked him up and stuffed the burned, scared animal in the back of his airplane, flying Boop to safety and pretty much breaking every FAA rule in the process.

"Haven't seen you in a while, Sen," Charley says, and I can hear it in what the cowboy pilot doesn't say. *Where did you go? Why don't we talk anymore?*

Charley might have traded in his rodeo belt buckles for airplane wings, but he's who he has always been. Someone very important to me. He's had dinner at our table more times than I can count, but I've been ducking him more and more the last year. I didn't want him to know how much I was hurting.

He's a shoulder I could have cried on. I just…didn't.

"I guess I just didn't want to make you have to choose," I say softly.

I know Charley doesn't have a lot of friends, and I don't want to be the one that costs him any. Charley interceded enough while I was still married, getting Micah sobered up before he came back home or giving him someone to curse at when things weren't going Micah's way.

We never talked about it, but Charley's always been protective of me. Even now, Charley regards me with intelligent eyes, taking in the items in my arms as if silently checking if I'm okay.

"I suppose if a guy had to choose, he'd be hard pressed not to choose the one in the right of things."

The softly drawled words are the Christmas gift I didn't know I needed. I almost hug him, but instead I stand there, grateful for the people who care. I don't have to say how much it means to me. Charley knows.

"You okay, Sen?"

My life has been a whirlwind this last week, but I start to smile as I think about the little girl back at home. "Yeah. I'm okay."

He clears his throat, then adds, "Jess said you met someone?"

I'm so not ready to answer this question, but Charley's looking at me curiously. "I'll get back to you on that one," I say with a bemused laugh as his radio buzzes at his side. "Tell Jake to hold his horses."

"Such a grump," we say in tandem, a running joke since we were all kids, then share a quick grin.

"Take care, Sen." Charley juggles his salt blocks so he can touch his hat brim, then the cowboy pilot heads toward his truck, grain bag resting easy over his shoulder and picking up his radio, buzzing again with Jake's annoyed voice.

For the life of me, I can't figure out how he's still single. That sweet drawl charms me every single time.

I go inside the store I used to own, heading for the clothing section. Emma's easy, because I've helped her put her shoes on and know what size she is. I even find a pair of sparkly purple muck boots she'll hopefully love. As for Guy, I have no clue. I really need to look at his shoulders less and his shoes a little more.

Sighing, I break down and send Guy a text. Shoe size? I ask.

I'm guessing you're a six? pops up on my phone immediately, followed by a smiley face.

I laugh out loud, then text back, No, you. Since the man emoji'd me again, I send him back a tongue sticking out. There's no way to be super subtle, but maybe Guy will be too busy to notice I'm asking specific questions right before Christmas.

Emma's a 10C and I'm an 11.5. What's up?

Yep. The hope was short-lived.

I send a "none of your business" GIF in reply, followed by a Christmas GIF. After a few moments, I get a sexy Santa winking at me. Oh dear. Things *must* be getting serious.

My face feels funny as I grab a pair of sturdy rubber muck boots from the rack in Guy's size, and as I pass by a mirror near a rack of work shirts, I realize I'm smiling wide enough to make my cheeks hurt. Since I'm there, I grab him a shirt in the same style he's been wearing to work.

Nothing says Merry Christmas to an overworked man like getting him more things to work in.

I grab a water from the soda case, then take my items up to the counter.

"Hey, Sienna," the checkout clerk says cheerfully, a nice kid named Dominic who's worked here since his sophomore year of high school. He's one of the best hires we...well, *Micah*...has, and I give him a friendly wave.

"Hey, Dom. How are your folks doing? Are they ready for the holidays?"

"Mom says it comes faster every year," Dominic says as he takes the security tags off the boots.

"Don't I know it."

He gives me a curious look. "Hey, is it true you're looking to hire a husband? Jess came by with an ad a couple days ago. It didn't last long on the board. The manager took it down because they thought the boss man might be ticked."

I just barely manage to smother my laugh. Of course Jess had the moxie to put an ad up in Micah's business.

"It was just a joke," I tell him. Then, because a secret never lasts long in this town, I add, "But actually, I did get remarried."

"You've got to be *kidding* me."

I go still at the voice behind me, closing my eyes briefly because his truck wasn't outside when I pulled up. Which means he came in because he saw my vehicle. There's no way Micah would have missed it.

I don't even have to see his face to know he's furious. Once, the man behind me used to take my breath away. Now I have to take a deep breath to steady myself before I turn around.

"Hello, Micah."

Sometimes, when I look at him, I still see the rowdy, fun-loving high school boy I fell in love with as a teenager. Micah was handsome then, and he's even more handsome now. The Hammonds have good genes, and I used to think we'd have beautiful babies. The problem with knowing someone too well is once the shiny exterior has been worn off by familiarity, you know too well the reality of what's underneath.

Maybe, if we were different people, we'd look at each other and not see so much ugliness. But a year's worth of arguing tooth and nail with lawyers in the room can take the polish off the best of them.

"I'll be out of here in a minute," I say in my best friendly but unengaging voice.

He looks at the items in Dominic's hands, and Micah's face flushes red with anger. I don't blame the kid for going still, but I'm used to Micah being mad at me.

I turn back to the clerk and nod at him to continue. "I'm paying with a card," I tell Dominic to redirect his attention.

"Sienna, we need to talk," Micah says from behind my shoulder, even closer now.

"Micah, not today, okay?" I tell my ex in a brusque I'm-too-busy-to-have-a-conversation tone. He should know it well; he used it on me all the time. "I just saw my dad, and I need to get back home and ride fences before it gets too late. We'll talk soon."

I swipe my card and type in my code as quickly as possible, then grab my stuff to go before Dominic has even bagged it.

"Damn it, Sienna, I'm not playing games here."

Micah's always been a big guy, and his naturally thick muscles have only increased through an adulthood of hard labor. When he steps into my way, I'm very aware of how large he is.

"Fine, we'll talk outside," I say, narrowing my eyes at him. "Dom's got a line, and we're holding it up."

At least this way the poor kid won't be stuck in the middle of us if this goes the way I have a feeling it will go.

Micah's truck is parked right next to mine, which ticks me off because it means he's looking for a fight. After seeing Dad, he might just be unlucky enough for me to give him one. I don't have a single reason besides my own peace of mind to play nice anymore. I'm trying so hard to embrace the Christmas spirit, but I'm about out of patience right now. Frankly, I have enough on my mind without having to deal with this.

"You actually got remarried."

The way he says it, you'd think I committed murder.

"You aren't messing with me with the insurance changes," Micah adds, sounding as if he can't believe his own words.

"Yes, I got remarried. And please don't cause problems with the health insurance. They need it."

The man looks poleaxed. I mean, I get why he's ticked. If he'd remarried the day after our divorce, I'd have been devastated.

I dig deep and try to find some compassion for him. "It's complicated, Micah, and it's not personal. It was just something that happened."

"Not *personal*?" He sounds even angrier. "How long were you seeing him?"

"I'm sorry?"

"This whole time we were separated, I didn't see anyone, Sienna. Not once. I thought it was cruel to you, but now I realize you were making a fool out of me."

I don't understand what he means at first, then it clicks. He thinks I was with Guy before the divorce.

"*If* I was seeing someone after we separated, I would've had the right," I tell Micah. "The day you moved out, you lost the ability to judge what I do or don't do. We were separated, and now we're divorced. My life is none of your concern."

"If you were sleeping with him when we were still married, I have a right to know," Micah snarls. I don't know if I've ever seen him this angry.

"I met Guy the day before he and I got married," I tell him through gritted teeth. "So no, I didn't date anyone before the divorce finalized. Even if I had, it's *none of your business*, Micah."

"It's my business when a stranger is sleeping in my bed, in my house—"

"*My* house," I snap. "My house, my bed, my dog, my animals. You wanted everything else, and you got everything else. What happens at the ranch is *my* concern."

I don't even realize I'm brandishing Guy's new muck boot until Micah shifts back so it doesn't bonk him on the chest. We're two seconds from screaming at each other in the parking lot, and I won't do this anymore. I got divorced so I didn't *have* to do this anymore. I hate how this feels, how my blood boils in my veins, but everything else feels cold, numb, and awful. Fighting with Micah makes me physically ill, and I don't want to do it anymore.

"We can talk when you've cooled down," I say, forcing myself into a state of calmness that has everything to do with emotional survival and nothing to do with how I actually feel. I turn and start to open my door.

His hand over my head pops it back shut.

Sometimes a moment feels like a lifetime. Especially ones like this, when we're a single word from everything flying apart. Then Micah grunts and backs off. "Sorry, Sen."

He's always sorry. He always does this shit anyway. Wordlessly, I get inside the truck, and I don't look in the rearview mirror as I drive away. I crank up the holiday music channel loud enough it hurts my ears, and I forget to turn the heater on until I reach the bridge. Just in case Guy and Emma are already home, I let the truck idle at the entrance of the ranch, watching the cedar sign swinging above me in the winter breeze.

"I will not cry," I tell myself as Bing Crosby croons all around me. "Just focus on what's in front of you."

I'm my father's daughter. I will not cry.

Chapter 11

It's a relief when I reach the cabin and no one but Barley is there, the old retriever curled up on his cushion in the living room. He opens one eye and then closes it again, turning his back to me just in case I'm tempted to disturb his sleep.

"Point made," I tell him, bending over and patting his head just to annoy him. "You're taking a personal day."

Since Barley's not interested in coming along, I spend the afternoon alone, riding the electric horse fence and checking for loose, droopy wires or broken plastic insulators. It's slow, hard work, and drifting snow likes to push my metal fence posts out of alignment. Legs's breath condenses in the cold, and every hour or so, I pause to wipe the ice crystals from his nostrils with my gloved hand. The distance I have to cover isn't far, but the deep snow on an increasingly steeper mountainside drops our pace to a crawl.

After the last couple of days, the silence feels deafening, but eventually it starts to become normal again. My brain rotates through a to-do list, unwilling to shut down and be peaceful, so I take comfort in mentally organizing my own chaos. It's better than focusing on angry exes or fathers who forget.

For a moment, I think about the rose Guy left me. It's in the center console of my truck, pressed between the pages of this year's *Old Farmer's*

Almanac. Maybe I'm being silly and romantic, but on a bad day, it's my something nice. In a year or so, when Emma has her kidney and these two have moved on with their lives, I want to remember them.

An image of Guy doing push-ups in my kitchen slips unbidden into my mind, and I have to smile at myself. He's not going to be an easy one to forget.

When we reach the high side of the horse pasture, where a tributary to the Salmon River below us creates a natural obstacle, I make sure to keep Legs away from the edge. What looks solid actually has rushing, ice-cold water beneath. An unexpected swim in here followed by a two-hour ride back down the mountain would be dangerous for both of us.

My small herd notices Legs and I as we head down the mountainside. Lulu whinnies at him, and Legs flicks his ears. She trots over, the copper-colored coat pretty as a picture against the snowy backdrop.

"If I had a camera, that picture would sell all your babies, Lulu girl," I tell her as she drops in behind us.

With nothing better to do, Dunkin and Paddlewhack follow suit. Herd animals are interesting. Once they start in one direction, usually they'll keep going if you seem like you have a good reason to. It's not dinnertime but close enough for them to follow us single file down the mountainside.

When I reach the barn, I pause, looking around in surprise. In the time I was riding the fence line, Guy's been busy. My stalls are clean. The water buckets have been emptied, scrubbed free of hay bits from the horses' breakfasts, and refilled with fresh water. He's also put two flakes of hay in each stall. True, it's the new hay instead of last year's hay, but it's the right amount. Bless the man, he even put an extra snow shovel scoop of wood shavings down for each of the animals in their stalls to replace what was cleaned out.

The ranch's extensive to-do list is copied on the chalkboard in the barn, ranging from the daily tasks like feeding and cleaning stalls to the weekly and monthly tasks. I notice that something lower on the list now has a checkmark on it, so I loosen Legs's saddle girth but drop a rein to the ground in a signal for him to stay ground tied—in one place—while I head outside to the lean-tos in the cattle pen.

When they'd first been built, we used galvanized nails to secure the brand-new corrugated metal siding to the framing. But like so many things in the Frank Church Wilderness, exposure to the elements has a way of wearing something down. The metal siding is weathered and bent from hoof kicks and scratching half-ton cattle butts, and the nails are starting to rust and loosen in places.

Sure enough, the loose piece of metal siding on the far lean-to has been secured down, and shiny galvanized screws replace many of the nails. Protecting my cattle from puncture wounds is important, but when I scan the snow, I don't see any nails on the ground.

Well, Guy did say in our coffee interview that he's a hard worker. The man probably hit the ground running the moment they got back from Emma's dialysis. What he's accomplished in a couple of hours would have taken some people most of the day.

I hear the front door of the cabin close, and I see Guy coming out across the yard, zipping up his jacket. I duck out of the cattle pen and meet him halfway, at the barn.

"Hey," he says when he reaches me, giving me that sweet smile of his in greeting. "I saw you coming down the mountain. I can't stay out here long because Emma isn't up from her nap, but I wanted to see if you needed anything."

"From the looks of it, you've been out here all day," I tell him gratefully. "How is she?"

"Dialysis went okay. She slept most of the drive home, and she's been out since noon. That was really cool, by the way." When I glance at him in confusion, he tilts his head toward the herd still lingering in the pad-dock. "The way they all followed you down the mountainside. Animals like you, don't they?"

"Barley might beg to differ," I joke as I start to untack Legs. "Hey, thanks for the flower."

Guy gives me a pleased look. "I saw the truck when we were headed through town."

"There's actually two other trucks in town the same as mine," I inform him with a little grin. "You might have really confused a couple people."

When Legs sighs a long-suffering sigh, Guy pats his nose. "It's kind of funny I live on a ranch now. I've never actually been on a horse."

"You're from Montana and you've never ridden?"

"We're not all cowboys," he reminds me.

I sigh in playful dramatics. "I married a townie. My dad will never forgive me."

"How was he?"

I don't know how to answer, so I just give Guy a tight smile and shake my head once. I get Legs settled while Guy hurries back to the house for Emma. Since he's gotten so much done already, I knock a couple more things off my to-do list before I feed everyone. I check the gates are all locked, then head back to the house. The scent of berries and vanilla waft through the cabin as I enter, and I find several dozen miniature muffins on the countertop.

Yep, the man definitely doesn't know how to take a rest day. Even now, he's scrubbing the countertops.

"Ooh, yum. Are these Emma-friendly?" I ask, because I've seen her list of allowed foods, and these look and smell far too good to be on a stage five renal diet.

"You think I would dare to make a treat under the same roof as my daughter if they weren't?" Guy jokes. "She'd never forgive me."

"Sorry." I flush, realizing my question could have been taken as criticism, but Guy just gives me a kind look.

"It's nice you care," he tells me. "And they're Emma-friendly in moderation. She can have one a day, no matter what she tells you."

"Christmas is a hard time to not be able to have treats."

"There's a lot of hard things about her life. It's why I'm so grateful for the time she's getting to spend here. Playing with Barley and making stockings for horses is a lot more fun than sitting in my truck on a jobsite with a tablet." This time, he pauses, clearing his throat awkwardly. "That didn't come out right. I know you do a ton of work around here—"

I lean over and steal a muffin. "Yep, which is why you are awesome for making these." I tear it in half and pop the treat in my mouth. "Should we just eat one too? To be fair to her?"

"We're adults, and these are teeny tiny. If I eat a fistful when she's in bed or playing in the other room, I won't tell if you won't."

"Snitches get stitches?" I say playfully as Guy slides over a small plate with two more mini muffins on it. "I would have married you sooner if I'd known you were this good around a kitchen," I tell him as I munch happily.

"You married me within twenty-four hours of meeting me." He flashes me a quick grin.

"Yes, and if you'd brought muffins, we could have whittled it down to a more reasonable time span." When I wink at him, Guy flushes a little.

"I got used to cooking on a hot plate in hotel rooms," he admits. "Having access to an actual oven feels like a luxury."

"Luxury until it comes time to wash the dishes," I say. "I never could convince Dad we could splurge for a dishwasher. Now he's in town, I feel guilty every time I consider installing one."

"Some of the hotels we stayed in were extended stays with kitchenettes, but there's been a few places where I was scrubbing dishes in a hotel bathroom sink. Trust me, Sienna, this place is a serious upgrade."

I step closer, looking up at him. "Thanks for everything you did today. Not just the muffins, but the stalls and the sheds too."

"Anything I can do, Sienna. I meant it when I said I'm here for you. Speaking of... I got a call from one of the guys on the site today saying he saw my brand-new wife shaking a shoe in her ex's face."

I wrinkle my nose at the humor in his tone. "It wasn't a shoe. It was a *muck boot*. And please tell whoever they are a big thanks for ruining my early Christmas present for you."

"Trust me, after what I waded through today, I don't need a surprise. I'm ecstatic for those boots." Guy's voice quiets as he asks, "Was he giving you a hard time?"

I hedge because Guy doesn't need to add Micah onto his already overflowing plate. "The store had what I wanted, and I was right there. I didn't see his truck, so I thought I could get in and get out without it being an issue. But I forget with Micah, everything is an issue."

"Sounds exhausting."

"Not my life anymore." I try to shrug it off, but Guy's arms fold around me, and I close my eyes. All the carefully erected walls I've built seem pretty strong, at least until Guy's nose dips and he places the softest kiss to the rim of my ear. It's the tiniest gesture of comfort, nothing more.

"I'm sorry you're still dealing with him."

For a moment, I can't pull away. I know I need to, but my hands hang on too long. Then I step back and clear my throat. "Okay, I suppose I need to grab a shower before tonight." Guy isn't the only one who waded through too much muck today. "Are you and Emma still okay with having dinner with Jess?"

"Wouldn't miss it," he promises me despite the tiredness in his eyes.

It's been a long day, and even though I love spending time with Jess,

I'm not feeling this evening at *all*. I'd much rather find a nice thick blanket and stay in. Since I'm dragging my feet, I linger in the shower longer than normal, and it takes a while to blow-dry my hair. I pick out a soft, cable-knit sweater dress from my closet, knowing it's my first Saturday night out with my sort-of-real-but-not-really-real husband. I should try to look cute, right?

I haven't worn this dress before, and it's been sitting in my closet for months. The fabric hugs me a little more than I remember, and it's thin enough I'll probably need a heavier coat. I'm not about to break a leg skating around in ice and snow in heels, but my best pair of dress boots has been gathering dust in the back of the closet for too long. As I pull on the delicately stitched fawn-colored boots, I can't remember my last "night out."

When I come downstairs, Guy is crouched on his heels in front of the fireplace, stirring the embers in the fireplace as if he isn't sure if he should add more wood.

"It'll be good until we get back," I tell him.

Guy turns his head at my voice, then the next thing I know, the poor man has lost his balance and almost takes a header into the fire. I wince when he catches himself on one of the metal screens, knowing how hot they get. He breathes a curse, jerking his hand away, then lunges to his feet.

"Daddy, you said a bad word," Emma singsongs from the top of the stairs, where she's still in her napping clothes.

"Emma, you're supposed to be getting dressed, remember?" Guy tells her, giving his hand a little shake.

"Sorry I startled you," I tell him, taking Guy's wrist and peering down at his reddened palm. "I think you're okay, but some ice wouldn't hurt. Come on."

He follows me obediently into the kitchen, and I pull a bag of frozen peas out of the freezer, holding it to his skin. I'm in his personal bubble, and I glance up to see if he minds. Guy's watching me, not his hand, and those tired, strained eyes soften.

"Want me to take this off?" he asks, glancing down at my shoulder. My brain decides to take a hard right at the suggestion, and the tiredness eases from his handsome features as he grins at the expression on my face. With his pinky finger, Guy lifts the price tag still attached.

Oh. Yep. Price tag. Gotcha.

"There's a pair of scissors in the drawer next to you," I tell him, feeling my face warm the air around me.

It's an oddly domestic moment between two strangers, when he's officially just learned my dress size, my preference for buying locally sourced clothing, and the fact that I will spend far too much for something sparkly. I learn he's careful enough not to nick the fabric and conscientious enough to remove the tiny plastic bit that gets caught underneath.

"Is what I'm wearing okay?" Guy asks me as he shifts back a bit to give us both more space.

I stop staring at his eyes—not an easy feat—and glance down. Worn jeans will always look great on this man, but I realize after the fact I've overdressed for what he owns. The collared shirt he put on has a little logo in the corner from a jobsite he must have worked on at some point. I hate when he seems uncertain, so I reach up to his collar, tugging it a little even though it was just fine.

"Okay, handsome, now you're perfect."

I could almost swear the man's eyes are getting more blue as he watches me.

Guy double-checks Emma's blood pressure and asks her again if she's feeling up to the evening. Dialysis is exhausting, but her long nap and the idea of meeting a new friend seem to have recharged her. Emma takes forever to decide what she wants to wear, and we're going to be late. Guy finally tells her if she doesn't make a choice, we will. It feels odd being included in this "we," especially because now "we" are getting the stink eye, not just him.

"I think I'm in trouble too," I murmur as he carries her out to the truck so the rainbow tiara princess with the dragon hoodie doesn't get her ballet shoes wet.

"This marriage is the Christmas gift that keeps giving," Guy jokes as he buckles her into her safety seat. "Is there anything special I should know for tonight?"

I get into the driver's seat and set the diesel truck into reverse. "Nope. Why?"

"You just seem a little tense."

I flinch, not expecting the phrase to come out of his mouth. In Micah's hands, "tense" was an attack, another word for bitchy, and when he used it, I always felt like somehow my emotions made me lacking in some way. Like I was wrong or annoying. When I glance at Guy, he's draped in the passenger seat, his eyes on me. And when he reaches over and squeezes my hand, I remember that whoever this man is, he's not Micah. I have a whole lifetime of triggers he knows nothing about, and I probably say the wrong thing to him half a dozen times a day.

"Whatever you just thought, I'd love to know what it was." His brow is furrowed, and I think maybe Guy is a lot smarter than I realized. Or at least he pays a lot of attention.

I offer him a tight smile as I turn the truck and head away from the cabin. "I'm tense because I'd rather have stayed in tonight," I admit. "Seeing my dad is always tough, and a run-in with Micah on top of it was…"

"Shitty?"

"Daddy, you said a bad word again." A cute little voice pops up from the back seat.

"You did say a bad word," I tease him. "An accurate word, but a bad word. Don't worry. Five minutes with Jess, and I'll forget all about it.

They're a lot of fun, and they've been bugging me mercilessly to meet you both."

Guy reaches over and takes my hand where it lies on the center console in between us instead of safely at ten and two. "Well, I for one am happy," he says, relaxing in his seat. "I'm out for a night on the town with my favorite ladies. Well, my favorite lady and my favorite rainbow dragon princess ballerina."

Emma dissolves into peals of laughter as he turns to tickle her dragon-y side, still holding my hand. I realize I'm grinning as I watch them in the rearview mirror, because they really do look happy.

Whatever else is happening, this right here? It's working.

Chapter 12

THE LOUSY KAYAKER'S BAR AND GRILL IS THE MOST POPULAR SPOT in Caney Falls on a Saturday night.

A shotgun-style bar and grill right off the main strip, it's just a few steps from the river and is the perfect location to get good food and better drinks and wander around the little niche antique shops and pastry shops lining downtown. The price tag is a bit steep, so it's definitely a splurge. When Jess suggested LK's, I pushed for something cheaper, but they insisted, because apparently, we're celebrating. If you want to go on a nice first date or celebrate a graduation, you go to LK's. A fancy business lunch? LK's. Introducing your best friend to the husband you've hired? LK's.

I'm used to the place being popular, but we struggle to find a parking place.

"Is it just me, or are there a lot of cars here?" Guy asks.

"They could just be busy…" I hedge, going down half a block to a parking lot next to the river. But I have a cold chill, hairs-on-the-back-of-my-neck-rising feeling that usually only happens when Jess has an "idea."

"I want Sen-na," Emma says when her father gets her out of the car, and Guy blinks at the unexpected request. This is a first. I don't want to hurt his feelings, but he seems fine as he passes her into my arms.

"It's just because I have Legs," I promise as he takes her rainbow mini backpack out and hooks the sparkly thing over his shoulder.

"Even Shrek liked donkeys," Guy teases as he closes the truck door.

"Daddy, Legs is a *mule*." The side-eye Emma gives him is clearly a "don't embarrass me" look.

I wink at him over her head. "I have one of those too."

I hadn't realized how much Guy stays out of my personal space until his daughter is in my arms. Guy is glued to my hip, and as we head across the street, he shifts between us and the headlights of the waiting vehicles, a physical barrier between Emma and any reckless driver who might get impatient. When we get closer to the restaurant, his hand brushes the small of my back, silently warning me as a pair of teenagers hustle past us from behind.

"Have you ever been here before?" I ask him.

"No, but the guys at work said it was good."

The sign on the outside says WE SERVE LOCAL BEEF, with several of the local ranchers' brand signs on it. The largest is a rocking H, with the words "Hammond Cattle" beneath it. I don't realize Guy knows my ex's last name until he raps his knuckles against the glass between us and the sign and says, "Should I get the chicken in solidarity?"

I grin at him as he holds the door for us. "I hear they make a great apple and honey salad here."

"I like honey," Emma tells me, and as I step into LK's, I wonder if she could eat a few bites of my meal instead of what Guy has packed for her.

You'd think I'd be more observant when all those cars are outside, but none of the customers are in front of the bar, waiting for a table. I'm so distracted by my new family, I'm completely unprepared for the sheer volume of the barrage of voices screaming "SURPRISE!" the second I pass through the door.

I yelp and twist, getting Emma in between myself and Guy, but other than his arm locking around us, he doesn't seem alarmed. Instead, he's grinning wider than I've ever seen him. We're a little town, but when you stick this many of us in a long, thin bar and someone gives us noisemakers, it's fairly traumatic, volume-wise.

"What is happening?" I say as I pass Emma to Guy and turn around, widening my stance to block them from whatever this craziness is.

"I think it's a surprise party for us, Sienna," Guy murmurs in my ear. "At least that's what the sign says."

Yep, among all the balloons and streamers and decorated tables, there is a massive Just Married banner stretching across the bar. And since everyone is staring at us, I'm guessing it's too late to sneak out of here. The place is packed all the way through the bar at the front and the tables at the back, and I can just barely see the outdoor patio lights lit up at the back of the bar.

I recognize all these faces, but I scan the bar for the person I want to see the most. It takes some effort, but Jess manages to push their way through the crowd and sweeps me up in a tight hug.

"You did this, didn't you?" I say, because Jess looks incredibly smug.

"Well, clearly you weren't going to do it yourself. Sanai helped too." They turn to Guy, nearly hopping with excitement. "Is this the new one?"

"Is this the wonderful person who sent me for coffee to meet my wife?" he counters charmingly. "I owe you a thank-you card."

Jess looks delighted. "Oh, you're already *much* better than the last one."

When they hug, I can see the effect Guy's easy friendliness and handsome smile has on Jess. We introduce them to Emma, whose eyes are wide as she looks around.

"Daddy, who is the party for?" she asks.

"It's for us, baby," Guy tells her, readjusting her lower because her little hand is gripping on to my shirtsleeve. "Because Sienna and I got married."

"It's for *all* of us," I tell her, leaning over and giving her a kiss on the top of her head.

"He's hot," Jess murmurs when Guy is momentarily distracted. "Needs a little feeding up, but I've got you covered."

Jess points to the middle of the bar, where the most massive Christmas-themed wedding cake I've ever seen is perched, one good drunken elbow away from getting knocked off. It's a tower of white icing, crystalized candies, and sugar-dusted strawberries. The bride and groom are sitting on the edge of the top layer in snow boots as they peer down at their cake winter wonderland. The whole thing is wrapped in sparkly snowdrifts of spun sugar, and it's too delicate and beautiful to be this large.

"It'll never survive," I say, because half of these people sound like they're already a couple rounds in.

"It will if they don't want to deal with my wrath." Jess steps behind us and nudges us forward. "Go. Be the center of attention."

I…don't know how. I don't really even understand why they are all here.

Jake and Charley are the first to step up and offer us congratulations. The pilots give Guy a handshake and then move aside, but not before Charley shakes his head, murmuring, "I should've answered that ad."

"It was just a joke," I promise him, and despite Charley's understanding smile, he looks a little glum. They think it was real.

Oh no. *Is it possible they all think the ad was real?*

Even though my heart wants to burst from how much I appreciate all of my friends turning out for me and Guy, I'm horrified. What are we supposed to tell people? There's literally nowhere to run to escape the eyes on us. I cast a frantic look at Guy and rise up on my toes. He bends his head down so I can whisper in his ear.

"What do we tell them?"

"Thank you for the cake, and please don't report us for insurance fraud?" He seems way too relaxed for this, and for once, his easy sense of humor isn't making me feel better.

"*Is* it technically insurance fraud?"

"Not on my side it isn't." Guy gives me a knee-melting smile and wraps his arm around my waist. "You didn't run an internet search on all this beforehand?"

"Of course I did," I insist, but my cheeks are on fire as I admit, "I just kind of got sidetracked by stalking you on social media. There was a very short turnaround, and I *did* still have chores to do."

His barked laugh cuts through the tension, and the next thing I know, I'm being herded toward the next group. Sanai finds us, and she admits she and Jess had been planning this since our wedding day. Those two have definitely been in cahoots; my instincts are always right. They've both done a fabulous job decorating everything, and the Lousy Kayaker's is open bar for the first hour, which explains why everyone seems to be on their merry way from sobriety. A vat of eggnog sits next to the cake, and bottles of iced champagne are tucked behind the bar, gleaming wet with condensation and ready for a toast. There's even a photo booth and lots of joke wedding-themed props for guests to pose with.

There's a problem though. Everywhere I turn, there are platters of decorated sugar cookies and caramel corn and pitchers of soda pop. The bar is closed for their regular menu and is catering burger sliders with mountains of cheese and salty, crisp fries for everyone.

I pull Jess aside, speaking quietly but quickly. "Okay, this is wonderful, and *you* are wonderful, but I haven't told you that Emma has stage five kidney disease. Meaning she can get super sick from eating or drinking things we don't think twice about. So you, me, and Guy are Team Emma tonight. Literally tackle anyone if they try to give her anything to eat or drink."

"I mean, I feel like I'd *normally* tackle a strange adult trying to give a child candy, but I hear you." Jess glances over at Emma, their voice softening. "Stage five is bad, right?"

"It's bad. Like, she needs a new kidney *now* kind of bad."

Jess nods, then they stand up straighter. "Well then, Team Emma it is."

I'm nervous about this whole situation, but Guy seems so calm. He's keeping an extra sharp eye on Emma though, because I'm not wrong about the food. She's staring at the plates of cookies with longing, and giving her grapes and her prepacked dinner is clearly not what she'd prefer. I think she's distracted, because the three of us are the center of attention all night long. In theory, this part is supposed to be fun, but I'm so worried I'm going to say the wrong thing. Every time someone new asks us how we met, my brain locks down, and I end up gaping like a fish fresh out of the river.

"Whirlwind romance," Guy supplies over and over, saving me from myself. "Couldn't help ourselves."

It helps that Emma steals the show, but once she decides hanging out with Jess is much more fun than with us, the adorable little distraction I've been hiding behind is gone. If anything, Guy seems utterly at ease, splitting his attention between where Jess and Emma are choosing the Christmas music and where I'm standing, trying not to make a fool of myself.

"If we're trying to pass this off as us being uncontrollably attracted to each other, I think at some point you're going to have to touch me," he finally teases me. "Otherwise, I might need to change my story."

"What would you say?" I rack my brain, trying to consider other options.

"How about the truth? My daughter is sick, and you swooped in like a knight in shining armor and rescued us."

I exhale a much-needed laugh at his joke, then I realize he's not joking. On instinct, I reach over and take his hand. "It's not one-sided," I tell him softly. The words stick in my throat, but I force them past. "It was lonely for a while."

"Longer than twenty days?" Guy's voice is gentle, and he dips his head, catching my eyes. The rest of my words stay lodged deeper in my chest, but I think he understands. He turns his larger hand beneath my palm and entwines our fingertips, smoothly changing the subject. "You said the other morning you liked to dance. If I asked my wife to dance with me, would she say yes?"

"She'd say 'Frosty the Snowman' is playing right now." I find myself smiling as he draws me toward the dance floor. Unfortunately, by the time we reach the patio, we start to get noticed.

"First dance, first dance, first dance," the room begins chanting. That's right. People. Lots of people, getting inebriated on an open bar and eggnog, and isn't that going to be an awful combination tomorrow morning?

"If they don't slow down, some of these guys are going to be puking their way back to their homes," I mumble.

Emma abandons Jess and comes running to us, lifting her arms in request, so Guy sweeps her up, pressing a kiss to her temple. "Having fun, baby?"

"*So* much."

The way she says it makes me laugh, and Guy's eyes twinkle in the holiday lights as he matches my grin. We have our first dance to Frosty, with Emma on his shoulders, the little girl dissolving into childish giggles each time Guy playfully spins around. The first dance turns into the second, then the third, and I'm happy and breathless by the time the three of us finally give in and sit the next song out. To be fair, there really is no way to dance to "Grandma Got Run Over by a Reindeer".

There's noise toward the front of the bar, but I'm not tall enough to see what's going on. "Is something happening?" I ask as Jess comes up.

"Jake and Charley are taking care of it," they say, waving off my question. "Okay, it's cake time!" Jess takes a picture, then adds, "For the paper. Tonight's party is going to be the front of page eleven."

Oh great, page eleven. The entertainment page. I'm imagining myself in ink, staring like a deer caught in headlights.

"Cheeseburgers, beer, and way too much cake." Suddenly I start to laugh. "You know who would have loved this?"

"Your dad." Jess smiles at the thought. "I asked the home about bringing him over here for the cake part, but the nurse on staff thought it would be too much activity. He might get confused."

"Dad sometimes recognizes me," I acknowledge. "He wouldn't understand why I was kissing someone else."

"That would require actual kissing," they murmur out of the corner of their mouth. "When do I get to hear the real story? You two might be making plenty of googly eyes at each other, but I'd bet my job you haven't jumped into full honeymoon status yet."

They aren't wrong, but other than a helpless shrug, I can't answer.

"Sen-na? Can I have some?" A little hand tugs on my sleeve, and I see Emma making moon eyes at the wedding cake. This is going to be a problem for Emma, and I look to Guy for help. He nods as if knowing what I'm thinking.

"As long as it isn't chocolate, I'll cut her a really small piece," he tells me. "I'll scrape the icing off too, which should help."

Nope, it's not chocolate, but there are a whole lot of strawberries and cream. Between the strawberries layered throughout the cake, we're able to get her a piece that's only a little cake and a lot of fruit. Emma's so excited she doesn't seem to realize her cake is tiny compared to everyone else's, but maybe it helps when Guy and I share a small piece, scraping the icing off too.

I appreciate not having cake stuffed in my face, although Guy cheerfully offers. He does dab a bit of icing on the tip of my nose to make Emma laugh, and when I wrinkle my nose at him playfully, he swipes it off and licks his finger, winking at me.

Oh, this boy knows how to give a really good wink. *Fake husband*, I tell myself. Don't focus on…that.

For some reason, it's getting louder in here, a chorus of clinking noises, which grows as more join in. Mouth still full of cake, I see the faces of people who claim to like me. Jess waves their hands and points at what's fastened to the string lights above us, the reason behind the clanging and smirks.

Yep. It's mistletoe.

I can feel my eyes widen when I realize what this means. We've never kissed, and I'm not sure if I'm ready for whatever everyone thinks is going to happen as they clang their dessert forks against their drinks.

Guy figures it out a moment after I do, and I see his jaw ripple.

Is he going to kiss me? Should I kiss him first? Do we have to do anything at all, since socially encouraged displays of intimacy aren't something we should feel forced to perform? I mean, yeah, he looks great tonight. If I'd had a couple of those eggnogs, it might be easier to decide.

Now I've hesitated too long, and it's getting super awkward.

Setting my fork down, I swallow down my bite and try not to look as panicked as I feel. Okay, first kiss in front of everyone. First kiss, and I haven't even decided if I want to kiss him. Who knows if Guy wants to kiss me? Then he's standing in front of me, his body so close his shirt brushes against my fingertips. Warm, strong hands take my face in between them.

"Breathe, Sen," Guy murmurs, his mouth barely ghosting over mine without any actual pressure against my lips. But his hands cradling my face make it hard to see, and when he pulls away, everyone's making catcalls and cheering.

It's not a kiss, even if they all think it was. Everyone turns away now the show is over, going back to their conversations.

"You good?" Guy's hands drop from my face, and as he cups my elbow, my palm rests on his muscled arm.

"Yeah, thanks for that."

The heat of his body warms my skin, and the slowly shrinking personal bubble of space we've maintained tonight is almost gone. His eyes drop down to my mouth, and suddenly I'm wondering exactly why it seemed like a bad idea to do this. When his thumb strokes a small touch on my arm, silently asking me to move closer, my body instinctively follows his request. I go up on my toes, fingers tightening on his shirt for balance as I wrap my hand around the back of his neck and tug his face back down to mine.

This time, Guy's lips brush over mine, then linger, as if waiting for me to decide. I close my eyes, bite my bottom lip, then nod. Guy's arm tightens around my waist, holding me to him as he deepens the kiss. He tastes like peppermint and cream, and despite the alcohol around us, I can smell his deodorant and, even fainter, the shampoo he used tonight. Those scents shouldn't calm my mind, but I find the party around us doesn't matter nearly as much as Guy does or the fact that he's here now.

His touch doesn't feel new. It feels...inevitable. As if it took me far too long to be exactly where I'm supposed to be. And when he presses the softest kiss to my jaw, it's not the end of this moment but a promise of the next one.

For the first time all night, this packed, hectic room quiets. I mean, it's a really good kiss. Why wouldn't they? I find myself grinning up at him, because as a first kiss goes, the Montana boy delivered. But Guy's not looking at me, and the arm cradling me close stays wrapped around my waist. I turn to follow his eyes to the sidewalk just outside the patio lights, and now I understand. There's Micah, standing there with a stunned look on his face. And until Charley and Jake all but drag Micah away, Guy's arm stays around me, locked down tight as we watch them go.

Almost as if this time, he's the one making sure *I'm* safe.

To Guy's credit, he never says a word about my ex showing up uninvited to our party.

Maybe he doesn't even know it was Micah, because Guy never mentions the man Jake and Charley hustle off down the street. He just takes my hand and dances with me and his daughter until Emma needs to call it an evening. She's fast asleep by the time we thank everyone and get home. Guy carries her up to bed while I make an evening gate check and animal check, then get changed into pajamas.

Yes, this was definitely the last way I would have expected tonight to go.

Despite what must have been an exhausting day for him, when I come down to tell Guy good night, I find him exercising in the kitchen again. He's got a portable pull-up bar hooked on the doorframe between the kitchen and the mudroom. Guy's listening to earbuds, and his back is to me, so he doesn't know I'm there. If I was a better person, I'd turn around and give him some privacy, but it's hard to beat this view.

Then I notice my favorite mug on the countertop, filled with milk and nowhere close to the Nalgene water bottle on the edge of the counter near him.

Apparently, I'm invited to this party too.

He's tall enough that he's got his feet tucked up behind him as he hangs from the pull-up bar, the muscles in his back flexing as he slowly raises his body up until his nose is at the doorframe, then just as gradually lowering himself back down again. I see his arms tremble a little at the last one, then Guy drops lightly to his bare feet. He turns to reach for his water bottle and then sees me.

"Hey," he says, shooting me a smile, pulling his earbud out. There's a little flush on his face, which might be from the exercise. Maybe. Or maybe he's thinking what I'm thinking. "Can't sleep?"

"I'm still a little wired from tonight," I admit. "Maybe I should do some of those."

Why did I say that? Is this me flirting? Oh, please don't let this be my version of flirting. It's been so many years, I don't think I know how anymore.

"Go for it," he says, stepping aside to make room for me.

I take a sip of my milk and then join him in the doorway.

The process seems simple enough. Grab the bar, hang there for a moment, hoist myself up, then repeat until I look as sexy and awesome as he does. The grabbing and the hanging part is easy enough, but when I try to do the pulling up part, my hard-earned muscles from years of backbreaking labor decide to just...not.

Huh.

A few wiggles and one serious effort might have pulled most of the muscles in my core, and I drop back to the ground, frowning at myself in annoyance. I look over and see the biggest grin on Guy's face, and I turn my frown his way instead.

"What?"

He holds his hands up innocently. "I promise I'm not laughing at you. It was just cute. You were glaring at your arms like they offended you."

"Well, they certainly aren't behaving. How can I unload a truck bed full of fifty-pound bags of grain but not get my nose to the doorframe?"

"Different muscle groups," he says. "Most people train these assisted until they can pull their own body weight."

I try again to no avail, then look around for something that could be an assist. "Like a chair?"

"You can use a chair to do a reverse pull-up," he explains. "Which will build the muscles up. Or bands can help too."

"Does baling twine count? I'm fresh out of exercise bands."

Guy shifts behind me, all extra tall and Montana-y. "I can give you a lift when you pull upward if you'd like."

"I don't want to hurt you," I tell him, and this time, I know he's laughing at me, if silently.

"I'll be fine," Guy promises, amusement in his tone as he takes my hips in his hands and helps me jump up. He supports me at the top, then eases his hold as I try my first pull-up.

This is a whole lot easier with the help, and at the top of my second try, he loosens his hands around my hips even more, supporting me less as I come back down.

"You barely need me," he says as I go for a third one, my arms shaking at the strain.

"I need you more than you think."

"It's a nice idea," Guy murmurs, and when I look over my shoulder at him, twisting makes me lose my grip. He's got me, his hands tightening to catch me, then he lets my toes touch the ground. "That's a good way to strain your neck."

"I'm surprised you didn't strain your neck carrying the leftover cake to the truck," I counter. The leftover cake is still sitting in the truck, in a box far too big to fit in our refrigerator. Even after convincing the party-goers to take extra slices home with them, there's just so much. "I don't know what we're going to do with all of it, and it's not fair for Emma to have to see it in the fridge."

I suppose I could put it in the freezer, in individually wrapped slices for us to sneak out when she's napping over the next decade or so, but that's assuming a lot of things about our future I simply don't know. The top tier is packaged up separately, supposedly for us to freeze and pull out on our one-year anniversary. I can't even begin to process what to do with that part.

"How about your dad's care facility? So he can be a part of the celebration too, even if indirectly?"

The tears well up in my eyes instantly, but a few hard blinks force them back. "Thank you. That's a great idea. Thank you for tonight too. I'm sure it was super awkward for you."

"Sienna, if you think walking into a party with the prettiest girl in the room was awkward for me, then we really do need to get to know each other better."

I bite my lower lip at his compliment, then laugh at myself. I can't believe he has me flushing this easily.

"No time like the present," I tell him. "Want to sneak out a piece of cake?"

We'd only had a few bites of a piece with Emma earlier, so we share a second larger piece instead of doing pull-ups.

"I'm destroying your stress-ercise session, aren't I?" I ask around my mouthful of frosting.

"Naw, I'm good. Tonight, I wasn't stress-ercising."

"So sometimes you just punish your body for fun?" When he flashes me the widest grin at my unintended dirty comment, I flush so deeply I feel the heat all the way into my chest.

"That might be too much of a get-to-know-you question," Guy teases. "How about this? If you could have one thing, anything at all, for Christmas, what would it be?"

"Besides the obvious?" I glance up at the mostly closed door to Emma's room. Emma's kidney, hands down.

"Besides the obvious."

I take a forkful of cake and stare at it, thinking hard. The thing about my life is I try to keep it reasonable, contained, and I don't ask for more than I believe I can attain.

"I'd like to get my dad's old work truck running again. The one tucked in the workshop behind where I park. Maybe take him for a drive in it on one of his good days." I smile wistfully, because this is a game, not reality. "How about you?"

His eyes glance up the stairs, just like mine. "Besides the obvious?"

"Along with the obvious," I say gently. "We can add Emma in too."

"I honestly don't know. A week ago, I was crying myself sick in a grungy motel bathroom every night after Em went to sleep, convinced she was going to be dropped from the transplant list. Now, I wake up and you're the first thing I see every morning, coming down those stairs."

His honesty guts me, and I don't know what to say. I almost make a joke about my morning breath, but the way he's looking down at our hands entwined together next to the dessert plate, the words catch in my throat. I don't even remember reaching out to hold him.

More carefully than any man has ever touched me, he lifts up my palm and presses a kiss to the inside of my wrist. I can't read what's in his eyes, but whatever it is, he feels it deeply.

"So, a little more of this?" I ask.

My husband is still holding my hand, and for a moment, the small gesture is bigger...*more important*...than anything has ever been before.

"Yeah," Guy says softly. "Just a little more of this."

Chapter 13

I STAY UP WAY TOO LATE, TRYING AND FAILING TO DO PULL-UPS AND having far too much fun hanging out with Guy. The following morning, I wake up from a dream where Guy is wearing a Santa hat and not a stitch else, watching me with those blue eyes of his as he fixes loose screws in Santa's sleigh.

Nope. That's not disrespectful at all.

I think he knows something is up, because I keep blushing when he looks at me over breakfast, and I know a smug male expression when I see one. Emma decides to hang out with me instead of her dad, so she rides with me on the tractor as I bring a fresh round bale of hay to the cattle pen. Barley wanders along after us, snuffling at the snow and looking stoically disappointed we aren't spending the morning in front of the fire.

"Why do the moo cows get these and the horsies don't?" Emma points at the big round bales, which are huge compared to the small square ones we keep in the horse barn.

"Because cows have tougher tummies than horses do. They can eat and eat, and it won't bother them. But if a horse eats too much hay or grain, they can get really bad tummy aches, which make them sick, and sometimes die."

"Kind of like me."

Her statement is so calm, so nonchalant, I sit there gaping. Unsure of what to say, I ease down the hay bale in the middle of the cattle herd. "Is that what it starts to feel like?" I finally ask her. "A tummy ache?"

Emma likes to wriggle, so I keep a snug arm around her as I turn the tractor and head back toward the gate. Sure enough, she wiggles around to put the toy reindeer in her hand in my curly hair. "Sometimes I throw up, but I try not to. Daddy doesn't like it when I throw up."

"No?"

"It makes him cry." Then she leans her head against my shoulder as she plays, ignoring the wintery world around us as she chooses to snuggle instead.

I can't get the image of a hurting, terrified Guy out of my head, trying to hide his tears from his sick daughter while she's trying to hide her nausea from him. I want to throw myself over both of them, but even a human shield can't protect them from the land mine going off in their lives. When we reach the gate, I set the tractor's emergency brake and wrap both of my arms around her, hugging her closer.

"Emma?" I say quietly. "Did you know that of all the things in the world, your daddy loves you the absolute most?" She smiles at me and nods as if, yeah, *of course* she knows. "Sometimes we cry because we love people so much. But he's always going to want to know about your tummy aches, okay?"

"Do you throw up?" Emma asks me as if we're having the most normal of conversations right now.

"Sometimes. When I don't feel good or if I'm too anxious about something."

"You should tell Daddy. He's nice to me when I'm sick. He'll be nice to you too."

I mean...I can't argue with her logic. Instead, I hug her until Emma starts to wiggle again, looking longingly at Barley. I can't blame her. At four, I'd rather have spent my time with a furry snout than a regular boring human too.

I double-check the gate is locked behind us, then we putter along back to the garage. When I park next to the metal siding, my normal spot when I know I'll be taking it back out again later, I see the sliding door is open. The telltale noises of a person working come from inside the garage, even though the last time I saw Guy this morning, he'd been up to his elbows in chopping wood for the wood-burning stove.

He's working on my dad's truck.

I stop in my tracks, trying to stuff the rapidly rising emotions down so I don't become a sloppy mess. It's just a truck. It's just a man leaning under the hood, replacing a corroded battery with a brand-new one. The dusty old radio on my dad's workbench is turned on, with '90s country playing in the background to the sounds of plastic scraping against metal.

"The battery in this is always a tight fit." I come up behind Guy, leaning a hip against the quarter panel. "Dad would cuss up a storm taking them out and putting new ones in."

"Then he and I have something in common," Guy says in a wry tone. "It's a good thing Em was with you."

He glances over his shoulder, checking on his daughter. Emma's playing just outside the door, with Barley flopped over on his back, all four reddish-gray paws sticking straight up in the air like he's a puppy again.

"Do you think it's just the battery?" I ask, peering into the engine block.

"Nope, but it needed one anyway, and I wanted to grab some other parts when I dropped off the cake. Everyone said to tell you thank you."

"You deliver the cake and I get the kudos?" When Guy winks at me, the memory of dream Guy in his Santa hat fixing things springs back up. I clear my throat, then laugh softly at myself. "You're sweet to work on this. You know you don't have to, right? You can take a day off."

"Says the woman whose been working since dawn." He doesn't say it unkindly. In fact, Guy sneaks an arm around my waist, giving me a little hug before refocusing on the truck. "Besides, this is fun."

I love that he's in a good mood, but I shift closer, lowering my voice. "Umm, I think you should probably know something Emma told me this morning. I guess she tries not to let you know when she's been throwing up."

His hands pause midtask, just for a moment, as he processes this. "Did she say if she has recently?"

"She didn't." I shake my head. "It's a bad sign, right?"

Guy takes a moment to answer. "Yeah. It's a symptom of the dialysis not working as well." He fiddles with the connections on the battery despite having finished installing it, his expression going bleak. Then he musters up a small smile. "I'm glad she has you to tell things to. Emma hasn't had a lot of women in her life who weren't doctors, nurses, or aides. My sister, Hayden, is great with her, but we only get to video chat once a week. It's not the same as having someone sitting next to you."

"Can I ask about her mom?"

The question has been on my mind from the very start, but he's never mentioned Emma's mother, and I wasn't sure it was okay to ask. Guy fiddles with the connections again, and I think he's not going to answer. Then he sighs.

"Her mom is a tough subject."

"That's fine. I don't mean to push."

"No, it's okay." Guy glances at Emma again, where she's moved on to tying pieces of baling twine like ribbons into Barley's tail. "Her mom's name is Becca. Some friends introduced us during my junior year of college. I was studying architecture, and she was an art major. We clicked right from the start. We had fun for a few months, but it wasn't anything too serious. Then she realized she was pregnant."

Some pauses are trying to know what to say, and some pauses simply come from being lost in memories. Maybe for Guy, it's both.

"I didn't pressure her one way or the other," he says quietly. "It was Becca's choice, and I knew she wasn't sure she wanted a baby. When she decided to keep Emma, I tried to do the right thing. I went to all the doctor appointments, and I took a semester off to work construction and get some money. I even proposed, although I was covered in sawdust and eating pizza at the time."

"Not the most romantic proposal?" I tease him lightly, earning a quick smile.

"No, but Becca was cool. Totally the type to appreciate pizza and a ring." His smile fades. "She said no, which I expected, because we weren't really together. More like friends who were having a baby. The delivery was rough, which I keep coming back to when I think about it all. Did I miss something? Did the doctors miss something? With either of them?" His voice drops even quieter. "Becca had never dealt with mental health issues before, and when postpartum hit her hard..." Guy's expression tightens. "I think back, and I try to figure out if I wasn't helping enough or if I wasn't understanding enough. If there's more I could have done. She wasn't bonding with Emma, and she was exhausted and scared and always crying. She used to tell me she just needed to sleep. I had a boss who understood things were tough, so he let me take Emma to work with me. I used to keep the truck running so she'd have air-conditioning, and I'd measure and cut boards next to the truck all day, so I'd be right there."

Guy stops, and I realize he's having a hard time continuing. When I take his hand, pressing my thumb next to his scuffed, engine-greasy knuckles, he squeezes tightly.

"I took Emma to all her doctor appointments. I didn't miss any, and I've double-checked a thousand times. Em was born with a congenital kidney defect, but no one knew it. The doctors say sometimes young children with CKD lose up to eighty percent of kidney function before they start to show symptoms…"

The self-recrimination is all over his face, and when I wrap my arms around his waist, he rests his chin on top of my head for a moment. Then he moves away, looking embarrassed.

"Sorry. The last thing you need is me leaning on you with this."

"Marriage of purpose, remember?" I remind Guy. "You get to lean on me all you want."

The looks he gives me sometimes make me bite my lower lip, wondering how much of this is actually in my head. Maybe he just looks particularly good in engine grease.

"Anyway, when we found out about Emma, Becca took it really hard. When no one in our families was a donor match, she spiraled. Her meds hadn't been working, and she needed more support than she was getting. She went to stay with her sister back east. I would have gone with her, but when she said she needed some space to try to process everything, I realized what was coming."

I close my eyes, my heart breaking for the younger version of the man in front of me, with a sick infant and nowhere to turn.

"How's Becca now?"

"She's doing better. She finished school, has a decent job, and met a nice person. She doesn't want to see Emma, even though we've talked about it a couple times. She says she can't get close to her while knowing…"

Knowing Emma's illness is terminal if she doesn't get a kidney.

"You've spent the last four years doing this alone," I say softly. "It must be scary."

"Yeah, but as time goes on, I'm learning how to mask it better. I sometimes wonder how I got so lucky, because so many people have helped us when we needed it most. Some more than others." Guy glances at me, and when our eyes meet, he gives me a sweet smile that matches his daughter's smile. "God's been good, and I've learned to appreciate when someone doesn't close a door in my face."

His ability to find something positive in this overwhelms me, and it's all I can do not to hug him again. "So, you're fixing my dad's work truck?"

"I'm *trying* to fix your work truck. Fair warning, I might not be successful. Try the engine for me?"

I slip into the driver's seat and scoot it forward so I can reach the pedals. The dashboard lights up, and the engine clicks a few times, but nothing. Guy makes a *tsk*ing noise but doesn't seem too bothered by it.

"Did Emma tell you anything else I should know?"

"Oh yes. Emma also said I should tell you when I get nervous about things. Not exactly in those words, but you know, when I have a stomachache too."

"Do as I say, not as I do?"

"Something like that."

"She's not wrong. You're my wife, Sienna. I took my vows seriously. When I said I have your back, I meant it. Can you try to rev the engine while I do something?"

I do as asked, and this time, the engine turns over. It isn't a healthy engine purr, but it's at least running. Then it promptly sputters and dies again. A word slips from his mouth, and I snicker.

"Yeah, my dad used to say the same thing all the time." It's easier to talk when there's an upright hood and an engine block between us, and my mouth unglues from what's been on my mind. "Hey, our kiss last night…" I drift off, uncertain how to verbalize what I want to say.

"Gave you a stomachache?" I can hear the humor in his voice as he comes around the side of the hood. Guy braces an arm on the roof of the truck, gazing down at me.

"Not exactly," I hedge, looking away. "But not *not* exactly."

He tips his head to catch my gaze. "I guess the question is, was the kiss for them or was it for you?"

"I might need to plead the Fifth on this one."

He barks out a laugh and then holds the door open wider for me to climb out. "We can't be forced to testify against each other. Your secrets are safe with me."

"Well, in that case, I maybe...*maybe*...did it for me."

"What did you do, Sen-na?" Emma calls over from the garage door.

"Yes, Sen-na, what *did* you do?" Guy teases as he gets into the truck and then promptly cracks his knee on the steering wheel. When another small curse escapes his mouth, it makes me giggle.

"Oops, sorry."

"Nope, it's all good." Guy slides the seat backward, shooting me a quick grin despite what must be a painful bump on the kneecap. "Just part of getting used to being with a very short woman."

"I'm not short," I protest.

"You're not very tall either." And when he winks at me, it occurs to me never once did it seem strange to have Guy in here, working with my dad's tools, in Dad's garage, making this his home too.

I think I like it.

———

When I go down that night before bed, Guy has transformed into a sexy Christmas Claus.

Not a sexy Santa Claus, because Santa never looked this good, not even in Santa's better days. But here he is, in bright-red flannel pants with Christmas toys all over them, which I know for a fact match the ones Emma's wearing to bed right now. The Maple family apparently takes their holiday pajamas more seriously than my "Christmas Eve and done" routine.

I'm far from a sexy Mrs. Claus right now. Per Emma's request, I'm rocking some neon-green Grinch joggers I had to dig out of storage, and she's given me a pair of felt reindeer antlers that have seen better days. One droops into my face, which might be why Guy keeps trying to hide a grin when our eyes meet.

Guy's still wearing the Santa hat she put on his head before her bedtime story, but he's ditched the boxy, shapeless matching flannel button-up shirt. Instead he's reclining in a seat at the kitchen island in a white T-shirt that shows his muscles to distressing detail and is a little snugger after getting three solid meals in for a few days.

He has to know he looks good. I swear the man is doing this on purpose.

There's a mug of milk and a brownie waiting for me on the seat next to his. I recognize this brownie. The special, Christmastime only, three-inch-thick, peppermint-dusted triple-chunk brownie from the bakery in town across the street from LK's. A slab of chocolatey holiday joy stuffed full of enough sugar to keep a girl running for a month.

"Is this for me?" I ask hopefully, sidling up to the counter, no longer focused on the sexy Claus. Because *nothing* is sexier than this brownie.

The little wink he gives me is cute. "What, this brownie?"

"That's my *favorite* brownie," I say, sneaking a little closer and sitting down in the stool catty-corner to his.

"Funny, that's what Jess told me last night when I was picking their brain for things you might like."

"Jess sold me out, straight up, huh?" I sigh lustily when he nudges the brownie my way. "Thank you, although I feel guilty eating treats after Emma goes to bed."

"Jess also told me you love puppies and snowmobiling," Guy admits. "This was the easiest to fit on the counter, but I could go to the rescue shelter…"

"Don't threaten me with a good time." Suddenly I realize this man would one hundred percent go to the rescue shelter for a Christmas puppy if I wanted to go. A rush of warmth for him floods through me, and I find myself grinning as I lift the brownie up and take an appreciative sniff. "Ooh, these get better every year."

"I forgot to tell you I grabbed the mail on my way in today," Guy says as I make doe eyes at my snack. "Do we normally get a newspaper?"

"Nope, I read the news online, like a normal human."

When he hands me an actual newspaper, there's a bright-green sticky note attached in Jess's handwriting.

"I thought you might want to keep this," I read aloud, then I groan when I see the front page. "'Christmas comes early for the Naples-Maple family.' Oh nooooo."

"Did we make the paper?" Guy seems surprised.

"We *are* the paper today. In a town this size, a rabbit hopping across the road makes the news. You and I getting randomly married is on the front page." I show him the picture under the paper's title page, then continue to read aloud. "Longtime resident of Caney Falls, Idaho, Sienna Naples wed Montana native Guy Maple in a private ceremony. The couple celebrated their whirlwind romance—" I pause and give Guy a look, which he responds to with that charming grin of his. "—whirlwind romance at LK's Bar and Grill. Sienna Maple (née Naples) and Guy Maple, along with daughter, Emma Maple, are the current caretakers of Naples Ranch, a thousand-acre private wilderness and gem of the Salmon River Valley." I hide my face in my hands, leaning on the island. "Jess! *Why?*"

Guy peers over my shoulder at the paper. "What's the big deal?"

"The big deal is that Micah is going to freak out. I never changed my last name to Micah's, which was a sore point for him. Like...a really sore point."

Guy thinks about it for a moment, and then his hands rest down on my shoulders, squeezing lightly. "You didn't change your name for me either," he reminds me. "You did it for Emma."

"Yes, but Micah isn't going to know. I swear I can hear him popping a gasket from across town." I get up and start wiping down the counter, despite it being clean. Guy settles into the seat I vacated, watching me for a few minutes, then he casually takes a little bit of the napkin beneath my brownie, tears it off, and wads it up. Then he sets it in the middle of the island, right where I've wiped down three times in the last thirty seconds.

"You looked like you needed something to clean," Guy tells me, those glacier-blue eyes sparkling mischievously. Then he starts to eat my peppermint-dusted, three-inch-thick, triple-chocolate-chunk holiday brownie.

He's eating my brownie.

"Oh, you brat," I breathe.

It's been a long time since I chased someone, but some things are worth it. Guy's faster than me, and he's overly confident, thinking I won't dare follow him out into the cold of the front porch. Not only will I dare, but I also grab for the freshly fallen snow on the railing, pack it up into a ball, and smoosh the sucker right into his face.

Hmm. Maybe this was a wrong move. Yep, definitely a wrong move, because I'm in my pajamas in the snow, and sexy Christmas Claus is chasing *me* now.

I squeal when I get a handful of snow down the back of my shirt, then dissolve into laughter as he picks me up in his arms, spinning me until I'm dizzy. Guy trips, and we both end up in the snow, although at least it's the soft, fluffy kind on the yard, not the hard, icy, packed-down stuff on the driveway. I'm sprawled across his lap, our limbs tangled, and I'm not sure the brownie made it.

"Brownie down?" I ask as his eyes gaze down at me in the bright wintery moonlight.

"There's a second one in the fridge," Guy tells me smugly. "I know better than to not get a backup brownie."

Oh, he's a smart man. A shivery, cold man, but a smart one.

"Aren't you supposed to be doing some sort of ridiculously sexy workout routine right now? Instead of getting frostbite on your entire back?" I ask, because Guy might be sitting in the snow, but plenty of it is still falling on us.

"I had to do something more important first." His voice gets softer and at the same time huskier. "Hey, Sienna? I'm glad everyone knows. When we walked into the restaurant last night, I have never been prouder. I like being married to you."

I close my eyes, then I exhale softly. "I like it too."

Guy's face dips down, his breath condensing in the cold air. "You said you had a stomachache after the kiss," he whispers. "I didn't have a stomachache."

"Maybe a stomachache isn't exactly the right wording," I whisper back. "More like a gut punch. The good kind."

Guy doesn't make fun of my description. Instead, he murmurs, "Yeah, me too."

His fingers curl through my hair, asking a silent question. Maybe, if a snowflake hadn't chosen this moment to land on the end of his nose, I would have been able to resist. Instead, I laugh at the way his nose wrinkles and find myself pressing my mouth to his smiling lips.

And when my fake-but-not-fake husband kisses me in the snowy moonlight, it's even better than peppermint and chocolate.

Chapter 14

My phone chirps at my side, and I can't help the silly grin crossing my face.

I'm finishing the last of the lunch dishes, so I don't check it yet, but I know who the text is from. I'm not sure when Guy managed to find time to work today, because we've been messaging each other little silly GIFs all morning. I sent him off to work with a lunch box filled with sandwiches again, resulting in goofy selfies of him eating each one with gusto. I never knew ham and cheese on whole grain could look so good in a man's hand, or maybe I just love seeing him happy. But I feel like I'm a teenager again, all excited when a boy texts me and unable to focus on my day job.

Admittedly, I haven't been trying to work much anyway. Emma and I spent the morning inside finger painting and waiting for the day to warm up enough to take her outside.

"Emma, do you want to go say hi to Legs and Lulu before your nap?" I ask as I dry my final glass. She doesn't answer, which isn't abnormal, but I hear a small gagging noise. When I turn, I see her sitting on the couch with her head bent down.

"Emma?"

"Sen-na, I don't feel good."

Then she promptly throws up all over herself, including the llamacorn

Christmas sweater she was so excited to wear today. The effect is instantaneous. The moment Emma realizes her sweater is covered in vomit, she immediately bursts into tears, bawling out my name.

"Oh, sweetie," I say, hurrying over to her. "It's okay."

This is a new experience for me, having a crying child holding on to me with vomit now on us both, but I know the power of a hug when you're feeling awful. I hold her tight until the sobs become sniffles, then I carry her into the hallway bathroom to get her cleaned up.

"It's really okay, Em," I promise her. "I'll throw it in the wash, and you'll still be able to wear it today."

"Really?" She looks up at me with red, puffy eyes, and I hug her again, extra tight.

"Really, sweetie. We'll do the quick cycle too, so you don't have to wait long." I'll even train Barley to do laundry if it'll make her feel better.

I start to help her change into clean clothes, then I realize it's not just her little eyes that look puffy… Her legs look puffy too. The tops of her socks look like they're digging into her skin. There's no way Guy would have dressed her in too-small socks.

"Emma, is it okay if I check your feet?" I ask her. When she nods, I press my thumb gently into her ankle. She's not just puffy; her feet are significantly more swollen than I realized. Guy checks her every morning and evening for symptoms, and he records everything. When I check her tablet, he's marked she has mild edema, but this doesn't look mild to me. These are some seriously squishy feet. I put a pair of my socks on her instead of her own, because too big seems better than making her uncomfortable with too-tight socks.

Barley's waiting for us in the hall outside the bathroom, and he whines pitifully until Emma is back in her room, where he can hop up next to her in bed. I'm about to tell him to get down, but she wraps her arms around his neck, burying her face in his fur, and the look Barley gives me is clear.

He won't be moving anytime soon.

"Good boy," I murmur, briefly touching his muzzle. Then I inhale a tight breath, because Barley's not the only one going gray. Emma is too.

When I call, Guy picks up on the first ring. "Sienna? What's wrong?"

"Emma just threw up, and she seems really out of it. Her feet and ankles are really swollen, and she's lost a lot of color in her face."

"How swollen?"

"Enough her socks don't fit. I put her in a pair of mine."

"Swelling and vomiting is a sign she needs dialysis." Guy breathes a soft curse.

"Didn't she just get it?"

"Yeah."

Emma makes another gagging noise, and I grab the trash can in the corner of her bedroom, pushing between her and Barley so I can hold it under her face. "She's throwing up again," I tell him, alarmed.

"Get her in the truck, and meet me in town," Guy says sharply. "I'll call her nephrologist."

He doesn't say goodbye before hanging up, and I don't blame him. I'm already scooping Emma up in my arms and rushing for the door. Barley is hot on our heels, but I bark at him to stay. He listens, but he doesn't like it. I run back in for Emma's bag, grateful for Guy's preparedness, because inside are green plastic vomit bags. Barley tries to follow again, so I shut the door with my foot before he can sneak out. He ducks through the doggie door, but this time he stays on the porch, ears flattened with stress, as I start the truck to warm it up for Emma.

Emma wants to lie down in the back seat, but I tell her she has to be buckled into her car seat. It starts a new wave of crying, but weaker this time. I hush her as best as I can, telling her we're going to get her daddy. She nods, clutching the vomit bag I give her like it's a stuffed animal.

I hate that I didn't remember to grab one of her toys.

Never has the drive from my place to the main highway felt this long. Every icy bump on the road makes me cringe, because now would be a terrible time to end up with a tire in a snow-filled ditch. I keep checking if my phone has reception just in case I get stuck out here with Emma in trouble.

She's sniffling in the back seat, and it's physically painful for me to keep both hands on the wheel instead of reaching back and holding her little mittened fingers. But I can't risk an accident. I talk to her instead in my softest voice because she's hurting. I tell her I love her and her daddy loves her and most of all, God loves her. I tell her when we go back home, we're going to make reindeer antlers for Legs. We can put Barley in a Santa suit because he's already red, even though he'll be grumpy about it.

Emma's still crying, but she giggles at the image. And when we finally turn onto the ice-free main road into town, I reach behind me and drive the rest of the way with her hand gripping mine.

Guy's waiting outside the jobsite with a little stuffed moose under his arm that must have been in his truck, and he jogs over to my driver's side door, opening it. "Her nephrologist wants to see her," he says, truck keys in hand. "I need to get her to Idaho Falls. Can we switch vehicles? The car seat takes forever to change out, and I need her there now."

"I'll drive you," I tell him. "I'd rather stay with you both."

I start to ask him if it's okay, but Guy's already hustling around the truck. He hops in the passenger seat, then turns around and takes Emma's hand. "Hey, baby girl," he says in his kindest, most gentle voice. "I brought Mr. Moose. He wanted to see you." When she ignores the moose, Guy's voice softens even more. "Having a tough day today?"

She nods, tears in her eyes, reaching her arms out to him. For a tall man, he's awfully good at climbing over the center divider, ditching the passenger seat so he can be next to his daughter. It's not safe to take her out of her car seat, so Guy sits as close as he can, wrapping his arms around Emma and cuddling her.

The drive to Idaho Falls is long, but it's never felt this long before. The stretch of highway lies in a valley between two parallel ridges, and in the summer, it's a pretty if remote drive. In the winter, it's two hours of nothing but snow.

I'm doing ten miles over the speed limit, but it feels like we're crawling. When Emma throws up again, I push it to fifteen. I wait until she falls asleep against Guy's shoulder, clutching a vomity Mr. Moose, before asking, "Was it the party? Did she get something we didn't see?"

"No, I watched her like a hawk." When I glance in the rearview mirror, Guy's expression is bleak. "This is just what happens. The dialysis isn't working as well anymore."

I don't ask if he's going to be in trouble at work. I don't think it matters.

It's been a while since I was last in Idaho Falls, but Guy knows these streets well enough to give me directions to the hospital without using his phone. When the hospital's concrete walls rise above us outside the truck windows, I should feel relieved. Instead, a new kind of fear washes through me. I follow the signs for the emergency department entrance, then pull up to the curb. Guy hops out and takes Emma from her car seat as I go to find a parking space at the most packed hospital ever.

It's been a long time since I've been to a hospital. As I scratch the door's paint job getting out because I parked too close to a concrete pole, I realize going to the hospital is Guy's and Emma's lives. Days like these maybe aren't the standard, but they sure are the norm.

By the time I get inside, Guy and Emma aren't in the emergency waiting room. "I'm looking for my husband and my stepdaughter," I tell the front reception desk, and I'm told they've been moved to the children's wing.

As I try to find my way to the children's wing, I wonder if it's confusing signage or simply my brain resisting this situation that makes it so hard to know where to go. Each long empty hall looks like the next. Beige vinyl tile, more beige on the walls. Gray plastic handrails and oversize pictures of benefactors from the last hundred years fastened to the walls.

Someone in green scrubs yawning while carrying a salad. Two coworkers in red scrubs laughing at a shared joke between them. The logical part of me knows this hospital is full of hundreds of people who need to eat and joke and walk down halls. They are the miracle workers trying to save Emma's life, the ones who will take care of her and hopefully one day put a new kidney in her. But in this moment, when I am scared and frustrated and lost, there's another illogical part of me that hates the salad for the normalcy it represents. A part that doesn't understand how anyone could share a joke when Emma's sick. Don't they understand? *Emma* is sick.

I pause, looking left and right, then close my eyes and lean against the plastic handrail, letting it briefly hold me up. I can't stomach the idea of calling Guy and telling him I can't even be competent enough to find them.

"Get it together," I tell myself roughly. "Be better than this."

"Do you need any help?" I open my eyes to see a woman in blue scrubs with CNA on her tag. Thank you, God.

"The children's wing," I tell her. "I think nephrology?"

"The kidney and transplant center?" She gives me a sympathetic nod. "This way. I'll take you there."

I don't know how long I'm taking out of her break, and I feel guilty for my earlier thoughts as I whisper a thank-you. I silently promise myself not to be upset at any more salads or laughter. We pass from the adult wing to the children's wing of the hospital, and the decor changes to an overly cheerful holiday theme. The walls are plastered with attempts to make this terrifying place resemble the North Pole. We turn left at the reindeer paddock, follow the hall of Santa's workshop, and I try not to let my eyes linger on the Christmas lists handwritten in crayon and taped to a giant snowflake cutout. There are so many Christmas lists, it makes my heart twist and drop somewhere deep in my gut.

I wonder how many times Emma's had her own Christmas list on a hospital wall.

"The waiting room is at the end of the hall," the CNA tells me. I thank her again and wonder how many halls like this have been in Guy's life. How many salads or jokes or kind people who sacrifice five minutes of their day to a stranger who is lost?

The holiday decor is only muted when I reach the waiting room at the end of the hall. Maybe someone instinctively knew the parents of these kids needed a break from the bright reds and greens and sparkles and smiles. Instead, there's a dull, scratched coffeepot and a basket of chocolate chip chewy granola bars.

Guy's the only one in the waiting room. His long limbs don't quite fit in the chair, and his shoulders are slumped. The man I first met in the coffee shop looks up at me with haunted eyes. There's a little more flesh on his bones now, but the strain crushing him then is still crushing him now.

"How is she?" I ask, slipping into the seat next to him.

At first, I don't think he's going to answer me, because it takes him so long to reply.

"They're giving her dialysis. Her nephrologist says it's not a good sign she swelled up so quickly. They're switching her over to dialysis every day." His voice is toneless, his eyes staring at the wall just over my shoulder, but a muscle in his jaw twitches, the only tell this man has. I don't know him as well as I want to, but I know this: Guy's terrified.

I take his hand, and when he doesn't squeeze mine back, I pull his arm over my shoulders. I slide my own arm between the seat and his back, gripping his worn leather belt and pulling him to my side. I'm not strong enough to budge him, not if he doesn't want to move. But until he tells me otherwise, I'm giving him something solid to feel, someone else to lean on.

It takes him a moment, and one more. Then Guy turns and pulls me into his arms, holding me crushingly tight. His face presses to my shoulder, his whole torso shaking.

And when he cries, I hold him right back.

———

We don't leave the hospital until they run blood work and are satisfied Emma's stabilized...for now. At least there's pediatric dialysis close by, because it's going to be every day from now on.

"Will they let a stepparent take her for dialysis?" I ask as we get closer to home. The bulk of the drive has been in silence. I don't know why Guy isn't talking, but I'm staying quiet because Emma is sleeping, and I don't want to wake her. He's been staring out the passenger window for the last two hours, except for when he glances back to check on his daughter.

"I don't know," Guy replies hollowly. "It's never been an option."

He doesn't say anything more, doesn't give me any hint of what he's feeling or what he wants me to do. My brain is racing as it tries to plan my way through this. What can I do, what does she need, how will this change things? I pull into the jobsite, and when I park near his truck, I move the driver's seat back to give him legroom. His truck keys are still sitting in the cupholder of my truck, so I pick them up.

"I'll follow you," I say, because I'm not separating him and his daughter right now.

Wordlessly, Guy nods and gets out of the passenger side.

Guy's truck is tidy inside, although it carries a light layer of sawdust, not unexpected for a man who works construction for a living. I'm grateful when the engine starts, because the temperature has taken a dive since nightfall, and I rushed out of the house without a coat this morning.

I give the engine a moment to warm up, fiddling with the driver's seat so I can actually reach the pedals. That's when I notice there's a photo of Emma taped to the dash with duct tape. The edges are worn and the color is faded, but her smile is still bright as ever as she holds a massive floppy-eared bunny in her arms. Then I realize there's a second, newer photo taped next to the first one. A photo of me and Emma in the photo booth at our surprise wedding reception, with us both making matching silly faces.

Guy's got a photo of us in his truck.

This hits me hard, because it's what my dad did: he kept a photo of me and my mom in his truck. I've always known, but suddenly I understand, really understand, what's happening right now. Emma is dying. The little girl in my truck, waiting for me to pull out of the jobsite so her daddy can drive her home, is *dying*. And her daddy, who loves her enough to keep a picture of her on his dashboard, is going to lose her.

I'm glad to be alone because I sob all the way to the ranch.

It feels like a lifetime has passed between when I left the house and when we finally park back in the driveway. Guy looks exhausted, even more than I feel. His strong arms hold Emma close, and I wonder how much of her life he's spent carrying her. He takes her up to bed, and I want to tell him that I can do it for him. I want to carry them both, despite it being physically impossible. Instead, I put on a jacket and go take care of chores, knowing the animals are all going to be very upset with me for feeding them late. I work fast, checking the water trough in the cattle pen for signs of freezing, making sure they have enough hay until tomorrow morning and that no one got hurt while I was gone. Then I get through the barn feeding in record time, because I want to be back inside with my family, not out here, wondering if they're okay.

My family. They aren't even mine, not truly, but in this moment, they feel like all the family I've got. I almost forgo checking the cattle gates, but a lifetime of repetition wins over.

When I get back inside, Guy is just coming down the stairs from putting Emma to bed. My heart hurts to see those broad shoulders slumped as he joins me in the kitchen.

He's not meeting my eyes, and I wonder if it's because he's too tired to deal with a stranger who isn't used to his life but is suddenly right in the middle of it all.

"Did you get anything to eat?" he asks me, and I blink at the question. Guy's brow furrows. "You look dead on your feet."

"I can't remember, but you definitely haven't." I return to my default mode: make sandwiches, and make Guy eat the sandwiches. His furrowed brow softens when I put the first sandwich in front of him. Peanut butter and banana today. I don't know if he likes them, but it's my comfort food.

"Thanks, Sienna," he whispers, and the way he holds my eyes for a longer moment, I feel like his thanks is for more than the food.

We eat in silence at the kitchen island, and I'm only finishing my sandwich when I realize I took the stool right next to him. I'm simply unable to stay out of Guy's personal bubble right now.

"Do you need anything before I call it a night?" He's so exhausted, his voice is a low, raspy version of his normal baritone. But in this moment, I realize Guy isn't just being polite. Despite today, despite so many days and nights like today, he's still willing to help me if I ask. Then he'll head to a broken-down couch I never got around to replacing, the one that probably hurts his back and he's never once complained about.

I don't have the heart to ask him to sleep there tonight. Guy's life is a train wreck not of his making. He shouldn't have to be hungry. He shouldn't have to sleep on a crappy couch.

"Will you sleep upstairs with me tonight?" I ask finally. "In case Emma needs anything?"

I'm aware I'm inviting him into my bed when I could have just offered to stay on the couch. The thing is, I'm not sure I'm okay with being far from Emma tonight. And maybe, if I'm being honest with myself, I'm not okay with being far from Guy either. I need to keep them both close, where I can make sure I'm there if they need me.

Guy looks at me as if trying to process what I said. "I was planning on sleeping on her floor or in the hallway."

Oh. It makes sense he wouldn't want to be far away. "We can take turns on her floor if you want. Whatever she needs, Guy. Whatever you need, I'm here, okay?"

We sit there silently, and I wonder if I made a mistake by asking. Then Guy closes his eyes and takes a deep breath. "I'm not thinking straight. Yeah, I'd love a real bed tonight. But if you decide at any point it's not okay for me to sleep next to you, I need you to verbalize it, Sienna. I don't trust myself to notice if something's wrong. I'll try, but my brain is scrambled."

"I'll say something," I promise. "If I get unsettled, worst-case scenario, I'll go sleep on the couch so you can be near her. Stop worrying about me, okay? Let's just focus on Emma. We're Team Emma. We're in this together."

And let me focus on both of you, I add silently.

His fingers are work-roughened, just like mine are. But mine feel small inside his as we climb the stairs together. He brushes his teeth in the hall bathroom and changes for bed while I do the same in my bathroom. Then he raps his knuckles lightly on the doorframe of my room in warning before coming in.

Guy's never been in my bedroom before, and it's a testament to his exhaustion that he doesn't look around. Instead, he pauses and waits for me to sit down on the side of the bed I'm used to sleeping on. Guy's careful to stay on his side of the bed, but he fills his side with long limbs and broad shoulders in a way that makes me feel like he's dwarfing me. The bed is suddenly much smaller with him next to me. I could flex my fingers and almost touch his arm. Instead, I tighten them into a fist and tuck them behind my back, willing them to stop shaking.

How many nights did Guy face this all alone? What could I ever say to make any of this okay? I'm in over my head, desperate to do anything to help when there's nothing I can do. I love that little girl when I never expected to love anyone ever again.

"Sienna?" His voice is rougher, and I don't know for sure, but he might be crying. "Thanks for being there for us today."

My fingers no longer shake, not when they cover his hand.

"I'm not going anywhere," I whisper in the darkness of the room. "We're in this together."

Chapter 15

SOMETIME AFTER MIDNIGHT, MY BODY BETRAYS ME, AND I TURN Guy into the little spoon.

I don't remember wrapping my arm around his waist, entangling our legs, and stuffing my nose in between the muscles of his shoulder blades. I should probably extract myself, but his arm is draped over mine, and his breathing is slow and steady. If he's finally getting some much-deserved rest, maybe I shouldn't move? Every muscle beneath his clothing is lean and solid, the product of hard labor and a harder life. I can feel every ridge and plane of his stomach, and my fingers curl into the deepest ridge.

Just when I start to think I'm feeding him enough…

A soft chuckle accompanies the movement of his abdomen beneath my arm. "Sienna, no more sandwiches. Not unless I'm making them for you."

Guy rolls and faces me, somehow knowing what I'm thinking. My arm is still around his waist, and as I start to untangle myself and scoot back, a warm, strong hand rests on my hip, silently asking me to stay. No problem. All the warmest parts of the bed are in the critical foot of space between us.

"Did I wake you?" I ask, glancing at the clock on my nightstand. It's only half past two, and Guy sounds much too alert.

"No, I've been awake for a while," he admits. "Did you know you talk in your sleep?"

"If I said anything incriminating, I plead the Fifth," I murmur. Like how his lower back seems to have invented some new muscles where most men just have normal flesh.

"You talked about cookies." The hand on my hip slides so his fingers span my lower back, a moment so foreign between us but not unusual between two people curled up together.

"I like cookies," I admit. I also like the weight of his hand, but I don't tell him.

"What kind of cookies?" Guy's question seems oddly specific after the events of today.

I huff a laugh. "Pretty much anything with sugar and flour is good in my book. Why do you ask?"

"I'm trying to sneak some more intel out of you. I know you like my daughter, Legs, and brownies."

"I like Emma much more than Legs. And I *really* like Legs."

Guy's expression changes, and in the dim glow of the woodstove, I see his eyes flicker down to my lips. "Duly noted," he murmurs.

"Should we go check on her?" I ask, because it's safer to focus on Emma than it is to focus on a low, gentle voice asking me about cookies. I swear even his body language is coaxing me closer.

"I checked Emma a little bit ago," he tells me. "Her vitals are good, and the swelling is better. She's sleeping."

"You aren't though, are you? Do you want me to leave so you have some more space?"

"That's the last thing I want." Guy hesitates, then he asks softly, "Can I hold you? I know it sounds needy, but it's been a tough night."

"It's not needy," I promise. "We're married, Guy. I know this is a marriage of…"

"Convenience?" he supplies with a tiny smile.

"Purpose. We have a marriage of purpose, and that's helping Emma.

There aren't any rules for how we do it. If midnight snuggles help you, which will in turn help Emma, I'm in."

Guy sometimes gets this look when I talk, and I don't know how to read what he's thinking.

I inhale a deep breath, then add, "It will help me too. Plus, since I already had you in a rear body lock tonight…"

He sighs with playful lust. "If you watch MMA, you just secured your place as my dream girl."

I snicker as I scoot over those important couple of inches closer to him, enjoying how the blankets are trapping heat in the space between us. Then I turn so my shoulders are pressed to his chest. His hand on my hip becomes a muscled arm looped around my waist, cradling me close without locking down too tight. Guy's a much better big spoon than me, and I allow myself a moment to experience being held by him. It's been a really long time since I've been held. It's…nice.

I'd almost forgotten what nice was.

The moon is bright tonight, and as we lie there in the pale wash of moonlight through the window, I'm overly aware of how close we are. I feel like someone should say something, so my tongue decides on the first random thought that pops into my head.

"Do you remember when I called you the first time, and you thought I was trying to get you naked?"

He smiles against my shoulder. "I remember thinking I knew better, because the wildly hot ones always get me in trouble, but I was sorely tempted."

"Wildly hot ones, huh?" I can feel my cheeks heating.

"You're beautiful, Sienna." His voice softens. "You might be the prettiest woman I've ever seen. I could barely open my mouth the first time I saw you."

This from a man who had me drooling from his first push-up.

"It's been a long time since anyone called me beautiful," I admit. "I think it was my wedding day."

"So, two and a half days ago?"

"Brat. No, my real wedding." My grin slips when I realize what I said. "I mean, not that ours wasn't real… I just meant…"

Guy makes a soft noise in his throat. "I know. I didn't take it that way. We're not doing this the usual way."

I look over my shoulder at him and see Guy's eyes sweep over me. "I've spent all night thinking about how grateful I am Emma has you."

"You have me too," I whisper, wishing my heart wasn't hammering in my chest because of how he's looking at me.

He doesn't ask if he can kiss me. The way his thumb traces my cheek is a silent question and one I know the answer to. When I nod, he dips his head, brushing the softest, slowest kiss across my lips.

"Like this?" he asks gently, and I murmur an affirmative, turning in his arms. The second kiss is even slower, somehow even softer, for all it sends my pulse frantically scrambling. "Or like this?"

"Now you're showing off," I decide, and the best thing happens. He grins, a real, happy grin, and I see a glimpse of the man he could have been if life had been gentler on him.

"You bring it out in me, Sienna. I can't help myself." One last kiss to the tip of my nose, then Guy snuggles in, as if holding me is just as good as any of the rest of it.

I daydream, just for a moment, that he's holding me from love and not convenience. A life with Guy would be a gentler life. Loving a man like him would have been safer than the path I chose for myself. The girl who picked the wrong boy because he looked cute on a horse and held on long after she knew she had to let go. Somewhere there's a version of me that's more than a shadow of who I could have been too.

I wish I had any idea of how to find her. I wish I could tell her I'm sorry this happened to her.

"Hey, Guy, I promise, okay? No matter what happens, you and Emma will always have me. No matter what we choose to do." Then I yawn and cuddle deeper into his arms, adding sleepily, "Since it's technically Tuesday now, we married six days ago, mister. It's too soon to forget our wedding date yet."

His low laughter accompanying a brief kiss to my brow is the last thing I know before sleep takes me. "Trust me, Sienna. I'll never forget."

———

Guy checks on Emma a couple more times throughout the night, and every time, the movement of him in bed wakes me. I offer to go check on Emma for him, but he just murmurs for me to go back to sleep. I do, but only after he comes back to bed, and I know Emma is still safe.

My mental to-do list decides to turn up the volume full force an hour before my alarm goes off, forcing away the last vestige of sleep I was hoping for. The list today is long, and there are two people and a lot of animals in my home who will need breakfast. Guy's boss told him to take today off, so if I move quietly enough, maybe he can get a little extra sleep. If Emma is feeling better, maybe I can coax her into eating something she likes after morning chores.

"Sienna?" A low voice thickened with sleep makes a hushing noise. "Come back to bed."

"I'm technically still *in* bed," I remind him.

"Part of you isn't. I can hear your brain running a mile a minute."

Guy's arm around me isn't a cage, but somehow, he manages to shift in a way that draws me deeper into his form, a place of hard muscle and heated skin. I move without consciously making the action, rolling to face him beneath his arm and snuggling in closer. The hollow of his large body fits around me perfectly. It's as if he's physically made to shelter others. Guy is honey on rustic bread, sweet and warm and a little rough around the edges. A safe place to hide for a while.

Except that's not his job.

Guy's eyes find mine in the dim light of the woodstove, his knuckles stroking my cheek in a brief, gentle touch. He's tired, I know he is, and there's still time for him to rest.

Then he sighs. "Okay, you win. I'll start the coffee."

I feed the animals while Guy works on getting Emma ready for the day, then we meet up for breakfast together. Emma's doing better, but she's cranky and makes it clear she's uninterested in her oatmeal. She keeps wriggling out of her seat as if unable to sit still for more than a moment or two. I don't know what it's like to be in kidney failure at four years old. I don't know what it's like living in her tiny, brave body, but I do know what restlessness is like.

"Emma, do you want to ride Legs today?" Guy's head comes up in momentary alarm, but I smile at him reassuringly. "We'll double up. He could handle all three of us if he had to, not that he wouldn't complain the whole time."

"Daddy, can I?"

"Can I say no when you're both looking at me like this?" he counters with a shake of his head. "But you have to eat your breakfast, Em."

"I'll go get him saddled."

"You have to eat too," he teases me as I start to get up with my mostly full bowl. "Girls and horses. You both have it bad."

"Horses, mules, anything with four feet… Emma and I know what's important." I smile cheekily at him, stuff a couple more bites in my mouth, then head off to the barn.

Not everyone is as happy as we are, especially when I break it to the mule he can't hang out with the others today and to Barley that he can't come with Emma. Oh, the *looks* we're getting.

Legs normally ignores me when I saddle him up, a standard form of passive-aggressive protest I find endearing. And true, he is technically ignoring me, but he keeps lowering his head to Emma, nudging at her pockets for treats and breathing warm breaths on her face. She giggles when he lips at her hair, the first smile I've seen from her in hours.

Horses—and mules—have this special relationship with kids. I never understood why, but having been the little kid with horsey breath on my face, hugging a nose larger than my torso, I get it.

To be fair, hugging them as an adult has never actually lost its appeal.

"Is he safe for her?" Guys asks, coming to stand by my side as I finish tightening the girth strap. "He's so tall."

"So are you," I reply, giving Guy a quick grin. "Are you dangerous?"

"Not to you," he promises, and for a moment, I feel his hand rest on my hip. "Never to you."

The hand on my hip slides to the small of my back. He gives me a brief squeeze, then Guy shifts away to give me room to finish my work.

"Legs is a troublemaker some days," I say because I'm not going to lie to him. "But he's the safest ride I have on snow and ice. I trust him to stay on his feet in a blizzard and get me back home in one piece. I can't promise he won't try to scrape me off under a few branches if I give him the opportunity. All's fair in love and trail rides."

Guy pats Legs on the neck. "Take care of my girls, big guy."

I don't ask Guy what he's going to do while we're gone, and as he lifts Emma up to sit in front of me in the saddle, I realize I never actually invited him to go too.

"There's room for one more," I say, because I don't want him to feel excluded, even if I hadn't thought beyond Emma this morning. "I could saddle Lulu for you."

"Naw, I know a ladies' day when I see one."

Guy watches us ride out, then he turns and bends down to ruffle Barley's ears. I think about turning around to convince him to come too, but Emma starts talking about what a ladies' day is as we wind our way up the mountainside.

The snow is falling in big, fat flakes, landing on Legs's neck and holding their shape until he shakes his head, snorting equally large snowflakes off his sensitive nose. I keep one hand on the reins, leaving them loose to stay out of his mouth, while keeping a snug arm around Emma's waist. It's a long drop from Legs's back, and while I do trust him the most in weather like this, the last thing Emma needs is a fall.

A ride in the snow before Christmas? That seems to be doing her good.

"Can we go faster?" Emma asks.

"You'll have to ask Legs," I tell her, loving the bright smile on her face as she twists back to look at me.

"Let's go, Legs!" she says, and I squeeze my calves into his sides at the same time as Emma calls to him. Legs picks up into a trot with the obedience of a mule much more satisfied in his life than Legs usually acts. It must be Emma. She's charmed him the way she's charmed me. I swear the grumpy old fool is picking his feet up higher as he trots on purpose. Emma's peals of childish laughter as the snow sprays around us are so good for my heart.

I hate that Guy is missing this.

We ride to the top of the peak, where there's a chance of phone reception. Far below, I can see the river and, nearby, our home. I make a video call, and to my pleasure, Guy's screen pops up on the second ring.

"Sienna? Are you two okay?" Guy's handsome face is lined in worry. I need to call him more, because he seems to associate my calls with bad things happening.

"Someone wanted to say hi." I angle the phone so he can see Emma and she can keep her hands on the saddle horn.

"Daddy, look! The snow is falling." Emma starts to babble to him about all the ways Legs has acted and all the things we've seen. And yes, I always enjoy my rides on some level, but seeing her excitement makes me sit back and look around again with fresh eyes.

"Are you having fun, baby?" Guy asks, and Emma nods emphatically. "*So much* fun."

"So much," Guy and I murmur at the same time, and I hear him laugh softly. "You girls stay safe. I'll have some apple tea ready when you get back."

As I tuck my phone away, I see Emma has her little mittened hands gripping Legs's mane the way she holds on to Barley, like she never wants to let go.

"Sen-na, do we have to go back?" she asks, turning big blue eyes—her father's eyes—to me.

As I look around at the perfect wintery world around us, the snow swirling in the evergreens while warm breath rises from Legs's nostrils, I hope one day the answer will be no. That one day, this will be hers to love without fear and restraint, where she can be just as safe and free as I've been. Where she can ride up and down these mountains and find her own paths and streams and favorite spots to show the people she loves.

Today, I'm going to have to turn around. Emma lives in a world where the adults in her life always have to turn around and take her back home.

But one day? One day, my answer will be "We can stay here forever."

Chapter 16

MY DAD WOULD KILL US IF HE KNEW WE WERE ALL SITTING AROUND the kitchen island in the middle of a perfectly good workday without a shoe in sight. I blame it on the apple tea and the fact that Guy looks so darn relaxed. I don't have the heart to tell him we need to be functional members of society.

I'm still getting used to eating what Guy and Emma do, but the man makes a mean mug of tea, and when he sweetens it for me with a little honey, it's perfect. Emma's tea isn't as hot as mine, and she can't have the honey, but she seems to be enjoying a drink that isn't water.

Guy's leaning back with the kind of lounging sprawl only a man as tall as he is can accomplish without falling off his chair. His favorite mug is in his hands, and every so often, his leg bumps into mine playfully, and we share a smile. Neither one of us can get a word in because Emma's spent the last hour telling him about our ride.

I think her happiness is rubbing off on both of us.

I'm on my second mug of apple tea when Guy takes advantage of a break in Emma's diatribe to turn to me. "I talked to my boss while you two were gone. They finished up the project this morning, and he's got work lined up for the crew after New Year's. So he's giving us all the rest of the month off."

It's a week until Christmas, and since his last job had shut down early and he'd scrambled to find this one, I'm surprised Guy sounds happy at the prospect. When he turns his phone my way, I understand why.

"He gave us all Christmas bonuses. I've never had anyone actually do that before."

"You mean someone treated you as a worker who's valued and respected? It should be the norm." I nudge his ankle with my toe, smirking over my mug. "Too bad your husband-for-hire job didn't offer a Christmas bonus."

"I was going to complain to OSHA about hazardous working environments and dangers of falling, but my boss looks really cute today." Those blue eyes seem to be laughing at me from across the kitchen island.

I wrinkle my nose at his flirtatious teasing. "Call OSHA on me, and you're back on the couch," I reply.

"I wasn't sure if I was officially *off* the couch. Good to know." He's definitely flirting with me. Shameless, these Montana boys. Then he shifts modes, tapping a finger on his phone. "How do you want me to handle this?"

I have zero idea what he's talking about, and it must show.

"Daddy," Emma pipes up. "Did I tell you Legs knows the best trees? He took us to the best trees, and we brought home pine cones."

"I have pine cones in my pockets," I tell him, tilting my head toward my coat hanging up in the mudroom.

"Better than some places," he murmurs out of the corner of his mouth, and when he winks at me, I nudge his ribs with my elbow.

"Ixnay on the irtingflay."

"Aybemay. Hey, Sienna. I'd really like to help with bills around here."

I think about it, pursing my lips. I don't want to argue with him, not when he's trying to be nice. "Okay, maybe we can have a grocery fund? I need to keep the ranch's income and expenses separate for tax purposes, but I'm all about you kicking in on food."

"Just food?" He folds his arms on the counter, and he's doing the thing where his shoulders are relaxed and his head tilted so he's not looming over me.

"Just food, laundry detergent, the kind of stuff we're sharing."

"Say I wanted to do more. Is that on the table?" He's not pressuring me so much as trying to coax me into letting him overextend himself. Which is *not* on the table. He's the one paying for Emma's medical expenses, and now that I know how much anti-rejection medications cost, I'm not taking a dime from him unnecessarily.

An idea pops into my head. "You can be in charge of the date-night fund. Emma and I require fun, well-planned date nights, preferably with Christmas themes. Barley's presence is negotiable."

"Sen-na, Barley isn't negoat-able," Emma pipes up. "He's goat-able."

Guy looks at his daughter fondly, then turns the same look my way too. "What my girls want, they get," he says.

As if he knew we were talking about him, Barley stands up out on the front porch and gives a loud woof, looking toward the driveway. I crane my head, because I'm not used to vehicles pulling into my driveway without knowing they're coming. There's no point in showing up unannounced when most people are out working on their property, so out here, visitors are few and far between and almost always expected.

I frown as a familiar Ford truck comes around the bend, and Barley gives a second, softer woof before turning around and heading back inside the house. He turns in a circle as if unsure whether to go back outside, then he comes to me, leaning against my leg for comfort even as his graying tail wags.

"Good boy," I tell him, resting my hand on his head reassuringly. Barley didn't understand when Micah left, and he hasn't seen him since. I'm not surprised he's happy but confused enough to come to me.

"Who is it?" Guy follows my line of sight out the window as Micah's truck rolls to a stop in his usual spot. Immediately, my shoulders tense because that's not his spot anymore. Nothing here is his anymore, and there's only one reason he would be coming by instead of calling.

"This is my problem," I tell Guy as I stand and set aside my mug of tea. "Don't worry about it. This will only take a minute."

I shrug into my heavy jacket, now heavier with pine cones, but only stuff my feet into my tennis shoes before I head outside. My toes might get cold, but I'm not planning on indulging this unexpected visitor one more minute than I have to.

Micah shuts the door of his truck too hard before stomping up to me.

"Sienna, we need to talk," he snarls.

I'm used to Micah's moods, but he's a big man, and I take a step back despite myself. There's nowhere to go as I bump into someone. A hand rests on my hip to steady me, then Guy's arm wraps around my waist as he moves next to me.

I didn't even realize he'd followed me outside.

"Who's your friend, Sienna?" His voice is mild, nonthreatening, but there's a tension in his arm I can feel. Micah is a big man, and right now, he's an angry one.

"Guy, this is Micah Hammond, my ex-husband. Micah, this is Guy Maple, my…" I stumble over the word because I haven't actually introduced him like this before.

"I'm her husband," Guy says in an easy, relaxed tone as he holds out his hand.

Micah doesn't shake it. Instead, Micah glares at Guy like he's a snake in the grass.

"You're letting him live here now? Have you lost your mind?" He all but spits on the ground at the last word.

"I don't know why you're acting so surprised," I tell Micah calmly. "You knew I was married when I sent in the insurance paperwork. You knew it when you showed up at our party, and you knew it when you drove out here today. Of course Guy and Emma are living here."

"I kept hoping it was some big mistake." Micah's eyes narrow.

"No. But it's also none of your business, Micah. This is my ranch, and what happens here is up to me and not up for public consumption."

He laughs, a hard, bitter noise. "Not up for public consumption? You're literally flaunting it in the newspaper, in front of our friends, and all around town. We *just* finalized the divorce, Sienna."

"It was a bit quicker than normal, wasn't it?" Guy smiles congenially at my ex even as he gives me a gentle tug into his side. I don't miss the shift of his body just ever so slightly in front of me, or the way he's positioned himself to jerk me behind him if this goes from uncomfortable to something worse.

"Quick?" Micah's fists ball up, and suddenly all the warmth in my veins is gone. "You were working her from the moment you stepped into this town."

"You're being ridiculous." I start to move between them, but Guy's arm is gentle but unyielding.

"Is there a reason you're here?" Guy asks, still sounding relaxed. "Or are you just trying to upset my wife?"

Well, that was blunt enough. Emma is inside, and I finally got her smiling again. The last thing she needs is her father to get in a fight with my jerk of an ex. Micah never laid a hand on me, but he's a bully through and through. I don't know why it took me so long to figure it out. I was in too deep when I finally realized the nice man I'd fallen in love with was petty and selfish on a good day and moody and aggressive on a bad day. The really bad days? I kept those to myself.

I never admitted to a soul that I locked him out of the house more than once, my shotgun on my knees until he sobered up out in the yard. Just looking at Micah now, seeing the flash in his eyes, makes me want to shift backward again, but there's no way I'm letting Guy stand between me and Micah.

"Guy, I just need to talk to Micah real quick. Can you go back to the house? I'll be inside in a moment." When Guy's eyes lock on me, searching my expression, I nod at him reassuringly. "Everything is okay, I promise."

I don't realize how close we are until he dips his head and presses a kiss to my temple. "Okay. I'm here if you need me."

When Micah snorts, Guy eyes him, and for a moment, I'm not sure my request is going to be honored. Then Guy smiles at me and stuffs his hands into his pockets. He heads back toward the house, whistling a little Christmas tune under his breath as he goes.

I only realize my heart is racing when Guy's retreat drops it down a notch. Micah watches him go with a flat expression of dislike.

"What do you want, Micah?" I ask him shortly. "If all you wanted to do was insult me, you could have just called."

"I did call, and I texted, and I tried to talk to you at the store. You won't answer me, and I deserve to know about this." He turns his phone toward me, opened to the paper's website. I'm not surprised at all that Jess's wedding article stares back at me. "You changed your name for him? You flat-out refused when we got married, even knowing how much it bothered me we didn't have the same name."

"You could have changed your name to mine," I remind him.

"That's not the point, Sienna." Micah looks so angry, and somewhere beneath the anger, he's hurt. Once, it would have bothered me a lot. But I have a child in the cabin behind me who means more than Micah's hurt feelings.

"I changed my name for his daughter. Guy was fine being a Naples. True masculinity is not being offended by outdated societal constructs forcing women into being subservient. Naples land, Naples daughter,

Naples hands. You knew why it was important for me to keep my name."

"I thought I knew," Micah growls back. "But now you changed it for some—"

"Watch it. If you utter even one breath of an insult toward my stepdaughter, I will cram my shoe so far down your throat your esophagus will herniate." Even I'm startled at how hard I snap the words at him. If I was Legs, my ears would be pinned flat and my teeth bared.

"Have you considered at any point here the asshole is playing you?" When I snort, Micah glares at the house instead of me. "I'm serious, Sienna. I know the divorce was just as hard on you as it was on me. You're hurt right now, it's almost Christmas, and your dad is sick. You're making rash, impulsive decisions that aren't like you, and the whole town is talking about it. I don't care if it pisses you off, but I'm not going to just stand by when a stranger suckers my wife into some sham marriage."

His wife. Like I'm not a person, just a possession. A toy he didn't want to play with anymore until someone else decided to notice me.

"I'm not your wife, Micah. And Guy might be a stranger to you, but he's not a stranger to me. The marriage isn't a sham. It was a...whirlwind."

I should know better than to use the line on him, because Micah knows me too well. His eyes narrow. He's not going to let this go, and if Micah truly thinks Guy's a danger to me, he's more than capable of causing us a lot of problems we don't need.

I look at the mountains, taking a long, deep breath. Then I tell him the truth. "It really was a whirlwind. Emma's sick, Micah. We got married to keep her on the transplant list. They're living here until Emma gets her kidney, which was my idea and my decision. I know exactly what I'm doing."

"And when she does? What happens then?"

"I don't know."

"So you *don't* know what you're doing." Somehow the anger in his voice was so much better than the pity. "You just picked up another stray."

He might not be as angry anymore, but I don't know if I've ever been so livid in my life as I am in this moment. I can't even speak.

"I'm sorry the kid is sick, but this isn't your problem, Sienna."

"Get. Off. My. Land."

"Sienna—"

I take a step forward, and I might be half his weight dripping wet, but Micah's pushed me too far, and he knows it. "I want you to understand something," I hiss. "From this moment on, you can hate me, you can hate Guy, and you can say anything you want all over town to anyone who'll listen. I can't stop you, and I don't care enough to try. But if I ever hear you bad-mouthing my stepdaughter again, I will burn you to the ground. Every secret, every mistake, everything I spent our whole lives protecting you from... I'll *destroy* you. Now *get off my land.*"

He's lucky I don't pelt the back of his head with a pine cone as he finally does what I ask.

"I still think you're making a mistake," Micah tells me as he climbs into the Ford. "Don't come crying to me when it bites you in the ass."

As if I could ever cry to him about anything. As if he had ever been a safe place for me, when our lives were centered around me having to be a safe place for him.

I stay right where I am, in between Micah's vehicle and the house, making him back around me. Only when the scent of diesel is replaced by the snow-dusted evergreens do I feel safe enough to take a deep breath, my shoulders slumping. When I turn, I see Guy still standing there on the porch, one shoulder set against the doorframe and his arms crossed over his broad chest.

"Technically, I went back to the house."

Guy waits for me as I climb the porch steps, those blue eyes scraping over me. I don't know what he's looking for, and I'm too unsettled by Micah's presence to be able to guess.

"I'm sorry," I say, walking past him, making sure to give him space.

Emma's playing in the living room, watching a show on her tablet, so I head to the kitchen and start making sandwiches. I use up all the ham on the first two and add a peanut butter as the third. I think they're apology sandwiches. *Sorry my ex is a jerk. Sorry your daughter is sick. Sorry life didn't give you better. Sorry I'm one more thing you have on your plate.*

Guy takes my stack of apology sandwiches and puts the peanut butter and strawberry jam one on a second plate. He sets it in front of me and leans back against the island counter next to me, facing the window, hip at my shoulder.

For the second time in a short span, a man is standing over me. But with Guy, it's different. I don't know why exactly, but like pine needles on the wind instead of diesel, his presence causes me to sag. I will not cry over Micah. I will not sniffle into this sandwich. I am a Naples, daughter to one of the toughest men in the Frank Church Wilderness. There's no room for weakness in these mountains. I will keep my head up and my back straight. I will be strong because there's no one to do it for me.

Guy's hand covers mine on the countertop next to my uneaten sandwich, fingers squeezing gently. I didn't even realize mine were trembling.

Chapter 17

THE NEXT MORNING, WHILE EMMA AND GUY ARE AT THEIR DIALYSIS appointment, I decide my stepdaughter is right: my Christmas tree is naked.

Technically she said "empty," but I think "naked" is a better term for it. Decorating the tree seems like something we could all do together, so I pull my Christmas ornaments out of storage and leave them next to my tree. I figure no one will mind if I string some lights on the front porch and hang my mother's Christmas wind chime, and I find myself humming along to the holiday music playing off my phone as I make my house feel just a little more festive.

I plan on asking Guy's help with the barn's massive wreath, because it's a task easier for two than one. But I'm seriously considering making a snowman to make Emma smile when my phone chirps with an email alert from Emma's kidney donation center. My gut tells me it's a bad sign I'm hearing back so soon. Sure enough, when I open the email, it says my blood type isn't a match for Emma's, and I'm welcome to make a follow-up appointment to discuss further with Emma's nephrologist.

Even though part of me expected this, I'm more upset than I'd realized I would be. I know dialysis is the last place either Guy or Emma wants to be this morning, and baking a Christmas treat isn't even close to being able to donate one of my kidneys. Still, I want to do something nice for them, so I flip through the Emma binder to the recipes section. The muffins Guy made were really good, and I decide to try some kind of cookie. Toward the back, there's a sugar cookie recipe that seems easy enough, and when I don't have all the ingredients, I find what I'm missing in the pantry supplies Guy brought.

He's tucked his things in a corner of the countertop, where they're out of the way. As I work, I add them to the pantry along with mine. This is his house too, and I don't like the idea of him feeling like he has to keep himself and Emma politely in a corner.

My Christmas cookie cutters are starting to rust, which might not be a sign of an impressive baking day yet to come. They used to belong to my grandmother, and I remember using them a lot those first few holidays with Micah, but at some undefinable point, like too many things that used to matter to me, I just stopped putting in the effort. They've sat so long in a ziplock bag in the garage that Rudolph's metal nose is starting to rust, and Frosty's bulbous snowman rear end is looking somewhat squashed. I decide we're just going to have round sugar cookies instead of cute shapes.

I'm not about to give a little girl tetanus with sprinkles on top.

Carefully following the recipe down to the letter, I weigh out the portion sizes to make sure I know exactly how much sodium, potassium, phosphorus, and protein are in each cookie. Since my cookie cutters won't work, I flatten each cookie into a circle and use a fork to score them like I would peanut butter cookies. And when they come out of the oven, I sprinkle them with the recipe's amount of colored sugar crystals so they look festive.

They smell *okay*. Not the cabin-filling Christmas wonderland I hoped for, but not terrible. Then, because my instincts are telling me something is off, I break off the corner of one to give it a try.

Huh. This is…different.

Maybe it's me. Maybe my overuse of salt in everything I eat, something I was never aware of until my unexpected marriage, has messed with my sense of taste. Maybe to people with low-sodium diets, these are delicious. I decide not to make any rash decisions, like scooping up my efforts and throwing them in the trash. But when I offer one to Barley, he sniffs at it with a dubious expression on his canine face.

"It's not so bad," I tell him.

Barley licks the cookie, then flattens his ears.

When Guy's truck pulls into the driveway, I'm teasing Barley by pretending to put cookies into his food bowl, and he's making all sorts of disgusted facial expressions. Guy gets Emma out, and by the way she leans on his shoulder as he carries her inside, I can tell the morning's been tough. Her little face is splotchy, as if she's been crying a lot, and her fist grips Guy's shirt.

"Rough morning?" I ask as they come inside.

"A little bit. Something smells good." Guy gives me a quick smile of greeting despite the strain on his face. "What's wrong with the dog?"

"He's just showing his age," I joke, quickly palming the cookie so they don't see. "You know, grumpy-old-man dogs."

Barley whines dramatically and rolls onto his back, shooting Emma a look of pathetic pleading. She barely notices, instead lifting her head and reaching her arms out to me. When Guy passes her over, Emma snuggles up to my chest, her face in my neck.

"Did you have a hard morning, sweetie?" I ask her, cuddling her close. She nods wordlessly. "I've got *Rudolph* ready for you before your nap. Do you want me to watch it with you?"

A second nod, followed by Emma mumbling, "Barley too."

At his name, he rolls to his feet with an agility that once made him an excellent, if unlikely, cattle dog. Barley barks once, then follows me up the stairs to Emma's room. We settle in on Emma's bed, and it only takes a few minutes before she falls asleep in my arms. I hold her for a while, not wanting to move until I know she's deeper asleep. Her hair seems thinner than even a week ago, and when I smooth my hand over it, extra strands shed loose. Her little ankles are still swollen despite getting dialysis every day now.

I don't want to process how it doesn't seem to be working well.

Emma's asleep, and there's a man downstairs who could probably use a hug too, so I extract myself from the pile of child and dog as carefully as I can, turning her tablet off so she isn't disturbed.

"Good boy," I murmur to Barley as he watches me go but doesn't move a muscle.

When I come downstairs, I glance through the windows to see Guy sitting out on the front porch steps. His head is down, and he's staring at the ground between his feet, not at the snowy wilderness of our home. Unsure of whether to leave him alone or join him, I err on the side of being too present instead of not enough. Leaving the door open a bit in case Emma calls down, I sit next to Guy on the steps.

"Is this where the cool kids are?" I ask as I playfully bump my shoulder against his.

"You forgot your jacket." His head is still down, but he gently bumps me back, leaning a little. He's got a cup of coffee and a little stack of cookies wrapped in a napkin, both untouched.

"I'm fine," I promise. "Besides, there's this big, handsome construction worker I woke up next to this morning who keeps hanging around the place. I bet he'll give me a hug if I get too cold."

Blue eyes find mine. As sad as he looks, how can he still manage to smile at me so sweetly? An arm wraps around my waist, and I'm the second girl today to lean my head on Guy Maple's strong shoulder. The difference is, he leans his head on mine right back, and my arm is around him too.

"It was bad today," he finally admits in a rough voice. "She didn't want to go, and she screamed the whole time we were in the office. I couldn't get her to stop. I had to hold her and force her to stay still for the treatment."

I tighten my arm around him. "That must have been hard."

"It was harder when she finally stopped and just wouldn't look at me." He exhales a harsh noise too bitter for a laugh. "I think she hates me."

"Maybe she hated this morning, but Emma adores you. You're her daddy, and you're a good one who makes her do hard things so she will be safe. Keeping his baby safe is a daddy's job."

"I honestly don't know what I'm doing anymore. You're lucky you didn't have to carry me to bed today and give me a show and a Barley dog." Even as he says it, the weight of Guy's body is resting less on me. His eyes are sweeping the scenery now and occasionally me but no longer on the ground.

"I would. I mean, we'd have to go get a puppy, because Emma's not sharing Barley, which would be way more drama than I want to deal with right now." I smirk as I add, "But it would be funny seeing the look of horror on Barley's face. If you think he's grumpy now, you should see him surrounded by puppies."

Guy laughs, a soft, real laugh, and it's good for my heart to hear it. The wind is a bit nippy, so I tuck my hands in between our legs for warmth.

"Did you still want to go into town after Emma's nap?" he asks me.

"And see your hard work? Absolutely."

He gives me a quick, shy grin. Guy doesn't talk about his job much, but after seeing how he's helped around here, I know he's skilled at it. Plus, opening night of the Christmas block party in town is one of the best parts of the holiday season.

"Also, I have a surprise for you during naptime tomorrow," I tell him. "Jess said they'll watch Emma for a couple hours while I take you to do something on the property. We'll be close by if Emma needs us, but it's kind of a Naples Ranch tradition. Only if you feel comfortable. We'll need to ride to get there."

"We won't be far?"

"Nope," I promise. "And the section of the property we're going to has good cell phone reception. It can wait, but the weather is supposed to be perfect tomorrow. There's a cold front moving in afterward that'll make everything gross and too frosty."

"It's a date."

When he looks at me like this, then brushes the softest kiss to my lips, I know it absolutely is a date. If it feels strange to be dating my husband, it feels awfully good to make out with him on the porch steps for a while. I'm shivery with cold and breathless when we finally pull away.

"I could do this all day," he murmurs as he steals one more kiss, then stands up, offering his hand to me. I gather his now iced coffee and the stack of cookies and follow suit. "But I'll actually get changed and get some work done. Do you mind staying around for Em while I hit the stalls?"

"Gee, hanging out in my nice, cozy house or scooping horse poop… Hmm…" I wink at him and then add, "I really need to finish clearing out the office. You need more space."

"Do I?" he asks softly. My hands are full, so he rests his fingers under my elbow, drawing me closer. His gaze slides over me, then he blushes as if embarrassed to be caught looking. He doesn't have to be, because I ogle him all the time. "Okay, gorgeous, I better get to work. I don't want to ruin this whole sugar-momma thing I've got going for me."

"What did you just call me?" I gape at him, and when Guy starts to laugh, I smack his arm playfully. "You are the biggest tease. And trust me, there's a *definite* lack of sugar happening in this house."

I may have sounded a touch plaintive on the last part. In my defense, I woke up to a lot of abdominal muscles on the other side of the bed this morning.

When Guy slides his hand down my back, putting the lightest pressure to ask me to move closer, I follow where he leads. How could I not? He's like the Christmas present I didn't know I wanted and for sure a present I never thought I needed. His lips taste faintly of peppermint, his mouth a slow caress over mine. Warm fingers slide through my hair, and when he deepens the kiss, I shiver.

"I'd do this every day if you let me," he tells me.

"Guy Maple-Naples, are you trying to seduce me?"

"Is it working?" Guy flashes me that quick, charming smile as he pops a cookie in his mouth. He chews…and chews. Then he seems to take a little breath, as if to brace himself, and then he swallows. The expression on his face is a little pained, confirming my hunch.

"They're awful, aren't they? I don't understand! I followed the recipe to the letter. These are exactly what they said to put in them."

"They're exactly right," Guy agrees. "The recipe just sucks, Sienna, which is totally not your fault."

I stare at all the cookies in dismay. "But it was in the book."

"Yeah, that's on me. I never took the recipe out. Thank you for baking for us." A light kiss presses against my cheek. "Happy one-week anniversary, Sienna."

I'm so surprised by his comment, I don't know what to say. Guy just winks at me and steps away, but not before tossing another cookie in his mouth as he heads for the door.

"Guy, you don't have to eat them. You hate the cookies!" I call after him.

"Yep, they're atrocious." Guy looks over his shoulder, adding sexily, "But you made them for us."

He doesn't have to say how much that means in his and Emma's world.

Chapter 18

SOME TOWNS HAVE CHRISTMAS PARADES. SOME HAVE FESTIVALS OR lots of lights. Some even have people drive from all over to ooh and aah over their decorations.

We have our snow globe.

I'm not sure who came up with it, but sometime in my childhood, a random person decided it would be fun to make a to-scale snow globe by the courthouse. It reminds me of a hot-air balloon, if the balloon was made of clear plastic inflated with holiday joy instead of burning gas. Even though there's plenty of real snow outside the snow globe, there's something fun about the big fake flakes swirling in the air as you duck inside the clear plastic door.

Each year, the snow globe gets bigger and better, partially due to reuse of the previous year's materials and partially from the money local businesses put into supporting our growing Christmas town. We've built up a small block party around the snow globe, complete with food trucks and carnival games, pony rides and vendors selling just about everything holiday related one could think up. It's a great place to hang out with friends and celebrate the Christmas spirit, and I've never missed a chance to drink a hot cider while watching my town mill about me.

As we head toward the snow globe this year, with Emma insisting on holding my hand and her eyes huge, it feels just a little more special than ever. Guy pushes her in a stroller despite her having resisted bringing it along, but we're going to be doing a lot of walking today. We don't want her to get too worn down.

We weave through the crowds of children running around with faces painted like Christmas trees and reindeer and groups of teens flirting and teasing each other. "Hey, Emma, did you know your daddy built this?" I ask her, indicating the three-story structure in front of us.

Emma's expression is awed as she looks up at the snow globe.

Everyone working on the snow globe is supposed to keep it hush-hush so as not to ruin the surprise for anyone. We've been so busy adjusting to our new lives together, I hadn't even thought to ask him what this year's snow globe looked like. It's bigger than ever, with second- and third-story walkways inside so everyone can look down from the top of the snow globe to the festivities below.

"Daddy did this?" She sounds impressed, and I can tell he loves it.

"A part of it," Guy says as he hugs his daughter. "I was on the walk-ways. Actually, those were my idea," he adds a bit shyly. "It was nice to dust off the architecture training."

"The place looks great," I promise him, and I love the proud, pleased expression on his face at the praise.

We wait in a line, which grows bigger by the moment.

"Is that a camel?" Guy asks, peering over the heads of the others and through the frosted plexiglass.

"I hope not." I shudder. "Last year, someone strapped reindeer ant-lers to the halters of a group of miniature donkeys. Which was *super* cute until the donkeys started having some intestinal difficulties." Emma giggles, and Guy shoots me an amused look. I add, "Hey, it wasn't my fault. I told them not to give minis green hay midwinter, but someone thought the alfalfa was prettier. Townies."

Several preteens squeeze through the line instead of going around, and Guy's large palm finds my back, shifting me out of the way so I don't get bumped. The unexpected contact sends a shiver of desire for him through me, despite the fact that we're in the middle of town. It's been a while since a man's hand on my back made me feel giddy. A while since I felt desired by someone who I want to desire me. The thought throws me all over again. I want Guy to want me. I'm just not ready to admit to it, let alone do anything about it. Or am I? Because I slip my hand into his and try to look everywhere else but at the man I'm holding on to.

Emma giggles, then is thankfully distracted as we reach the front of the line and go through the ornate snow globe entryway, decorated with glittering white and blue paint over swirled wooden designs to replicate parting snow. We enter the ground floor, and Emma oohs and aahs as she looks around and up to huge, twinkling snowflakes suspended from nearly invisible wires above our heads. Paths wind through the globe, lined with candy-cane guardrails to separate piles of faux presents and local actors waltzing together as if part of the original snow globe's scenery.

I'm not sure who thought it would be a good idea to substitute an alpaca for the nativity scene's camel, but I'm guessing it took a lot of pushing to get the sucker in the door. By the widening of its oversize eyes, it isn't going to be leaving any easier.

At the center of the snow globe is a massive Christmas tree. Since everyone who goes into the snow globe gets to hang an ornament on the tree, I've come prepared with a paper-and-puffy-paint ornament Emma and I made the night before. Guy picks her up and sets her on his shoulders so she can reach up and hang her ornament higher than almost anyone else's.

Emma *loves* it.

After exploring every inch of the snow globe and listening to Guy's playful stories about building it, we end up wandering around the block party. We find a Santa's sleigh–themed bouncy house for kids under six, and despite Emma being frailer than the other children, she's desperate to bounce too. I don't like how energetic the other children are, but I don't feel like I can say it's a mistake when Guy lets her go in without one of us in there too.

"This is worrying you, huh?" he suddenly asks as we let Emma abandon her stroller and race into the bouncy house.

"Are you always going to be this good at reading my mind?" Hmm, that might have come out a bit grumpy, but Guy only smiles.

"You're really cute when you're protective of us. But Emma's tougher than she looks. Plus, it'll embarrass her if we go in too. Em needs to feel like a normal kid sometimes, and only the toddlers have a parent in there with them."

I nod and try to trust him. Maybe it shows on my face more than I realize.

"Sienna?" My husband's voice pulls my attention. "You can talk to me. We may not be the same as everyone else, but we're partners. It matters what you feel about situations regarding Emma. I might not agree with you, and I might choose to go against what you want, but I know you care about her. I respect you, Sienna. It matters to me what you think."

"Respect and communication? Guy Maple, you're making this sound dangerously close to what a real marriage should be," I tease. "And we never had a honeymoon."

"Yet." When I glance over at him, he adds, "God willing."

We share a grin, and when I lean against the railing to watch Emma in the bouncy house, Guy angles his body next to me, keeping one eye on her and one on the crowds milling past.

"Do you actually believe in God?" I ask as Emma lets out a peal of giggles as she bounces.

"Yep," he says, almost too easily, as if saying yep, he likes pepperoni on his pizza.

I'm silent, swallowing my next question, because my curiosity isn't worth his peace of mind. Emma's happy, and he is too.

Guy glances at me, one corner of his mouth quirking up. "Are you wondering if I'm angry at God?"

"The thought crossed my mind," I admit. "After seeing how difficult Emma's life is and all the things you've gone through with her... It must be hard not to be angry."

"'Raging-fucking pissed' is the phrase I used to use," he says. "And if I focus too hard on the unfairness of what's happened to my daughter, the feeling comes back. Like it's just waiting to strangle me and cut me off from my faith. It took me a long time to realize I could be terrified and lonely and angry at God or I could be terrified and not as lonely, because He's with us through all the bullshit. I try to accept that for whatever reason, Emma isn't going to have the life I want for her. I don't understand it, and I'm never going to understand it. I lean on my faith though, and I pray my ass off, just in case God wants to change His mind." Guy glances at me again. "How about you? Are you angry with God over Micah and your dad?"

I try to answer, but the words catch on my tongue. "It's complicated" is what comes out, and I'm disappointed in myself.

Guy just nods. "Honestly," he says, voice quiet, "the thing I'm scared of is that God gave us you to help us through these days. Not because things were going to get better, but because we have someone Emma and I care about when things get worse. I'm scared I have an answer to my prayer...just not the one I was hoping for."

When Guy clears his throat, I lean into his shoulder. The fact that he leans back a little helps the lump in my own throat dislodge.

"I'm not angry. I just felt like I'm a disappointment. Like if I'd kept things together better, maybe I'd have made more of my life. I wouldn't be the divorcée in the bathtub drinking too much wine and buying naughty rubber ducky shower curtains on her phone."

"Is that how you feel now?"

Emma's childlike laughter fills the air as she and another little boy bounce together, and I shake my head. "I feel grateful I get this time with her."

"Just with her?" Guy teases, and I nudge him with my elbow.

"Brat. And with you. I don't pray much, but when I do, I pray I won't mess this up."

For the first time since Emma went in there, Guy takes his eyes completely off her, just for a moment. His large fingers cradle my face, and he murmurs, "Sienna, I honestly don't think that's possible."

"Daddy! Sen-na! Look!"

Emma's made a friend, and we spend the next half hour watching her and the other child as they play, making polite talk with the little boy's grandmother. They get matching face paintings before we part ways. I'm the proud stepmom of the cutest Rudolph the Red-Nosed Reindeer who ever graced the state of Idaho.

We see Jess running around with their camera and a Santa hat, interviewing people for the *Caney Falls Daily*, and we make a stop at Sanai's pop-up coffee shop tent for coffee for us and ice chips for Emma.

Guy knows more people than I realized, and when he sees his boss across the crowd, he brings Emma and me over. I know just about everyone in this town, but it's brand new to be introduced as part of our little family. When the two start to discuss Guy's new job in January, I pick up Emma in my arms and shift away to look at a booth of quilts, giving them privacy.

I can't help but be grateful his foreman appreciates Guy's hard work. Knowing he has a job lined up after New Year's is going to help him be able to relax over the rest of the holidays.

"Look how pretty this is," I murmur to Emma as I shift her higher on my hip, admiring the blues and yellows of the handmade quilt in front of me.

"There's ice cream. Sen-na, can I have some?"

"Oh, I'm sorry, sweetie. We can have one of the treats at home." I move to the next quilt, then notice Emma's face is all scrunched up. At first, I don't understand what's happening. She was so happy just a moment ago. "Emma, what's wrong?"

"I want ice cream."

"Oh, Emma, I know, but we can't—"

Midsentence, she lets out a high-pitched scream right next to my ear, so loud I almost drop her from shock. Boy, did I underestimate Emma's lung capacity. She shrieks again that she wants ice cream, and a little mittened fist smacks me right in the nose. For a moment, I wonder if I'm going to have a black eye or two for Christmas. Then Guy is there, appearing at our sides as if out of nowhere, taking Emma out of my arms and marching toward the truck. Her screams change pitch, and I'm bizarrely impressed when she finds another octave to hit. I follow with the stroller, feeling eyes everywhere on us.

I'm not embarrassed, but it's clear from the tension in his shoulders that Guy is. I glare at the people around us, daring them to keep looking as Guy unlocks the truck and sits Emma in the back seat.

"I don't *want* to go," she bawls as he puts the wriggling, fighting child into her car seat.

"I don't want to go either," he says firmly. "I'm not the one who decided to pitch a fit."

"I think it's my fault," I start to say, but Guy gives a hard shake of his head.

"Emma knows not to yell, and she's choosing to do it anyway. Em, is this getting you what you want?"

She shakes her head even as she keeps sobbing.

"And did hitting Sienna get you what you want?"

She only sobs harder. Emma is having a complete meltdown, and I have no idea what to do to help. And boy do I feel guilty, despite knowing that saying yes to ice cream would have been a much worse decision.

Guy's tougher than me. I'm ready to hug her until the world is better, but he stands there, foot on the doorjamb and shoulders rounded so they are at the same height, holding eye contact with his daughter.

"I want…ice cream," Emma sobs. "Everyone else…has one."

"Not everyone. Do you see me with one? Or Sienna?"

Emma's lip is out, and it quivers as she shakes her head.

"Baby girl, I know it's hard. I know, okay? We have to take this one day at a time, and we have to be nice to each other. Is screaming and hitting Sienna nice?"

"No."

"Are you sorry?"

She nods her head.

"It's okay, Emma. I'm not mad."

When Guy checks to see if I mean it, I smile at him reassuringly despite the fact that my eardrum is still pounding and my nose feels a little stiff.

"She bopped you good, huh?" he asks.

"What happens in a quilt stand stays in a quilt stand." I lift my chin. "Didn't anyone ever tell you snitches get stitches?"

"Can we go back?" Emma sniffles. "I want to go on a pony ride."

Guy hesitates, then glances at me. It's the first time I've seen him do so, as if he's silently asking for my opinion.

"Emma's had a long day," I say quietly, despite the fact she's hanging on our every word.

"Yeah, that's what I was thinking too. I just hate…" He trails off, and

I get it. Emma doesn't have a promise of next year. She doesn't even have the promise of next month, and I hate to take her away from something she's enjoying.

"Emma?" I ask. "The pony ride line is really long. Would you rather stay here for another thirty minutes or go home and go for a pony ride on Legs?"

"He's not a pony," she says, affronted on Legs's behalf.

"True, but Legs doesn't know it."

In the end, she decides she wants to go back to the block party. We make another pass through the snow globe, and even though she's worn herself out with her fit, she seems happy to pet the alpaca again. I don't tell Guy that despite her smile, Emma's looking wan and pale in her stroller. No one can look at her at this point and not be able to tell that Emma's a very sick little girl.

And there's absolutely nothing either of us can do to change it.

———————

That night, we reheat the previous night's dinner, and afterward, Emma looks at the cookies, a hopeful expression on her face. "Can I have a cookie?" she asks.

"If you want, baby," Guy says, but I catch Guy making a little gagging face at her. There are no secrets in a household with a four-year-old, because his sneaky warning is followed by a fit of giggles from Emma.

"Your dad's muffins are better," I promise her.

"Daddy ate them all after you went to bed, Sen-na. When he says he's stress-ercising, but he only does it to get you to come down for milk. Right, Daddy?"

By the expression on his face, Guy just got totally busted. This time, I'm the one giggling.

"Daddy's a sneaky muffin monster," Emma singsongs.

There's no way to explain himself out of this situation, so Guy opts to pretend to chomp his daughter's belly, tickling her until she's laughing all over again. Tickling is not conducive to getting small children to bed on time, and Guy reads Emma several stories before she falls asleep. By the time she's down, I've finished cleaning up the kitchen, and I've been past her room twice to say good night, because she keeps asking for me.

I'm dangling off Guy's pull-up bars, trying to see if I can figure out the trick of it, when he finally comes downstairs.

"Soooo…" He gives me an abashed look.

"You're a sneaky muffin monster?" I find myself grinning at him. "And you've been setting me up with the evening workouts to show off your pull-up skills?"

"If you think I'm going to apologize, you're *wrong*." He adds playfully, "A guy does what he can to get the pretty girl to notice him."

"Oh, the Guy does, does he?"

"You lasted so long without a name pun," he sighs lustily. "Longer than anyone else. You're my dream girl, Sienna."

Then he scoops me up off my feet, and I'm just as bad as Emma, dissolving with laughter as he pretends to chomp my neck, as muffin monsters do. Except I have to bite down on my giggles so I don't wake Emma up all over again.

He drops down to the living room recliner with me still in his arms. We fall quiet, and when I rest my head on his shoulder, Guy's hold on me shifts so we're both more comfortable. He turns so he can press a soft kiss to my temple, then Guy dips his face and kisses the sensitive place behind my earlobe just as softly. The pressure of his lips against my skin is ticklish and makes a light shiver roll through me.

"Those cookies are really bad," I whisper, because the other option is acknowledging my skin has gooseflesh and my toes are actually curling at a third kiss a little lower on my neck.

"Those cookies are atrocious," he murmurs against my skin.

"I can't believe you ate four of them." My fingers thread into his hair, tugging him closer even as I tilt my head to give him better access to my neck.

"I ate *five*. It was rough. All to impress a girl."

"Technically, we're married. I'm not sure you have to impress me."

"Oh, you're so wrong. Trying to impress you is the fun part."

Mid kiss, I wince at the change in position of my neck. Guy's hands immediately still. "I'm okay," I promise before he can start to worry. "I just have a bit of a headache."

"Em really did thump you good, huh?"

"I have no idea what you're talking about." I know where my loyalty lies. Guy's strong fingers begin to massage my shoulders in a special form of wonderful.

"You know it's dead sexy when you protect my daughter, right?"

I hum noncommittally because I'm completely focused on how good his touch feels.

"We're in a rustic cabin in the woods. It's pretty romantic when you take the cows out of the mix."

"Speak for yourself," I tell him. "I think cows are extra romantic."

Guy chuckles, then moves to the tense places on my neck. "If this was our honeymoon, what would you want to do?" When I start snickering at Guy's innocent question, he laughs, fingers pausing on my shoulders. "Well, other than the obvious."

"Right now, I'd say let's lie on the beach in bikinis and listen to the waves, baking ourselves into warmth and oblivion."

"I've never worn a bikini," he admits, "but I could try."

I share a grin with him, but the movement causes my neck to tweak. "Ow."

"There?" he asks, fingers probing, and I groan in answer, pressing into his hands. The man is melting me like chocolate. I'm turning into actual goo in his palms.

"What about you? What would you want to do on a honeymoon?"

"Other than the obvious?"

"Stop making me laugh. It hurts my head," I complain, tilting my neck to try and crack it.

His murmured apology isn't contrite in the least, and those skilled fingers skim down my sides. "I'd like to see you in a bikini," Guy says, somehow managing to sound wistful instead of pervy. "And I'd drink a cold beer."

"That's all you want?"

"There's a lot of things I want, Sienna. I just try to keep my daydreams achievable."

"Are we actually married?" I rest my hand on his leg, feeling off-kilter from my own question. "I know it's legally real, but are we really real? Like, actually have a honeymoon real?"

Guy's arm wraps around my waist, anchoring me to him. "You and Em are my family, Sienna. That's as real to me as it gets."

Warm breath ghosts over the nape of my neck.

"So…really real?"

"Really real."

"I better buy a bikini."

"Me too."

This time when I look up at him, it doesn't hurt my neck. Or maybe I don't care if it does because I want to see him. Fingers capable of hauling around two-by-twelves brush featherlight against my cheek before threading into my hair. Our kiss is soft, slow, but full of a promise I'm only starting to realize.

———

At some point in the night, Guy reaches for me. At first, I don't think he knows he's doing it when he draws me close to his warm, strong form. Then I open my eyes and realize Guy's not as asleep as I'd thought. I don't know how he manages to curl around me so perfectly, as if his arms are made to hold me and his legs to tangle with mine.

"I'm running out of reasons why I should stay on my half of the bed," I murmur to him, because it's easier to admit the physical attraction than it is the desperate relief I feel from being with him.

Guy's low, masculine laugh rumbles his chest beneath my cheek. "Because the only thing keeping me on my half of the bed is knowing the other half is yours," he replies.

Dreamy. He's freaking *dreamy*. When did that happen?

"I mean…we could reallocate." When I straddle him on his side of the bed, the sound escaping his throat is dangerously close to a purr. Maybe if a lion was purring.

"And this is you…"

"Examining the real estate," I promise.

"In case you're wondering," Guy tells me, "the view is *really* good on my side of the bed."

Why does he have to say things like this? Why does he have to know just how to run his hands along my skin, drawing me closer to him with each stroke?

"Tell me what you just thought," Guy murmurs, hungry and yearning.

"I think you're going to be a problem" is the best I can verbalize, because yes, those hands are really good. He knows it too.

"Mrs. Maple, are you trying to seduce me?"

"Is it working?"

"It's about time." Guy sits up with me wrapped around him, slowly turning and laying me back in the bed. In the middle of the bed.

No-man's-land. And when he runs his thumb along my upper rib cage in silent question, I wrap my arm around his neck, kissing him deeply.

I'm not sure where this is going to go, but Guy doesn't seem to be in any rush. I feel like he's memorizing me, finding what makes my breath catch and what makes me press against him for more. He's taking his time, waiting for me, which is good, because even as I'm tempted to draw him closer, I can feel part of myself shying away.

We're teammates, partners, and I like to think we're friends. But letting our attraction go further can complicate things. There's a very sick little girl across the hall who needs us not to mess this up.

The thought is a cold bucket of water over my rapidly beating heart. So, I pull away and murmur that we should get some rest. Guy nods in acceptance, and after one last lingering good-night kiss, he shifts over so I can sleep on my side of the bed alone. Our pinky fingers stay hooked, but he's giving the rest of me space as if instinctively knowing I need it.

As I lie there, watching the flickers of shadows playing over his skin in the low firelight, I wish I could snuggle closer. I want to press my forehead to his shoulder and just lean on him, just *be* with him, but this wasn't the agreement. Guy never promised me love, just respect and commitment. I can't fall in love with him. Love has never been part of the deal.

"Sienna?" he murmurs into his pillow. "You looked real pretty today."

He's making this so much harder than I ever thought it would be.

Chapter 19

"YOU REALLY HAVEN'T EVER RIDDEN BEFORE?"

Guy looks dubiously at where Legs and Lulu are standing saddled and tied to the horse pen fence, waiting for our date. "Do pony rides count?"

I snicker and pat him on the shoulder before untying our mounts. "I highly doubt you have ever been short enough to ride a pony. Here, you're on Legs." Guy takes the reins and follows me and Lulu out to the gate. Sometimes I forget not everyone grew up on horseback the way I did, so I add, "We can ride double on Legs if you're uncomfortable."

"And risk the other animals seeing? I don't have a reputation to maintain, but I'd rather not destroy yours."

I smile at him because it's adorable how hard he's trying. The reality is that Legs is strong enough to carry both of us twice over, not that I'd ever ask him, but it would be better for my grumpy pants of a mule to only have a single passenger. I adjust my stirrups to fit Guy, then I hold Legs as he climbs up with only a little awkwardness.

"He'll know where to go," I instruct Guy. "Just fall in line behind me and Lulu, and if he gets too close to her tail, bump the reins. Don't pull back hard, because he only needs a little bump. And if something happens to me on the trail, turn his nose down the mountain, and he'll take you home."

"If something happens on the trail, the last thing I'm doing is turning tail and leaving you." Guy almost sounds a little grumbly there.

He's cute, so I wink at him. "Remember that when it's bear season."

"Is bear season going to be a thing?" he asks as we lock the gate behind us.

When I follow his glance back at the cabin, I see Jess waving at us enthusiastically. They've agreed to hang out at the house for a couple of hours while Emma naps after dialysis, and after going through the Emma binder, Jess is well prepared for an emergency. Still, I can tell it's hard on Guy to leave, even if just for a little bit.

"We don't have to do this," I tell him gently. "I won't be mad."

Guy hesitates, legitimately considering it. Then he sighs. "No, I need a break. I don't want to leave, but I like Jess. We won't be far?"

"Nope, and there's a shortcut back if we need to take it. I have a sat phone in my saddle, so Jess can get ahold of us, and we'll never be more than a fifteen-minute ride straight down the mountain to reach her. Ten minutes if I take Legs. He can handle terrain Lulu can't and at a faster speed. You'll be closer to her than if you went into town."

I wait for him to nod, accepting my reassurance, before getting on Lulu. We both wave back to Jess before heading up into the mountainside.

"Is this the path you usually take when you're riding fences?" Guy asks as I turn Lulu's nose toward a stand of fir trees.

"No, the path this way is prettier. Once we're over the ridge, you'll see what I mean." I let Lulu pick her way through the snow, turning back to look at Guy and Legs behind me. "You've been here for almost two weeks, so it's time you got the grand tour of your home."

"I like how that word sounds," Guy says, gazing at me warmly. "It's been a long time since Em and I had a real home."

A real home. I've been lucky. The thing they don't have is something I've been blessed with my entire life. Unable to keep myself from sharing,

I start pointing to little spots along the trail, places where I got bucked off as a kid or my dad was chased by a cow into a tree. The path stays tight as we head up the mountain, then it opens up on the ridgeline. I hear Guy suck in an impressed breath, and I pull up Lulu, turning her so Legs and Guy come to a stop next to us.

"And this was where I had my first kiss," I admit. "Although that's probably too much information."

Guy turns in the saddle, and between his height and Legs's height, he has to dip down to brush his lips against mine. "It's perfect information. I like knowing where I can sneak one of these."

I lean over, secure knowing Lulu will stay still, and brace my palm on his chest. Our second kiss is more heated, until Legs snorts and shakes his head vigorously as if disgusted.

"Yeah yeah, we know," I say as I shift Lulu over a step so Legs has his personal bubble back again. "You're not a willing participant."

"So this is all yours?" Guy asks as we gaze at the world around us. Snow-covered peaks rise above our heads, and below, the icy Salmon River snakes through the countryside.

"Not mine," I say softly. "It's just where I'm lucky enough to live. Indigenous people were forced to leave here against their will, and it's too special of a place to treat it as a possession. This land is something to take care of, not something to own."

"A lot of people don't think that way," he replies.

"Don't I know it." I check Guy's face for the same flicker of financial opportunism I used to see in Micah's eyes. Instead, I just see acceptance. "I've taken Emma up this path a lot," I admit. "One day, I'll show her every inch of these mountains. It would be nice if you could come with us, but it's okay if horses aren't your thing."

"I don't know. I'm kind of digging this guy."

Guy pats Legs on the thick neck as we start off again, and I swear I see Legs roll his eyes at me. The man looks good in a saddle, which is a weakness of mine, and he's got a natural sense of balance, which doesn't surprise me at all.

"You're one of those people who is good at everything, aren't you?" I compliment him. "I never would have guessed you don't ride."

"The reason I look like I can ride is because Legs doesn't want to embarrass you by letting me fall off." The very thought makes me laugh. "I'm serious," Guy insists. "Every time I lose my balance, he moves underneath me until I get it back. He's a Cadillac."

I angle Lulu closer and reach over, giving Legs's mane a little tug. "Don't listen to him, big guy. He's trying to win you over. This man's a sweet talker."

"I can prove it." Guy leans over. With a sigh of annoyance, Legs shifts toward Lulu to get back beneath him, so close our stirrups bump. When Legs steps back to his preferred path, Guy rests an easy hand on the back of his saddle, holding the reins in one hand, body relaxed as if he rode horseback every day. "See?"

"Be nice to my mule's back," I tell him with a *tsk*. "You're not a hundred pounds soaking wet, mister."

"Yes, ma'am." His eyes twinkle at me, and I feel my cheeks heating up.

We ride higher, and the ranch comes into view below. The house looks tiny from up here, but I think being able to see the building where his daughter is sleeping helps the residual tension in Guy's shoulders. I send a text to Jess to make sure everything's still okay, which they report back to immediately, including a pic of them watching *Prancer* on the couch because Emma and Barley are still asleep in Emma's room. Jess would have texted when Emma woke up anyway, but I wanted to show Guy we have good phone reception and a responsible babysitter.

Guy doesn't call me out on my not-so-subtle act of reassurance, but he does aim a grateful look my way. As we crest the next ridge, a whiff of sulfur tinges the air.

"Hey, Sienna? Is that a hot spring over there?"

I look to where Guy is pointing. A slow, sinuous plume of steam is rising from behind a clump of rocks, blocking the hot spring from view.

"Hot Toddy? Yep, that's him."

Guy snickers. "You named your hot springs after a drink?"

"Actually, we named him after someone my grandmother thought was attractive in school. Made my grandfather grumpy every time he went for a soak."

"How hot is it in there?"

"Not melt-your-feet-off hot, but definitely warm enough to make it a whole lot colder when we get back out again." Our eyes meet, and I find myself grinning. "You still have bikinis on the mind?"

"I forgot to pack mine, but I'm game if you are."

I hesitate, because I'd planned on riding a little farther to my favorite lookout, sharing a mug of hot coffee, and then heading back. I knew we'd go past the hot spring, but I hadn't given it much thought. The steamy water is just too tempting. Or maybe the temptation is Guy, because he's already swinging down from Legs's back, and on a day this cold, the idea of relaxing in the hot springs with him sounds wonderful.

And maybe just a little bit scary.

"Believe it or not, I didn't think to pack a swimsuit," I tell him as I loosen girth straps and tie off the animals on the far side of the rocky outcropping, where they can rest out of the wind. Some seriously good making out in bed in pajamas is different from stripping down to nothing and hopping into a hot spring together.

Guy just shoots me a sexy wink. "I'll leave my boxers on so you don't get any naughty ideas about me."

"Too late," I murmur as he unzips his jacket and peels off his sweater and cold-weather undershirt at the same time. The man doesn't even flinch at the cold air on his skin.

Montana boys.

"Why do I have the feeling you've spent more than your fair share of time in hot tubs?" I joke as I disrobe more slowly, leaving my jacket, sweater, socks, and jeans next to Guy's clothing. I'll just have to stuff any waterlogged clothing in my pack before we leave, because no one wants to ride with a frozen-solid bra and underwear.

"Hot tubs, no, but hot water, definitely." His eyes linger just a moment longer than usual before he glances away to give me privacy.

The hot spring isn't the largest one on the property, but it's the least stinky. Plus, the view is incredible this high up in the mountains. We brave the snow on our bare feet crossing to the spring. If this weren't the middle of winter, I'd ease into the heated water, but it's way too chilly to linger. Guy slips into the spring after me, then dunks under the water. One of these days, I'm going to have to stop objectifying him. The problem is some men just really pull off water droplets rolling down their skin, clinging to hard, defined muscle, and he's one of them.

"If I took a picture right now, I bet I'd sell a lot of Naples Ranch catalogues."

The grin on Guy's face only makes him more handsome. "Be careful, Sienna. I might think you're flirting with me."

Would it be so bad? Whatever this attraction is between us, would it be so wrong to ease up on the choke hold I've been keeping on my feelings? It's been a long time since I longed for someone. Yet here I am, my bra soaked with spring water, steam turning my skin several shades redder than normal, and I want him. I'm longing for him.

He's not very far away, and I'm absolutely overwhelmed with how to cross the distance between us. I don't even know if I'm supposed to. Taking care of Emma was the goal of all this. Not filling the empty half of my bed. What if he thinks this is something he has to do? Is the attraction real, or does Guy feel like he has to flirt with me for Emma's sake? I've never forgotten how we met: a proud, scared, exhausted father answering a humiliating ad in a desperate attempt to save his daughter's life. I'm the one who crossed no-man's-land last night. I'm also the one who pulled away.

Clearly, I don't know what I'm doing. I'm over here heartsick for the man, and Guy looks like he's never been more comfortable, his arms draped on the edge of the spring as he leans against a rock.

His eyes are closed with blissful appreciation, so he must have some secret superpower when he smiles slightly and says, "You're thinking too hard about something."

Maybe.

"Want to talk about it?"

Yes. No. Flip a coin, because I'm so unused to someone wanting to hear what I feel or think. Yet he always asks, and it's getting harder not to answer. *Just use your words, Sienna*, I chastise myself. The alternative is an awkward soak or going back into the snow barefoot, and I'm only starting to warm up from the ride.

"Guy, you know you don't owe me anything, right?"

He tilts his head, and when he opens his eyes, I wonder if those glacier-blue eyes can see right through me.

"I think I owe you a lot." Guy stops me when I start to disagree, saying, "Big things and small. Sienna, whether it means getting something you can't reach off the shelf at the grocery store or recognizing you jumped into this marriage with good intentions, even if you weren't emotionally ready, I owe it to you to be good to you."

"Am I so obvious?"

"Sienna, half the time, you look at me like you want to drag me into the hayloft, and the other half, you can barely meet my eyes."

This hits me hard because it's true. I'm embarrassed, and I don't even know why. Guy's speaking gently to me, the way I would to a frightened calf.

"Sen, you hold on to me at night like you're afraid to let go, but then you pull away. It's as if you don't trust me, but I haven't done anything to deserve it. Micah did that. I can't fix what I didn't break, but I can be here for you. I can let you hold me and sneak in holding you when you aren't looking."

"Is that what you've been doing? Cuddling with me on the sly?"

Guy nudges my calf with a playful toe. "More or less. More when you let me, less when I can't convince you to stop working for a minute or two." His expression grows serious. "Sienna, no matter what caused us to sign that paper, I take you being my wife very seriously. Getting to see how great you look soaking wet with the backdrop of the mountains behind you... It's just a bonus. A really great bonus." Guy tilts his head and catches my eyes before adding, "You're my family. Even if you decide today this isn't working for you and you want a divorce, you're still going to be my family. I owe it to you to be kind to you."

"It would be an annulment." I clear my throat awkwardly. "Since we've never had sex, it would technically be an annulment, not a divorce."

What is wrong with me? The man has basically declared his heart to me, and I'm babbling about sex or the lack thereof.

"Uh-oh, you said the *s* word." His playful tone makes me exhale a small laugh, easing nerves I didn't realize had strung so tight.

"I wish it was easier to say what I'm thinking." I watch the steam rising in front of me, playing my fingers through it. "It's so easy for you."

"I've had a lot of therapy," Guy admits. "I needed it to help me deal with Emma's illness, and I've learned to verbalize the things that are important to me. You're important to me, so I'm talking about this. Trust me, I don't go to work and do much more than grunt at a few people."

"Did you get teased about the snowman sandwiches?" I ask, because I've wondered about it a few times.

"If I did, it was worth it. Someone cared about me that day, and that means more than you realize."

He's not flirting with me. He's being open and honest and emotionally available. So I take a deep breath, sink deeper in the hot spring, and take a leap of faith.

"It just sometimes seems like you're too good to be true." I can't risk a glance at him, not when I'm finally being open and honest too. "You're a great dad, and you try so hard every day. It just feels…"

I don't even know how to finish the sentence because I'm terrified of hurting this good, kind man.

"Sienna, you're over there wondering why someone would be good to you, and I'm over here wondering how in the world that man wasn't." He opens his mouth to say more, then seems to reconsider. Instead, he says gently, "What were you thinking so hard about that made you worried?"

"I was worried I'm pressuring you. For…this." Guy tilts his head again, and I know he's trying to understand. I feel my cheeks heating even more than the hot springs has caused and gesture my fingers in between us. "Like last night. Which wasn't part of the deal."

I can't meet his eyes after admitting it. I don't know if I've ever been this embarrassed.

"Sienna?" The way Guy says my name feels like warm honey, sweet and rich on his tongue. "For what it's worth, I'm really hoping pretty soon any chance of an annulment will be off the table."

Oh. *Oh.*

"I'm happy to prove it to you right now if you're interested. The view's even better over here." Guy holds out his hand to me, and when I raise my eyes to his, the way he's looking at me takes my breath away. Patient, always patient. But hungry and yearning too.

A week ago, I wouldn't have had the guts to cross this hot spring. Maybe even a day or two ago, I would have hesitated. Right now? I touch my palm to his, watching our fingers press against each other before entangling together. A soft tug of invitation is enough to draw me closer.

I'm not the first Naples to wind up in Hot Toddy in a man's arms. I'm probably not even the first person this season to be in here, considering how often teenagers sneak up here for some alone time. I'm pretty sure no one else has looked as good as Guy does, relaxed against the rocks with the backdrop of the mountains behind him. He draws me over his lap, and my hands move to his chest to balance myself. I don't need to worry about slipping though. Guy clearly has this handled.

He touches my face and combs his fingers through my wet hair before tilting my face down to his. I shiver despite the heat of the spring. Or maybe the way his hand traces lazily down my spine is what has me shivering. I don't know.

"Relax, Sienna. I'm just a hot Guy in a hot tub."

"That was an awful joke," I tell him, giggling as he presses his lips to where my shoulder meets my neck.

"Yes, but it made you laugh." Guy presses another, softer kiss to my collarbone. "I know when we met was terrible timing for you. I know you weren't even ready for a rebound. But what this is, what we have, it's good. I'm not going to mess us up, no matter how much someone else messed up everything else."

"That's the first time you've used the word. Us."

"You, me, and Emma… You're my family. But you and me? This right here? *Us.*"

We fit each other better than I ever could have hoped for, as if we were made for being this close together. When I tighten my knees against the muscles of his waist, his eyes sweep down over me again, lingering. Guy is always waiting for me, leaving it as my decision. This is the first time I've truly understood how hard it is for him. It's been too long since I've felt like this, and Guy is making a very good case for why *us* is a good word. But even as I start to reach for him further, I can feel myself holding back.

If we take that next step, I'm very afraid he'll officially have what's left of my heart. The thought is terrifying.

Guy tangles our fingers, then kisses my fingertips one by one. "If you're not ready yet, it's okay. You're worth waiting for, Sienna. No matter how long it takes."

"Even if you turn into a prune in here?"

Guy's grin will never be less than beautiful, especially now I've seen him in pain. The fact that he can still smile like this makes him all the more precious to me. Someone to protect. Someone to cherish.

"Even then," he promises. "I've always wanted you, Sienna." His hands trace my curves, and the way his eyes follow his hands makes his point clear. "When you're ready, you let me know. Until then, I'm more than happy to take this slow. I love what we have right now."

Resting my forehead to his, I whisper, "I love what we have too, and I don't want to mess it up. I don't want you to feel like a rebound."

And I really don't want to break my own heart by falling in love with someone as great as him before I'm ready. When I bite my lower lip, worrying it, he kisses me and steals my lip away. Guy nips it far more gently than I did before placing another kiss to my earlobe. I'm already melting into him.

"Just remember, Sienna," he whispers in my ear as those strong hands start to move. "I can't be a rebound if I don't give you back the ball."

Chapter 20

THEY SAY WHAT HAPPENS IN A HOT SPRING STAYS IN A HOT SPRING. As I sit across from Jess and Sanai at the coffee shop, buying Jess coffee as a thank-you for watching Emma, I'm tempted to start waxing poetic. Even hours later, I still feel the languid relaxation that comes from a man who knows what he's doing.

And *boy*, does the man know what he's doing.

"Okay, spill. You look like you have stars in your eyes." Sanai grins at me from around the lip of her drink, and I know I'm busted. Sanai's hired help is on the clock, giving her a chance to join us.

Jess leans forward, waggling their eyebrows. "Have we reached the actual honeymoon stage of your total-sham-but-actually-not-a-sham marriage?"

"There may have been a visit to Hot Toddy," I admit. Jess sighs, their eyes glazing over dreamily, so I quickly add, "But it didn't go—"

"Nope." They stop me before I can finish my sentence. "Just let me have this moment to envision my best friend and her hunky new partner having the kind of romantic experience she deserves instead of the table scraps you were trying to make do with."

I try and fail to smother my snicker, because Jess is right: sex with Micah was terrible by the end. But I know I never complained about it to them, so I arch an eyebrow.

Jess just smirks. "Can't. Fool. Me."

This time, I do laugh and tap my coffee cup to both of theirs. "Let's just say this is not the same. No more table scraps. We're dealing with…a full sandwich."

"Like a couple slices of ham on rye or a full meatball hoagie?" Sanai asks as I try not to snort my coffee into my nose, and this time, they're both grinning at me naughtily.

I'm not going to answer…but it's really tempting to. "How was watching Emma?" I ask Jess instead.

"She's adorable and twice as smart as anyone in this town, and unlike you, she gave me all the good gossip on you and Guy. Barley's head over heels, isn't he?"

"He's a grumpy curmudgeon until she's in the room, and he turns into a lovestruck puppy." I smile thinking about my stepdaughter. "If any little girl deserves full-blown canine adoration, it's her."

"I see it, you know," Jess says, breaking off a corner of the gingerbread scone we've been sharing. "At first, I thought you were making a really reckless decision, but I can see how easy it was to marry him. The boy has some serious puppy-dog eyes, and when you pair the two of them up, your stoic, take-one-for-the-team savior complex never had a chance."

"I think there was a compliment in there somewhere, but I'm not sure."

"We're just saying Barley isn't the only one hot on someone else's heels," Sanai adds cheerfully.

"For now, anyway." When they both look at me askance, I sigh. "Things are getting complicated. I think Guy wants it to be a real marriage."

"You're a hottie." Jess shrugs. "Can you blame the man for wanting sex?"

"No, I mean, I think he wants a relationship."

"Well, duh." I blink as Sanai openly laughs at me. "Please tell me you're not this dense. All Emma talked about at the block party was how much she and her daddy like you. And while you were holding her, Guy could not stop staring. The boy is smitten."

I drink my coffee and try to sort through the thoughts in my head. My friends wait, knowing sometimes it takes me a while before I know how to verbalize what I feel, even to them.

"Right now, he wants this," I agree slowly. "But Emma could get a kidney any day now, God willing. I pray for it every night, because I want that for her and Guy more than anything. I have no illusions about why we're married. I know it's to help Emma, and it's not fair for me to ask Guy to stay with me when all this was about saving his daughter. If I had feelings for him—"

Jess snorts. "Which you clearly do. Not that you're admitting to it."

I sigh, burying my head in my hands. "Okay, let's say if I have feelings for him, it's not right to push them on him. Not when a month from now, his nightmare could be over, and he could go back to his life the way they want it to be. He might want to be with me at Christmas, but by New Year's, everything could change. I can handle annulling the relationship after knowing we got what we wanted and Emma is okay. But I know me. I know if I let this be too real…" I close my eyes briefly. "I'm just not ready to get divorced again."

Sanai and Jess share a look, and then they each take one of my hands, giving me a chance to fight off the wave of hurt the thought brings up in me. And I know my friends held my hand through Micah, and they'll hold my hand through Guy too. I just don't want them to *have* to.

Taking a deep breath, I squeeze their hands, then lean back in my seat. "So yeah. That's why I'm holding back."

"So let me get this straight," Sanai says. "You're worried you're falling for your husband."

"Yes."

"At Christmastime," Jess adds, and I can see them trying to keep a straight face.

"Yep."

"And you're trying to decide if you should tell him before his daughter gets a kidney and they don't need you in their lives anymore?" Sanai's eyes sparkle with humor.

"Right-o."

"So very Hallmark of you." I roll my eyes but exhale a small laugh because Jess has got me there. "Sienna, why don't you just *tell* him this?"

"Because that would be far more emotionally healthy of me than slugging copious amounts of caffeine." I wrinkle my nose. "I just feel ridiculous. Like…okay, he does these exercise things at night, and I just stand there and stare at him like he's the star quarterback and I'm the water girl with horse crap on my boots."

"Which matches up with most of the people in this town. You won't believe what we mop up in here," Sanai says with a sigh. "Speaking of customers, Roman's about to get overrun."

A wave of teenagers are coming in, ruddy faced from holiday shopping, so Sanai gives us both hugs and disappears into the back.

I sneak the rest of Sanai's piece of gingerbread scone before Jess can get it first.

"Can I ask you a question?" Jess says. "A real, just-be-honest-with-yourself question?" When I nod, they lean in on the table. "When you close your eyes and imagine what their life is going to be like once Emma gets her kidney, do you see yourself there? Her next birthday? Five Christmases from now? Are you going to be pulling up to my house with her every Halloween because I pass out the good candy, until she's embarrassed to be seen with you? Do you want to still be sneaking up to Hot Toddy with this boy when you're both old and wrinkly and sun-damaged, because we both know you never remember to use sunscreen?

If you do, I'm here for it. I'll make these two an emotional room in my life, because if they matter to you, they matter to me."

"Micah didn't get a room," I remind them.

"He didn't deserve a room. Boundaries are our friends."

I don't have to close my eyes to imagine the rest of my life with Guy and Emma. I imagine it all the time. "Yes. I just don't know if they do."

"Then, my friend, there's only one person who can answer that, and it's not me."

———————

Jess sends me home to think about what I've done. Namely not admitting to Guy how important he is to me. I've already texted him that I'm on my way, but as I pull off the main highway, I get a call from Guy.

My heart skips a beat as I see his name pop up on my dash, and for a moment, my body is back in the hot springs.

"Hey, you," I say in greeting, smiling at the memory. "I'm crossing the bridge as we speak."

"Did you close the gate after you left?" Guy says instead of his normal hello. He's stressed, the kind of stressed I've only heard him be when Emma was involved.

"Is she okay?" I demand, muscles locking down instantly.

"Yeah, Em's fine, but we went out to get a jump on chores before you got home, and I just found a cattle pen empty of cattle. I was about to drive down to make sure the front gate is latched."

"The gate's closed. Are you sure the herd aren't on the far side of the hill? Sometimes they pack in tight by the clump of firs to get out of the wind. You might not see them unless you hike up there."

I let myself through the gate, locking it behind me, and listen to Guy's breathing deepen. My guess is he's hustling to the top of the hill, not an easy feat through knee-deep snowdrifts.

"No, I don't see them. I don't see any fencing pushed over either—" He breaks off and lets out a low curse. "Sen, the gate to the pass is open. The small one. Could a cow get through?"

"A whole herd could get through if they wanted. It's why I keep it double latched."

I normally don't drive on the lane very fast, but this time, I push my foot to the accelerator a little harder. When I park out front, I can see Emma playing at the kitchen table through the window. I give her a wave, then hurry around to where Guy is pacing on the porch.

The expression on his face is strained, and he's clearly upset. "I don't know what happened." Guilt and self-recrimination fill his voice. "I've never even used that gate."

"Stay with Emma," I say as I give him a brief hug. "I'll check it out."

I start up the ATV and drive around the barn, out toward the cattle pen. Sure enough, my cows are gone. I don't understand what happened because I distinctly remember double-checking the gate as Guy and I rode in today. Yet there it is, wide open, with all my income gone up the mountain. At least the newly fallen snow makes their trail easier to find. Even a herd as small as mine leaves a substantial swath of tracks. I check the gate for signs of damage, but it's not only fine, the little backup chain is hooked properly to keep it held open. Then I notice a different set of tracks in the snow by the gate.

Very cute little snow boots with stars on the treads make those kinds of tracks, with Barley-sized paw prints right next to them. Partners in crime.

I return to the house, and Guy's still on the porch, looking even more distressed. I hate what I'm about to ask him. "I noticed some boot prints by the gate. Was Emma over there this afternoon?"

"Yeah, when I was cleaning stalls. She was playing with Barley out-side the barn, and I told her not to go any farther because the gate was within eyesight. When I was done, she came back, and we went inside the house to get warmed up. I never went to double-check the gate." Guy sounds panicked as he closes his eyes. "Sienna, I never checked the gate."

"I wouldn't have either. She likes to build little snow people over there, and she knows not to open it."

Guy looks sick as he turns back to the house. "I'll go ask her."

I catch his hand. "Take a beat first. Deep breath, then relax, because she picks up on you being upset. The cattle are out, there's no changing it, and I don't want her afraid of being around the animals because of this."

Guy nods, then he turns back to me. He loops his arms around my waist, taking a slow, steadying breath. "Yeah, you're right. Thanks. I needed that. I can't upset her just because I'm stressed."

"We're a team," I tell him, hugging him back. "I can go talk to her if you need a minute."

"No, I'm okay. Let's go ask Em."

She's moved from playing at the table to playing on the couch when we go inside. We leave our dirty boots in the mudroom but don't change. When Guy sits down on the couch next to her, Emma doesn't look at him, choosing instead to focus on the Frosty the Snowman toy in her hands.

"Emma, I need to talk to you. Did you let the cows out of the pen?" Guy asks.

Emma shifts uncomfortably, and she's holding on to Barley's coat with her little hand, not meeting either of our eyes. It takes her a moment before she says, "Yes."

Guy must have been hoping we were wrong, because he exhales heavily. "Emma, you know not to open the cow and horse pens. Why did you do it, baby girl?"

"They wanted the food on the other side." Her face gets this frustrated look. "They should get to eat what they want."

"Did you do it because you didn't get to eat ice cream at the block party?"

She still won't look at him, and tears start to gleam in her eyes, even as she stubbornly fights them back as she plays. I settle down to the floor next to the couch so we're not both looking down at her.

"Emma? It's okay to get disappointed when you don't get what you want. I do. Your daddy does too. It's okay for the cows to be disappointed too."

"Daddy gives you milk."

Guy starts to say something, but I glance at him, silently asking him to let me answer. He nods, then leans back on his hands.

"I'm new to your family, Emma," I tell her. "Just like you and your daddy learned which hay to feed the horses, I'm learning what foods not to keep in the house. I'm sorry I drink milk when you can't. If it bothers you, then I won't do it anymore."

"Milk is bad for us," she says determinedly.

"No, Emma." Guy smooths his hand over his daughter's head, then he hugs her, the child almost disappearing beneath his arm. "Milk is bad for *you*. It's not bad for me and Sienna. There are going to be a lot of people in your life who might get to eat or drink or try things you want. But it's important to know what's not good for you, baby girl."

When she sniffles, burying her nose in his rib cage, it breaks my heart.

"There have been things I thought I wanted, but they weren't good for me," I tell her softly. "Your daddy is helping me learn that. I'm like you, sweetie pie. We're a little stubborn when we think we're right. Unfortunately, you can't let the cows or horses out without an adult. There's too much that can hurt them, like too much food or bad weather or predators. Part of living here means taking care of them, even if they want something they can't have."

Emma turns red-rimmed eyes to me. "Did I hurt the cows?"

I don't have an answer for her, not until I go get the herd. "I'm going to go see if I can find them, and hopefully they will be fine."

"They won't come back like the horsies?"

"No, baby. They've gone up into the mountains. When cattle wander away, they don't usually come back by themselves."

Emma glances down at the dog resting his head on her lap, staring up at her with sad eyes. Barley always was good with crying women. "Barley will get them back," she decides. "He can do anything. Daddy can help."

I look at the aging retriever, his white muzzle barely speckled with red. If I drag him up this mountain in December to try to work the whole herd, I'm not going to have a Barley dog left coming back down. Barley's a good boy, the best boy, but he's not enough. And it's one thing to take a new rider on a trail Legs is familiar with, but it's another to take Guy out into the mountains in the dead of winter. He doesn't know how to work cattle, and this is a bad time to learn.

"Sienna, I am so sorry." Guy puts a hand on my shoulder, and his voice sounds devastated. "This is all my fault. How do I make this right? I'll do anything you need."

I stand up and head to the window, looking out at the mountains rising above us in the distance. It's too late to go after them now. We're already losing light. Unfortunately, as cold as it is, it's only going to get colder tonight and tomorrow. Without the donkeys with them, the calves are more at risk for hungry predators, but I'm the most worried about the weather. Bad visibility in bad country means serious falls for animals and people alike. My stomach twists, but I know what I need to do. This isn't about any of us. It's about getting those cattle back safely. There's only one other person who knows this dangerous landscape as well as me.

"Guy," I tell him quietly. "Neither of us will like this, but there's something I have to do."

Chapter 21

I MAKE THE CALL, AND MY HELP AGREES TO SHOW UP FIRST THING the next morning.

Ours is a sleepless night as I stay up late gathering the supplies I need and planning for the next morning. Guy keeps apologizing, clearly riddled with guilt, until I give him a hug and ask him to stop. I know he feels terrible about the cows getting out, but there's nothing we can do to turn back time. I'm not angry with him or Emma, but I am stressed and worried. I care about my animals' safety and health, and I need every single one of my cows to make this ranch stay afloat. More than anything else, I don't like knowing what—and who—the next day will bring.

As much as I appreciate Guy taking responsibility for Emma's actions, I can't juggle his emotions right now. I need to process my thoughts on my own, and eventually Guy falls quiet, doing what he can to help me prep for tomorrow and staying awake with me even when there's nothing he can assist with. We finally crawl into bed, dozing fitfully for a mere two hours before it's time to get back up again. We feed the animals and are standing ready on the front porch when Micah arrives at dawn.

I remember the days of pulling into a ranch in a Ford F-450 dually, a truck closer to a semi than the other Ford trucks driving around town. I remember the truck pulling a brand-new fifth-wheel horse trailer with living quarters, fully loaded down with horses, as if the weight wasn't even there. I remember the soft purr of the engine instead of the rattle of my current ride, with butter-smooth leather interior and automatic warmers for the bucket seats.

I don't miss the man, but some days, I do miss that truck.

To his credit, Micah didn't give me a hard time on the phone the night before. We might be in a bad place emotionally, but he's a third-generation cattle rancher. If anyone knows how much trouble I'm in, it's him. He doesn't show up alone either. When Micah climbs out, two of his ranch hands follow suit. I don't recognize them, but I do recognize the trio of cattle dogs who hop out of the back seat after the hands.

"Hey, babies," I say in greeting, kneeling down and hugging them. I raised these three from puppies, and I try not to think about how much I miss them or how they were considered property to be traded, like all the other animals I loved.

Micah introduces me to the ranch hands, and as they unload their horses, we discuss our plans. He knows every inch of this property, and it's pretty clear the two paths the cattle should have taken. Whether they *actually* did remains to be seen.

Micah eyes Guy as he stands there with Emma in his arms, and the expression on Guy's face is strained. I know he would saddle up with us in a heartbeat. Even if he doesn't know how to drive cattle, he'd still try and, in the process, in snow this deep, end up getting his or his mount's necks broken. Either way, Emma's not well enough to go where we're going, and Guy needs to be here.

That doesn't mean he has to like it.

Guy sets Emma down on the step next to Barley as I mount up on Legs and ride over to the porch. Lulu might be a better cattle horse, but I need Legs's strength and stamina for this ride. Paddlewhack is absolutely dwarfed by the sheer bulk of Legs, but the donkey has food for us and the animals and my tent loaded on his back.

Guy meets me at the bottom of the stairs, then rests a hand on my thigh as he looks up at me. "I'm sorry," he tells me quietly. "I'll make this up to you."

"There's nothing to make up. We'll be back down as soon as we can, but it might be tomorrow, depending on how far they got." I don't tell him how much I'm not looking forward to a night in Micah's company in a tent on the mountainside. "Don't be surprised if I don't check in. If the herd went into the gorge to get out of the wind, reception sucks in there."

I don't tell him the gorge is the most likely...and most dangerous... place for them and for us. Guy doesn't need me to say it, and the tension in his face increases. His thumb curls into my leg, and I can see him eyeing the rifle strapped to the back of my saddle, the same as the other three riders.

"Are you expecting any predators?" he asks quietly.

"I'm just staying prepared." The last thing I'm going to say in front of Emma is that the gun is for the cattle in case any of them didn't make it safely through the night.

My eyes flicker to her, and Guy notices. He closes his briefly, then nods. "Come back safe, Sienna."

I lean down to hug him goodbye, and I get a brief but warm kiss in return. Then he retreats to the porch with Emma as we ride off.

I don't know if Guy sees Micah fall in next to me, but I think Micah does it on purpose because we're not even out of eyesight of the house. Legs snorts at the presence of a different horse, but we ride in silence. This is what we were best at, being in the saddle next to each other. On horseback, we seemed to have everything figured out, even when we were kids at the local barrel races. It was when our boots hit the ground that everything always fell apart.

"I didn't see a broken fence." Micah breaks the silence first, like he always does. "How did they get out?"

"I left a gate open."

"You've checked those gates twice a day every day for your entire life, Sienna."

"It's a gate," I say. "They get left open sometimes." He glances over at me, clearly not buying it. I can already feel my neck start to ache from the tension in my jaw. "My gate, my responsibility."

Micah snorts. "Yeah, you used to cover for me with all the crap I did too. But hey, I never left the gate open. The kid let them out, didn't she?"

"My *stepdaughter*, Emma, made a mistake. She's four, Micah. Four-year-olds make mistakes."

"So do adults."

He's not wrong, although I don't know if he's talking about me or himself. At one point in my life, I would have driven myself to distraction trying to decipher his comment, but today, I just want to get my cows and get back home. The strained set to Guy's shoulders is playing through my mind, and the last thing he needs is more to worry about. If I can get the herd home safe and sound, then no harm, no foul.

"Can he ride?" Micah asks, as if following my train of thought.

"Yes, but Guy can't be in two places at once, and Emma can't be out in this. He doesn't know the terrain like I do, so I'm going. Give him any crap about it, and I will run you off this mountainside and get the cows myself, even if it takes until New Year's."

"Even if they all end up frozen to death?"

"Even if."

As I say it, the wind picks up, blowing hard into our faces, and I know this is going to be a bad ride. Bad for the horses, bad for the cowboys, and bad for the dogs. I'd planned on the dogs picking up the trail, but wet slush joins the bitter winds, wiping out the trail the farther we go into the high country. If we get hit by a storm, it's going to be nonnegotiable. We'll have to wait it out. I'm not killing these men for my cows.

"Did you check the weather?" Micah asks, even though he knows I did. We always check the weather out here.

"I did before we left."

"You still going to be mad at me when we're done?" He almost—*almost*—sounds apologetic.

That question is a better one.

I watch Legs's right ear rotate, and I instinctively glance to the right to see what caught his attention. We're all out here looking for cattle, and Legs is just as likely to notice them as I am.

"I don't have a lot to care about, Micah. When you go after the things I have, you're going to get a fight. I just don't know why you want to fight with me. Haven't you had enough?"

"We weren't fighting anymore." When I look at him, confused, Micah gives me a tired, bittersweet smile before explaining. "It took me a long time to figure it out, but when you stopped fighting, it meant you didn't care anymore. I actually thought things were getting better. Clueless me, huh?"

He clucks to his horse, picking it up to a trot as he rides up to join the two hands.

I ride alone and in silence, even though we make plenty of noise as we head into the high country. It's past noon when the little brindle cattle dog barks an alert she's found the herd. I'm grateful, because even Legs is struggling with slogging his way through the snow and the wind up and down these mountains. Dark forms wind in and out of the trees, hooves kicking at the snow to search for grass, but not enough. I frown as I angle my way toward the herd…or this part of it at least.

"How many did you say were up here?" Micah calls over to me. He's been riding with his men the last couple hours, which has been a welcome reprieve from his presence.

"Sixty-one, including the bull."

"I've got forty-three," Micah's cowhand says, and Micah nods in agreement.

I nudge Legs into a trot and circle on the left flank of the herd, staying as quiet as I can to keep them from moving. They're hard to count, with snow caking their backs and the steers huddling tight together.

Forty-three. Dang it.

"There's eighteen more somewhere up here," I tell the men. "If I can take one of the dogs, I'm going to keep looking for them. If you all head down, you might get in by tonight. At least you'll get to lower ground."

Micah tilts his head to the two ranch hands, indicating for them to do as I suggested, then turns to me. "I'll go with you. They're probably in the gorge, and it'll be easier for two of us to get them down."

He's not wrong, but I don't have to like it.

It's dark before we reach the gorge, and the area is just too dangerous to ride at night, even in the best of weather conditions. We make camp in a stand of trees, where the animals can get as much shelter from the weather as possible. Paddlewhack brays in annoyance until I feed him and Legs, but I leave Micah to tend to the dog and his mount. We each brought our own tent, but we set them up close together as a much-needed windbreak. Another thing I don't have to like but will deal with because it's better for everyone to stay warm out here…as warm as we can be anyway.

Of the many, many things that got shipped off to Hammond Farms, included was my favorite trail blanket. Micah's got the thin but toasty-warm plaid blanket draped over his shoulders as we huddle near the fire, trying to thaw our hands around cups of coffee.

"It's warmer over here, Sienna." He flaps the edge of the blanket at me.

I just look at him, hoping my eyes convey what I'm thinking: I will literally freeze to death, and I mean *literally*, before I crawl under a blanket with my ex-husband again.

"It's not as warm as you think," I finally say.

"You always were the most stubborn thing in these mountains, and that's saying something." Micah chuckles, then gives his head a shake before sipping his coffee. "My momma warned me about taking up with a Naples girl, but you had me hooked the first time I saw you ride."

"That was back in peewee classes at the county fair, Micah."

"Yep."

"Is there a point to all this?"

"I'm saying despite what went wrong with us, we've got history, Sienna. How long have you got with the guy back at your place? A couple weeks, max?"

"It took a lot for me to call you for help, Micah. It was humiliating, and while I appreciate you coming through for me, I asked for help to keep my cattle safe, not to get grilled on my love life."

"So you love him? The loser with his boots on your couch right now?"

"I barely know him." Even as I say it, the words feel wrong on my tongue. I look up at Micah, and there's an expression on his face that says he thinks he's won. Won what, I don't know. And maybe I do know Guy. I might not know his best friend from middle school's last name, but I know when he's happy or when he's scared. I know he'll be strong when he's exhausted and he'll be good to us, even when things feel really bad.

I know I love him.

As I look across the fire, I realize something very important. Divorcing Micah was the best thing I ever did.

"A thousand paper cuts," I say quietly. "That's what being married to you was like. A thousand smug smirks, a thousand little looks, a thousand snorts of disapproval. You were an aggressive drunk, which scared me a lot more than I ever admitted. But being married to you was bleeding out on my feet from a thousand paper cuts. And it hurt worse than I could even describe."

"Sienna—"

"No, I'm not done. You might be the guy on the horse who knows how to help with the cows. But the *loser* at home? He's the one patiently waiting for me to figure out what I want, when I want it. You tell me, Micah. Which one of you is the real man?"

He watches me from across the fire, and it's been a long time since Micah didn't look mad at me. He just looks discouraged. "You know, Sienna, if you'd fought half as hard for us as you just did for him, we'd still be together."

"Then that would have been sad for both of us." I almost feel bad for him when I add gently, "I don't want you back, Micah. You don't want me back either, if you're being honest with yourself. It just embarrassed you when I moved on. Normally it would be one more paper cut, but honestly, I have enough on my plate without worrying about what you think or want anymore. That part of me belongs to Guy now. I just want to get these cows and go home. I miss my family."

Micah is silent for a long time, then he nods and gets up. Before he goes into his tent, he offers me the blanket, but I shake my head. I have everything I need. And the things I lost? Well, they just aren't so important anymore.

Chapter 22

THE NIGHT DROPS DOWN TO THE COLDEST IT'S BEEN ALL WINTER. Even Legs is shivery when we start toward the gorge at first morning light, and I'm an icicle all the way through.

We keep searching, and the longer we look, the less I think I'm going to find them.

"This is my fault," Micah tells me when we pause to try to warm up and regroup. "I was so mad, I made sure you didn't have two pennies to spare when the settlement was done. You'd have tracker tags on them if it wasn't for me."

His words grate on my ears, but I choose not to indulge his comment or let this turn into the Micah show.

"Dad never needed GPS to find his cattle, and neither should I," I reply instead. The past is the past, and I can't change what is or isn't on my cows' ears. "I don't want to stay out in this another night, and we're low on food. If we don't find them in the next two hours, we need to head back down."

Micah doesn't have to say he agrees with me, because I know he's thinking it as well. His own mount is just as cold as Legs, and the dog needs to get inside too. We range wide from each other to cover as much ground as possible while we still can. Then a sharp whistle says Micah's found what's left of the herd. At first, I have hope, but when I ride up, my heart sinks.

It's worse than I had expected. He's only found three heifers, and the rest of the herd—including Jerkface—are long gone.

As a cattle rancher, I understand ultimately these animals are meant to feed us. They aren't pets, no matter how much I care about each and every one of them. I've never liked sending them to be butchered, but it's part of this job. But to lose an animal due to an accident or neglect? That's another thing entirely. My cattle need to be down at the ranch because of the warmth of the shelters and the safety of being off the mountain. Jerkface might have lived up to his name, but it hurts especially hard to admit I've lost him to the mountain this winter.

Legs is shivering, and I have other animals that need to be cared for. I'm ready to accept defeat, knowing we've done what we can and it's time to go home.

We ride down the mountain in silence, driving the three heifers between us. We meet up with the ranch hands halfway home, and I learn they spent the night in the living quarters of Micah's trailer instead of heading home for the night. They were on their way back to try to help us find the rest. I'm grateful, but the search is done for now.

My sixty-one head of cattle are now down to forty-six when we reach the homestead. Guy must have been watching for us because he meets me at the gate. His eyes are bleak as he opens the gate for us and watches us ride in with the three cattle.

"The others?" he asks, sounding sick.

I shake my head. "We lost eyes on fifteen after we found these three in the gorge. It's bad country out there. I'll keep searching for the rest… maybe hire Jake or Charley to fly me around to look for them. It's possible they'll find their way down on their own."

Possible, but not very likely.

"I'm so sorry, Sienna." He rests a hand on my shoulder, and I lean briefly into his touch, then straighten. Later, I'll let him comfort me, but not in front of these men.

"I'll put some coffee on," I say tiredly to the group, but Micah shakes his head.

"Thanks, but we'll get gone. Sorry it didn't end better, Sen."

The other two touch their hats as they follow Micah to the Ford. As I watch them, I realize I don't want the big truck or the shiny trailer anymore. I'd take my dogs back in a heartbeat, but I can't pretend I'm not glad to see them load their horses and the whole rig go.

I just want a hot shower and some time to process the loss.

"How much were they worth?" Guy asks me in a low, rough voice. "This is my fault, and I'll pay to replace them."

"We can work it out later," I say, but when the strain in his eyes only worsens, I add, "The steers would have been sixteen hundred a head this spring, maybe more or less depending on the value of beef. Jerkface will be harder to replace, but we have until springtime to figure it out."

I don't want to get into how the bull is the worst of it, because he was one of the best from years of cultivating the herds. All of them hurt, and not just financially. Thankfully, Guy doesn't press me.

There's work to do even now, so I check over my remaining cows for injuries, feed everyone, and triple-check every gate. The big gates are far too heavy for Emma to open, but I notice the smaller gates all have new, heavy-duty, screw-locking carabiners on them, something her little fingers would struggle with opening. Guy's not been idle as he waited for us to come home. He stays at my side with every chore, and the second body is deeply appreciated. Hauling hay and opening grain bags is heavy work, especially when the molasses inside each bag has started to freeze.

"You took good care of everything while I was gone," I finally say as he hooks up the hose to the water pump so I can top off the horses' heated water buckets. "How was Emma's dialysis this morning?"

"She's pretty tired today, and she was quiet except for asking about you. I think it scared her when you didn't come home last night, and I know she missed you at bedtime."

"I'll check on her when we get done," I promise. "I missed her too."

I start to peel off my gloves so I don't get them wet, but Guy keeps hold of the hose and does it himself. Even now, he looks good with a hip to a stall door, his fingers plucking errant bits of hay swirling in Lulu's bucket as cold water runs in.

"You're smiling," he says, and I don't realize I've closed the distance between us until his damp fingers pluck hay bits out of my hair now instead of a bucket.

"I missed sleeping next to you last night," I admit. I haven't shared a bed long enough for this feeling, but it's true.

Guy wraps his hand over the end of the hose, folding it so the water is blocked off to a trickle. Instead of moving to the next bucket, he cups the back of my head and kisses me. I must stink from two days in a saddle, and I wouldn't want to kiss me, that's for sure. But he doesn't seem to mind.

"I slept on the couch last night," Guy tells me quietly. "I hated not having you next to me." Then he wraps an arm around my shoulders and hugs me into his body. "You're dead on your feet and frozen through," he whispers. "It's okay. Go inside, and let me finish."

Guy's been taking care of everything here the last day and a half, and he knows what to do. I hesitate, glancing longingly at the house. "Yeah?"

"Yeah." He kisses me again, then uses his arm to turn me gently toward the barn door. "Go. I'll be done here soon."

"You'll double-check the gates?" I ask softly because he's right. The prolonged exposure to cold and wet has stripped me of my energy.

"Honey, I'm going to be double-checking those gates the rest of my life." He shakes his head with a tightening of his eyes.

I'm halfway to the house when I realize it's the first time he's used a pet name for me. It's also the first time Guy's mentioned what we have as being a long-term situation. I'm too tired to process what that means for us and instead kick off my boots in the mudroom and gratefully strip out of my riding gear. When I go inside the house, I find Emma on the couch, watching one of her shows on her tablet, with Barley stretched out behind her like a fluffy child-size sofa.

Other than a lazy thump of his tail, he ignores me. Emma does the same.

"Hey, Emma," I tell her, giving the child her space. "I'm going to take a shower if you need me."

She nods but still doesn't say anything. That's okay. I'd rather get cleaned up and get my head on straight before she and I talk much anyway.

I turn on the water to cool, but it still burns when I get in the shower. I shiver, letting icy skin and protesting toes get used to the temperature change before cranking up the heat. I could probably have stayed in there forever, but eventually me and my billow of steam decide to listen to my gurgling stomach.

I honestly don't remember the last time I ate anything, and I must not be thinking straight because I realize belatedly the shirt I grabbed from the footboard of the bed on my way into the bathroom is actually Guy's. Maybe some women look cute in their partner's clothes, but his shirt goes to my knees, not a sexier part of my legs, and it looks particularly baggy when added to the fuzzy blue fleece penguin pajama pants I snagged on my way.

Any thoughts of changing leave my head when I realize there's a little girl sitting on my bed. Emma has Mr. Moose in her arms, and she still isn't meeting my eyes, which isn't normal for her.

"Hey there." I sit down next to her, and when she leans into my side, I smooth my hand over her hair. "You okay, Em?"

"Sen-na?" She blinks big blue eyes at me. "I'm really sorry."

"It's okay, Emma. It was an accident. I know you won't do it again." I wrap my arms around her, which seems to give her the permission she needs to climb into my lap. She's crying, so I hug her close, murmuring soothingly. "Sweetie pie, this is a ranch, and on a ranch, sometimes accidents happen. Cows love to get loose. It's part of the fun of being a cow. Some of them just chose the wrong way to go."

Maybe I should be mad at her or at Guy for it happening in the first place, but I just can't. I care about them too much, and I can't stand to see either one of my little family upset.

Emma's still crying, albeit softer now. "Daddy said no more cows came back. Did they die?"

I can tell by her tone she's having a hard time with this. Death is difficult for any child, but for Emma, it seems to be hitting especially strongly.

"We don't know if they're hurt. They're probably just wandering around, playing in the snow. Hopefully they'll find their way to someplace warm with food, but I'm still going to keep looking, okay? I have a friend who can fly airplanes, and I'm going to ask him to help."

"What if they don't find any food?"

I see Guy's shoulder appear in the doorway, and I know he's leaning on the other side of the wall. He could come in here and handle this better than I could, but he's waiting for me. I wish I knew what to say, so I try to think about what my mother told me and what her mother told her.

"No one gets to be here forever, Emma. But it's a gift to be happy. It's a gift to have people care if we're happy. Jerkface loved to jump and run, and I bet he's having a lot of fun right now. He has a good life, and it's all any of us can ask for."

"Do you have a good life?"

"I have you, and you make my life the best life ever. You make your daddy's life the best life ever. We're so much better than good. We're the best."

She nods, then Emma puts her little arms around my neck and gives me a butterfly kiss on my cheek. "I love you, Sen-na."

It's maybe the best moment of my life, because I can honestly, truly say, "I love you too, Emma."

Oh, sweet child. If only you knew how much I love you too.

Emma's already had dinner, so I curl up in a chair at the kitchen table with a warm blanket, slowly eating what Guy hands me. He waited to have dinner with me, which was nice of him, even though I'm quieter than normal. I pick at the last half of my veggie burger, not because of the taste but out of sheer exhaustion.

"Do you want something different?" he asks before taking my bowl.

"No, I'm fine. Sorry, my appetite is shot." Me and my blanket follow him to the kitchen, where Guy starts on the dishes. I lean back against the countertop next to him as he works, finding myself wanting to be close to him. His voice drops so little ears can't hear us.

"Sienna, I am so, so sorry."

"I know. It was an accident, Guy. I'm not angry."

"I have no idea why you aren't. I'm furious with myself for doing this to you. The last thing you needed—" he starts to say, but I interrupt him.

"The last thing I need is you making yourself sick over this. We need you too much." I'd meant to say "she needs you" but the "we" slipped out. Even as I say it, I know I mean the words completely. I need him to be okay.

Guy hesitates and then murmurs, "We need you too, Sen."

Silence falls between us, the kind of silence that feels like a shoulder to lean on instead of the tightrope of tension the last two days have been.

"Thank you for being kind to Em," Guy eventually says as he scrubs our bowls. "You have every right to be upset, but I appreciate you being gentle with her. She's been beating herself up over the cows since yesterday. It broke her heart they didn't all come back."

"I know, the poor kid."

He's watching me out of the corner of his eye, and when I glance at him, Guy's blue eyes flicker away. As soon as I look away, I can feel him watching me again. The weight of his attention tonight is too strong to ignore, especially when there's only a few inches between my shoulder and his.

"Are you okay?" I ask him, cautiously feeling out what might be causing him to…well…hover a little. He's been hovering since I got back, now I think about it.

Strong hands linger as he wipes the bowls dry an extra time. "I'm trying to figure out if I'm allowed to ask you the same thing."

I don't understand, and it must show on my face.

Guy clears his throat. "Ever since I started the new job and people learned I married you, I've gotten nothing but warnings about Micah being trouble. I didn't say anything because I didn't want you to feel like you had to protect me. Which you try to do every second of every day."

He might have me there. I lean my head into his shoulder, and Guy turns and wraps his arms around me and my blanket.

"I stood there like a fool, watching you go up into the mountains with the same guy everyone's been telling me isn't safe, and I couldn't think of a single thing I could do to stop it. It's my fault you had to spend a night alone with him, and it's not my place to ask you if anything happened."

I start to pull away at the last sentence, but he makes a hushing noise.

"Not like that. Although if it *were* like that, I'd do my best to deal. I vowed I would have your back, even if you choose someone else…"

Guy pauses, his hands tightening around my waist, and when I touch still-cold fingertips to his tensed jaw, he leans his face into my hand. "Seriously, Sen, seeing you with someone else would gut me."

"Then it's a good thing the only one I'm getting into any hot springs with is standing in this room."

Guy smiles, his eyes heating with shared memories. Suddenly I'm not quite as cold as I was a moment ago.

"I care about you more than you realize. If your ex upset you, I can talk to him. If Micah..." Guy trails off mid-sentence, and a muscle in his jaw flexes.

"Was the aggressive bully you're worried about?" I pat his arm reassuringly. "I promise it was nothing I couldn't handle. He and I will always be at odds, but I think the anger he feels over us is getting resolved." Then I frown. "Who was warning you about him?"

Suddenly Guy laughs, and the arms around me squeeze me almost breathless. "See? You're determined to protect me and Emma."

"So? It makes me happy."

His mouth presses the softest kiss to the side of my neck, his voice wistful. "Yeah?"

"Absolutely."

"I really like you being happy." Guy's breath is warm on the rim of my ear, his body heating mine. "And I love you in my clothes."

"Now that I've successfully reassured you that you don't have to pick a fight with my ex...want to make out for a while? Because it would make me *very* happy."

Guy's breath is warm on the side of my neck, and the tiny nips of his teeth are causing gooseflesh to rise on my arms. I'm not sure whether to laugh, groan, or just dig my fingers into his shoulders. I give up and do all three. Those glacier-blue eyes gaze down at me with enough heat to melt all the snow in these mountains.

Suddenly two very warm, very strong hands squeeze my bottom, then hoist me off my feet. My arms wrap around his neck for balance as Guy holds me up in his arms, my legs winding around his waist. The blanket hits the floor, but I couldn't care less.

"Does this count as your exercise tonight?" I ask him breathlessly as he carries me into the living room.

"I think it's considered accessory lifts," he teases. "Which I've been sorely lacking."

"I have zero idea what those are, but I trust you."

"I trust you too, Sienna." He only needs one arm to hold me up. The other is tangled in my hair, drawing my head down to his. Guy's voice is quiet, sure, and calm. "I know what I have, and I'm not going to blow it. Do you have any idea how incredible you are?" He reaches the couch, then puts a knee to the cushions, laying me down. "I'm completely convinced there's nothing you can't do."

As I wrap my arms around his neck, pulling him closer, I'm fairly certain there's nothing he can't do either.

"Daddy? My movie is over."

Except maybe continue this. At the sound of Emma calling from her bedroom, Guy groans softly into my neck, hands stilling on my rib cage.

"Did you forget we have a daughter?" The teasing words slip out of my mouth, then I realize what I said. His palm lingers over my stomach, his eyes hot and hungry, and I know he's not angry about my slipup there. Not even close. "We're a family, right?"

"We're a family, Sienna." There's more he wants to say, then an annoyed voice calls for him again.

"*Daddy.*"

"I'm coming, baby." With one last kiss, he leaves me on the couch under the soft glow of the Christmas tree lights and so glad to be home with my family.

Chapter 23

I WAKE UP WITH TWO EXTRA BODIES IN THE BED WRIGGLED IN between myself and Guy. One is little and has morning breath, and the other's tail keeps thumping lazily against my knee. Guy's arm is long enough to wrap around all three of us, and I'm the only one not squirming.

I don't even remember getting to bed the previous night. The last thing I can recall is Guy going to change Emma's movie while I cuddled up to wait for him on the couch. I must have passed out, and at some point, he carried me to bed.

I'm kind of sad I missed that part.

"What time is it?" I mumble, not wanting to look at the clock next to me.

"An hour after you usually get up and fifteen minutes until you'll be mad if I don't wake you up." Guy's voice is husky with sleep but more awake than mine. He pats Barley's rib cage before briefly squeezing my hip. "I was willing to risk it."

"You're a brave man." When I roll over, I can't help but smile across the heads between us. His sweet smile in return makes my heart thump so hard in my chest, it feels like bursting. I cover by hugging Emma, who yawns some of the absolute worst morning breath in my face. When I wrinkle my nose, she dissolves into peals of childish giggles.

Guy gets a sneaky look on his face, then suddenly scoops all of us into his arms and rolls. Man, woman, child, and dog all end up in a pile of blankets and pillows and paws. I can't even begin to extract myself, and Emma's high-pitched laughter is right in my ear as Guy tickles her. Barley gives up being polite and escapes by scrambling across my chest, and I'm pretty sure I'm going to have a paw print on my breast until New Year's.

I honestly can't remember being happier.

A good night's sleep has done me a world of good, and I want to check on my cows again. I head out to start chores while Guy feeds Emma some breakfast, then they join me as I'm going over Legs to make sure he's still sound after our trek up the mountain. The mule's body is so large that when Guy leans on the stall door, he can only see my rear end, where I'm bent over cleaning out a hoof.

Yep, he's whistling again, a little Christmas song that makes it clear he's as happy as I feel today. I crane my neck around, a mule tail swishing against my shoulder.

"Why do I get the feeling you're enjoying the view?" I ask, raising an eyebrow.

"Just a perk of the job." Guy shoots me a cheeky grin. "Speaking of perks, what can I do to help after Em and I get back from dialysis? Since you left, I've cleaned every surface in the house, fixed every piece of equipment in the garage, and restacked the hay. I'm running out of ideas."

"You got through all the hay?" I ask, surprised. "How did I not notice?"

"You were dead on your feet yesterday," he tells me. "I moved last year's hay to the front so you could put your ATV in the corner next to the tack room, like you'd talked about doing. If I screwed up, I'll move it back."

I find myself smiling because he definitely did not screw up. "Don't you dare move it back."

I set Legs's foot down, finished with my task, and join Guy at the stall door. I rest my hands on his arms and go up on my toes so I can kiss him in thanks, and I'm breathless when we finally pull away, steadying myself by gripping his forearms. Even beneath his winter jacket, I can feel the muscles there.

"Thank you for the hay. Did you eat enough while I was gone? I have this mental image of you stress-ercising too much and forgetting to take care of yourself because you were focused on everything else."

He flushes, looking slightly guilty. "I might have been a little distracted." When I *tsk*, Guy steals a second kiss. "It's cute how you've been stuffing food my direction every time my hands are empty. It hasn't gone unnoticed, by the way."

"You were thin, Guy. Gorgeous, but thin."

"I was exhausted from worrying about her." His eyes flicker toward where Emma is playing with Barley by the barn door. She seems happier today, if lower on energy than usual. "I still am, but it doesn't feel quite so hopeless anymore."

"Don't give up hope." I slip out of the stall and hug him around his trim waist. "It's Christmas. This is the time for hope and wishes."

"What if I hope you'll kiss me good morning again?" I laugh as he sneaks a third kiss, this one briefer because it's clear Emma is watching us curiously.

"Actually, I was hoping to ride in with you and Emma this morning if it's okay. I'd like to spend some extra time with her, and I might go see my dad during part of her dialysis appointment."

Montana boys must never need to wear gloves, because Guy runs a bare hand over my hair, kissing my forehead briefly. "I'd love to meet him. Is that a possibility?"

I hesitate. "Dad usually doesn't remember me, but if he does, he won't understand if I bring you instead of Micah." I add, "But it would be nice if he did remember me. This time of the year was so special for my family. My mom loved Christmas, and after she passed, he tried so hard to carry on her traditions."

"Like what?"

"Like making stockings for the horses," I admit with a small laugh.

"The first thing you did with Emma." Guy hugs me close, resting his chin on top of my head. "We'd love for you to come with us, and I really would like to meet the man who created the legend."

I nearly choke. "The legend?"

Guy winks at me. "You don't know what they call you in town, do you?"

"That hussy who married a man the day after my divorce finalized?"

"Sen-na, what's a hussy?" Emma asks as she and Barley move their game in front of Legs's stall.

"Yes, Sen-na, what's a hussy?" Guy grins as I hedge, trying to think of how to escape this one. Then he saves me by adding, "The people I've met all say you faced down a team of sharklike lawyers and the richest family in the state to defend a piece of property beautiful enough it should be protected from development forever. They say you're as tough as the mountains themselves, and no one better get in your way when you walk into a room."

Now I'm the one who's blushing. "Which might be a *slight* exaggeration."

"I don't know. As the man lucky enough to get to walk into the room with you, I'm pretty sure they've got you pegged." An alarm goes off on his phone, and Guy glances down at his daughter. "Speaking of walking into rooms, if we leave now, we have plenty of time to go see your father before Emma's appointment. We could all go together as a family."

As a family. My family.

I want to be with them, at dialysis or Christmas shopping or in a pile of blankets early in the morning. They are my favorite people, and I want to spend the holidays with them.

"Okay," I say. "Let's go introduce you to my dad. Do you want to take your ride or mine?"

"Actually, I have an early Christmas gift for you." When Guy reaches into his back pocket, my breath catches in my throat. I'm instantly overwhelmed with affection for this man, because in his hand, he's got my dad's keys. He gives me a hopeful smile. "Want to take his truck?"

———

Emma's paler than normal, and her blood pressure is lower this morning, so Guy leaves a message for her pediatrician before we head into town. Despite the rougher ride of the old Dodge, it's fun being back in my dad's truck. It even still smells like I remember: years of dirt and hay and sunshine permeating the cloth bench seats.

Guy drives and I kick back in the passenger seat, my foot up on the dash like I'm a teenager again. He winks at me as we drive along the Salmon River, and when he rests a warm hand on my thigh, I absolutely love it.

Emma falls asleep on the ride in but then perks up when we pull into the long-term care center. As we're parking, Guy gets a call back from Emma's nephrologist, so I grab her bag and take Emma out of my dad's truck so she doesn't have to hear them discuss her case. She insists on bringing her toy moose and a folded piece of construction paper she drew on while I was finishing morning chores.

We wait for Guy just inside the front entrance, because I don't want to take her inside without her father's presence. Long-term care facilities aren't always easy places to be for anyone, not the people living there or those who come to visit them. Memory-loss units are especially difficult, which is where my father stays.

"Daddy says your daddy is sick. Is he sick like me?" Emma hugs me, and it takes me a minute to realize she's hugging me for me, not for herself. I snuggle her against my chest, resting my cheek on the top of her head.

"Yeah, sweetie, he's sick," I explain, grateful I have her to hold. "But not the same as you. He's got something that makes it hard for him to remember things."

"Does he remember you?" Emma asks, touching my hair the way she always does when we're sitting close together.

"Sometimes. Sometimes he forgets me though."

She nods, then looks down at the construction paper in her hand. "When I die, do you think Daddy will forget about me?"

I go still, then I close my eyes. "Sweetie pie, your daddy thinks about you every moment of every day. There's nothing that's ever going to make him forget about you."

I desperately want to tell her she's not going to die. I almost say it, but I don't know what Guy would want me to do here. Instead, I open my eyes, and I look down at her, holding her gaze.

"Emma, did you know the Naples family is the toughest, strongest, most stubborn family in Idaho?"

She shakes her head.

"That's us. And as tough as my father is, do you know who was even tougher? My mom. And her mom, my grandmother. My grandmother once rode from southern Texas to the Canadian border just to prove she could. And my great-grandmother built the house we live in with her own two hands. And do you know what my mom once did? She beat breast cancer twice. Because Naples women are the toughest women in the world." I take her hands and squeeze them. "Emma, my name is Maple now, but I'm still a Naples woman. And you're my stepdaughter, which means you are one of us. You're one of the toughest, strongest, most stubborn women Idaho has ever seen. So don't you give up, Emma. You stay tough, you stay strong, and your daddy and I are going to be right here with you."

Emma doesn't answer, but she does snuggle a little deeper for a moment as we watch Guy climb out of the truck. He's carrying a tension in his shoulders that wasn't there before the call, so I pick up Emma and meet him at the entrance.

"Is everything okay?" I ask as we head inside together.

"Her pediatrician wants us to go see her cardiologist," Guy murmurs. "I left them a message, but I'm guessing it'll be hard to get an appointment until after Christmas."

"Not if I'm standing outside their office with a pitchfork," I mutter back, bringing a smile to his handsome face.

"It's nice having backup. Hayden texted when I was on the phone. She wants to meet you. Maybe we could do a video call on Christmas morning?"

"'Tis the season to meet the relatives," I say with a quick smile, but I'd be lying if I said I wasn't a little nervous.

Nervousness shifts to discouragement when we learn that my dad's having a tough day. The staff warns us he hasn't left his room the last two days and doesn't want to come sit in the common area or be around the other residents. He's been getting mad when anyone comes in to feed or bathe him, and he's becoming more verbally aggressive.

Which is the absolute last thing I want to expose Emma to.

"I don't think this is a good idea," I tell Guy as we stand outside my father's closed door. "I don't want Emma to be frightened."

Guy's hand rests on my waist, a solid, steadying touch. His voice is achingly gentle as he says, "There aren't going to be a lot more days left, are there? Will this be his last Christmas?"

I won't let my lip tremble like I'm a child. I will be strong because my father deserves it from his only daughter. "They don't think it'll be much longer now."

He nods, and his thumb runs soothingly across my hip. "We all have bad days, Sienna. It doesn't mean we don't deserve love and respect. I'd really like to meet him if you'll let me. I promise I won't think anything but the best of him."

"We can go in separately and take turns with Emma?" I suggest, but Emma tugs on my hand.

"I want to meet your daddy too," Emma insists, getting a look on her face like she's going to dig her heels in if we refuse. So I finally nod in agreement.

Guy presses a brief kiss to my temple and knocks lightly on the door. When there's no answer, Emma opens the door herself, takes my hand, and heads inside. As I follow behind my stepdaughter, I wonder if these two are the bravest people I've ever known.

I don't know what to expect when we see my father sitting in the corner on a recliner, wrapped up in a blanket and a heavy sweater despite the warmth of the room. He's looking out the window at the snowflakes falling outside, eyes unfocused, but when Emma walks around the end of his bed, Jeff Naples does something I haven't seen in a very long time: he smiles.

"Well now, look who came to see a boring old man," my dad says, his tremulous voice stronger than it's been for months.

"You're not old," I say out of habit, because that's how my father always used to greet me. But he's not looking at me. He's looking at the little hand I'm holding.

"Hi," Emma says, looking around the room before letting go of me and walking over to my dad.

"Hey, honey," Dad says. "Shouldn't you be in school?"

"No, it's Christmas. We took your truck. It smells funny."

I can't believe it when my dad actually laughs.

Guy quietly closes the door all but the last inch, remaining near the doorjamb instead of coming forward. At first, I don't understand why he's staying back, and then I realize what is happening: my dad thinks Emma is me. The last thing I want is for Emma to be confused or scared, so I start to step forward to intercede. But instead of being scared, Emma crawls into my dad's chair next to him, arms full of her moose and her picture. She snuggles into his arm as if he's her new best friend.

"I drew this for you." Emma holds up her drawing proudly. From where I stand, I can see she's drawn a picture of all three of us and Legs and Barley, although the latter two are both in purple and look fairly similar to each other. Candy canes and Christmas trees decorate both sides of the paper, and on the back—where my father can't see—it says, "To Grandpa."

The title makes my eyes instantly water with tears. I cover as best as I can, wiping them away with a quick swipe of the heel of my hand.

"Well, this is real nice," my dad says, taking the picture in his right hand and keeping his left around Emma so she doesn't fall off the chair. I know how bad his eyesight is, but he looks down at her drawing as if it were a precious Picasso or the ceiling of the Sistine Chapel. "Real nice."

"I know." Emma nods with all the confidence in the world.

I bite my lip to stifle my laugh as Guy and I share a smile. My dad is ignoring Guy completely, because Emma has all his attention. And maybe that's why I miss this man so much. I knew when he looked at me, he really saw me. That I mattered more than anything to him.

A low whistle escapes his teeth. "I'm not sure I've ever seen a drawing this good." And I would bet a twenty he means it completely.

This right here is my daddy. The man who always saw the best in me. Who was always proud of me, even when I was at my worst. A man who would declare my drawing the best he'd ever seen and not just mean it but be willing to throw down with anyone who dared tell him differently.

"Why aren't you out riding, girl?" Dad asks her in that gruff, teasing tone he used with me so much of my life. "We don't have all these horses just for them to sit in their stalls."

"I have to go to the doctor's," Emma says as she plays with Mr. Moose.

"Why's that now? You look fine to me."

Emma shrugs, then hands her toy to my dad. "Mr. Moose doesn't like going, but we always have to."

"I don't like going to the doctors either, but she's always making me," my dad says, eyes twinkling as he shoots me a smile. "She's always stealing my truck too."

My dad doesn't just think Emma is me...he thinks I'm my mom. Heart in my throat, I decide to play along.

"Because you're too stubborn to go if I don't," I say, my mother's words coming unbidden to my tongue. It was the same joke they always had between them.

"I'm pretty sure the stubborn one in here ain't one of us," my dad murmurs to Emma, and she giggles.

"You can have my moose for when you see the doctor."

"Well, that's real nice of you. I'll do that."

Then she stands up next to his hip and presses a kiss to his age-spotted cheek. "I love you."

His eyes water—the big softie—and it would be a lie to say mine aren't watering too. "I love you more than the whole wide world, kiddo."

I inhale a hard breath and out of the corner of my eye see Guy lean a little toward me, even though he doesn't move away from the doorway. A soft clearing of a throat pulls our attention to the nurse waiting outside.

"It's time for his medicine," the nurse says apologetically from the hallway, where my dad can't see her yet. Remembering what they said about how he's been with company, I take Emma out of my dad's hold and press a kiss to his cheek.

"I'll see you later," I promise in a thick voice, and for the first time in so very long, my daddy wraps his arm around me and gives me a hug.

"Now don't cry. It's just an appointment. Nothing to worry about."

"I know," I whisper and hold on to him just a little longer.

"You take care when you're driving," he says to me. "I wouldn't be nothin' without my girls."

"We will," I say, then I pause and whisper, "Merry Christmas, Jeff."

"Merry Christmas, honey."

For once, I leave my father with a smile on my face. And yes, I'm still trying to keep it together, but in a much better way than usual. It feels like the Christmas gift I didn't know I needed.

"Thank you, Emma," I tell her when we leave the memory-loss unit and sit down on a bench outside. "You were very nice to him."

"Can I have a snack?"

I blink back the wetness from my eyes and nod. "Yeah, you just have to take your binder first."

I dig the medicine out of her bag and then give her a pill and her little Tupperware of grapes. Guy doesn't speak until after we get Emma in the car seat and shut the door behind her.

When I turn to him to see if maybe his silence is because he's upset, Guy quietly says, "Jeff is the only grandparent she's ever had. He's a good man, and I'm glad we got to meet him. Thank you, Sienna. It means more than you realize."

As he opens the door for me to climb into the driver's side of truck, suddenly I know being a Naples woman is nothing compared to what I am now. A Maple. Emma's stepmother. Guy's wife.

And this temporary marriage of convenience? In my heart, it is absolutely, one hundred percent real.

Chapter 24

EMMA'S BLOOD PRESSURE IS LOW ENOUGH THAT SHE ALMOST DOESN'T get approved for dialysis. She doesn't want to sit still for it, even though the dialysis nurse warns she could end up with bruising on her fistula. After a very long three and a half hours of trying to keep her in her seat, we finally start for home. Emma says her chest hurts when we're almost at the ranch, and she starts breathing faster than normal, which worries us enough we turn around and start back toward town.

Halfway back to Caney Falls, she falls asleep, her breathing seeming to return to its usual rate. We decide to take her into the emergency room anyway, just to be careful, and they offer to keep her overnight for monitoring. But other than recommending she see her usual doctors for follow-ups, the emergency doctor doesn't have much to add. She's a sick little girl on a lot of medication in renal failure. She's puffy with edema, and her blood pressure is lower than a normal child her age. She's tired, but she's also getting dialysis every day, which is exhausting.

She's spent most of the afternoon in dialysis or the hospital, which is even more exhausting.

At the idea of staying the night away from Barley, Emma pitches an absolute fit, which causes her breathing to worsen again. It gets better when we finally calm her down, and Guy and the doctor decide it's best to take her home. The less stress on her system, the better, and she's happier at home. We can always come back if we need to do so, and Emma will rest better in her own bed.

So home we go.

I take care of feeding and checking the animals while Guy gets her bathed and ready for bed. He looks worn out from the day, and even though I'm tired too, I volunteer for Emma's bedtime story. She has a tough time settling down, even though she's happier with her arms wrapped around Barley's neck.

Halfway through my second bedtime reading of *A Moose's Majestic Christmas*, Emma tugs my sleeve. "Sen-na?"

"Yeah, Em?"

"Do you want to be my mommy?" The way she asks the question makes it sound as if she isn't sure of my answer, and her eyes don't quite meet mine.

It takes a lot of bravery to ask someone if they want to love you.

For a moment, I sit there, wondering what Guy would want me to say. He's downstairs doing what he's now dubbing "relax-ercise," and ultimately, my relationship with Emma is because of him. Except... I love this little girl. Even though all this started as a complete confusing mess, I love her from the tip of her nose to each of her tiny pink-painted toes.

"If you want me to be your mommy, I would love to be. But you get to choose."

There's a lot in her life Emma doesn't have control over, but this one is something she gets to decide. The worry smooths from her brow, and she nods, snuggling into the bedding. "Daddy likes you."

Despite my best efforts, I can't help the goofy smile that comes to my face. "I like your daddy too." And then we go back to reading. Apparently three times is the charm, because her blue eyes finally start to grow heavy-lidded. Emma yawns, then reaches her arms up to me for a hug.

"'Night, Mommy."

My heart does this flip-flopping thing, and I blink rapidly when my eyes suddenly sting. I lean over and kiss Emma's brow. "Good night, sweetie. When you wake up, it'll be Christmas Eve."

When I start to stand, her little hand catches my sleeve again. "We get to open a present. Remember? Daddy said one present on Christmas Eve."

"I remember."

"And go ride on Legs," she adds, eyes closed already and half asleep.

I laugh softly and smooth her hair. "And ride Legs. We can all go for a ride together as a family. I love you, Emma."

"Love you too."

She snuggles into her pillow with Barley curled up on the end of her bed, watching over her like the good boy he's always been. I don't mind I've lost my dog to Emma, because if any little girl needed to be loved by a big, fluffy dog, it's her.

Guy's in the hallway, hands stuffed into his pockets. By the relaxed set of his shoulders as he leans against the wall, I can tell he's been there a while. His eyes lock on to me, and I hesitate, biting my lower lip.

"I know we didn't talk about it first," I say in a rush. "But she asked if she could call me that and I—"

His fingers catch mine as Guy gently tugs me a step closer, cutting me off. When I look up at him, his eyes are reddened, the way they always are when he's been crying. I reach up to touch his face, and he leans his jaw into my palm.

"It's just been Em and me for a long time," he says quietly. "You have absolutely *nothing* to apologize for." There's still moisture on his cheek, and when I wipe it away, he drags his wrist across his face in a rough motion. "Sorry. It just got to me more than I realized it would. She just hasn't had... I tried to be two parents for her, but I knew she wanted more."

"Now she has both of us." I hesitate, then lean into him, adding, "As long as you two want me, I'm in. And you have nothing to apologize for either."

Guy's head dips down, and his mouth brushes across mine, once, twice, then he deepens the kiss. Our fingers tangle, and his body somehow manages to coax me closer with only the softest touches. When he pulls away, I'm breathless and yearning, wishing it hadn't stopped.

"Sienna?" Guy murmurs. "You asked me what I wanted for Christmas."

"And you said more of this," I breathe in reply. There's a look in his eyes I understand, and when he cradles my face in his hands, stealing my lower lip from between my teeth, I know what he's silently asking me. "No more annulment?"

"Let's take it off the table, gorgeous."

I'm melting beneath his touch, the way his breath is warm against my neck, the way his body is nothing but hard muscle and soft caresses. I never truly knew what it was like to be in a man's arms until him. As if nothing can touch me when he is.

"Guy? Are you sure? I don't want to pressure you."

His lips curve against my skin as he laughs softly. "You stole my line."

We usually keep the door open a few inches for Emma, but tonight Guy reaches behind his back and closes it. I should go build up the fire so it doesn't go out in the middle of the night, but for once, the cool air feels good on my skin. The chunky sweater I'm wearing is too thick, and when I start to peel it over my head, Guy's hands help pull the fabric free. His T-shirt follows suit, and both end up balled up on the floor. I'll never get tired of looking at this man shirtless, but allowing myself to run my hands over him is still very new. Hard muscles contract as my fingertips brush over his stomach, and his own hands are sliding down my back, tracing my curves, then squeezing gently as they tighten around my hips.

"Too many clothes?" I ask breathlessly, pressing into the heat of his body.

"Definitely too many," Guy agrees, his voice the low, husky tone he gets when his attention is one hundred percent, completely on me. His fingers undo the button on my jeans, and when I wiggle out of them, kicking them off to the side, Guy sinks to his knees. His mouth presses soft kisses to my belly, and I close my eyes, threading my fingers into his short hair. Those strong hands trace my curves like I'm made of glass, as if I'm far more delicate than I've ever felt before.

I like being special to him. I like being someone he's careful with, because he's very good at taking care of the people who matter to him.

I'm overly aware of what we're building up to here, what we've been building up to since the first moment we locked eyes over the cup of coffee in my hands. I don't know how long it's been for him, but I definitely know how long it's been for me. I'm already shivery and breathless with need.

When I wrap my arm around his neck, Guy easily picks me up and heads toward the bed. Instead of lying us down, he turns and flops backward, making me laugh as we both bounce.

"We're going to break the bed," I warn him, giggling, and Guy threads his fingers through my hair, pressing a soft kiss to my lips.

"Don't tempt me," he murmurs. I love the way his voice gets when his hands are on me. Low and soft with just a little bit of a growl that is oh so sexy.

Then he flips us so I'm on my back in the bedding. When I reach for him, there's a moment when his eyes half close, then he steals my hands, kissing the tips of my fingers before moving to the inside of my wrist.

"Slow down, Sienna," Guy whispers against my skin. "We have all night. I want to see where it takes us."

Good places. Considering how skilled this man is with his lips, his tongue, and soft nips of his teeth, I know we're only going good places. I settle in, for once riding shotgun and not having to take the lead. Guy's too good at this, making me feel like I'm the endgame. As if I've always been the endgame.

And as this beautiful man's mouth moves down my body, for the first time in a very long time, I feel like being me is absolutely good enough.

———————

I don't know why I keep turning Guy into the little spoon when he's clearly a much better big one. Yet somehow, I wake up with my nose in the back of his rib cage, my left leg hooked over his and my left arm wrapped around his torso like he's a man-size teddy bear. My hand seems to have decided to do inappropriate things of its own accord while I slept.

"Hmm." I wriggle my fingers. "This is new."

"I'm considering it an extra Christmas present," he says sleepily, and I can hear the smile on his face even though I can't see it. "You've been groping me all night."

"Should I apologize?" I wonder, earning a low chuckle and my little spoon rolling over to face me.

"You should definitely apologize," Guy murmurs, threading his hands into my hair and kissing me.

"I have mouth breath," I protest, but he laughs and blows a raspberry against my breast.

"I like your mouth," he promises. He likes other things about me, but before he gets too distracted, I remember there are many ways to wake up in the morning. Since Guy's been missing out on a lot of the best ones, I decide to remedy the situation. The look he gives me afterward is so heated, I'm pretty sure we could spend all day in this bed. Unfortunately, I need to—

"Hey, Sen?" A warm hand strokes across my stomach, then squeezes my hip. "Want me to feed the animals while you rest?"

The noise that comes out of my throat at his offer isn't PG rated at all. Guy grins as he untangles us from the bedding, looking more relaxed than I've ever seen him. "Are you sure?" I ask. "Because if you're just teasing me, it's very mean."

"I'm never going to be mean to you," he promises me. Then he sneaks a handful of rump, kissing my neck where I'm ticklish and making me giggle. "Unless you ask me to, and only if you ask nicely."

I grin at him and wiggle the rump in question. But behind his teasing, I can hear the promise to his words. He knows where I've been, and I close my eyes, sighing softly with the relief of a promise I never have to go back there again.

This is the moment when I finally accept it. The man in the corner pulling a pair of jeans over his hips is the best decision I'll ever make.

Guy stirs the ashes in the woodstove back to life and then squeezes my pinkie toe, the only part of me not underneath the covers.

"Everyone gets their supplements at night, so grain only. Last year's hay in the turnout, check the water heater. Sleep, Sienna. Or at least spend the morning in your pajamas *not* working for once."

"Mmm. I'm not technically in pajamas."

"Oh, trust me, my gorgeous wife, I know." Guy pauses, and his hand trails down my torso, his palm resting over my belly. "You were the most beautiful woman I'd ever seen the day we met. I didn't understand why in the world I wasn't in a line out the door vying for a chance for your time."

"Now you've seen me up to my knees in cow crap," I joke, but whatever hard edges I have directed at myself are soothed by the look in his eyes.

"Sienna? You were the most beautiful woman I'd ever seen, and that was before I realized you were the kindest one I'd ever met. And after last night... We may need to talk about this. I'd like to make sure we're on the same page."

I start to sit up in bed, pulling the blanket up my chest and wondering if I've misunderstood things.

"Not that page." Guy kisses me, a slow, lingering kiss full of unspoken promises. "*Never* that page. A guy who feeds your horses isn't on that page."

Every step of this, he's put himself out there, and I finally feel safe enough to do the same. I watch him finish getting dressed, then I say, "Hey, Guy? A girl who makes you breakfast while you're feeding her horses isn't on that page either."

When he gives me that boyish, charming grin of his, it melts me every time.

We'd checked on Emma multiple times during the night, and other than her edema and blood pressure, she seemed the same. Bruised on her arm from wriggling too much during dialysis, but the same. But I'm not surprised to hear Guy checking on her again before heading down the stairs.

"Emma, start waking up," I hear him say across the hall, and her sleepy mumble in reply. After a moment, I hear him again. "No, you need to sit up, baby. It'll make you feel better." Guy pokes his head back in the room. "Hey, Sen? Her blood pressure is a bit lower, but I think it's because she was sleeping. Can you retake it in twenty minutes? If it's still low, we might be driving back to Caney Falls."

"Sure."

For fifteen blissful minutes, I lie in bed, soaking up memories of the night before. Then I get up because I can hear Barley whining from Emma's room. He probably needs to go out to the bathroom, although I know for a fact Barley's perfectly capable of nosing a door wider and getting out.

"Hush, floofy boy," I say to him softly. "You're going to wake Emma."

Then Barley starts barking in alarm, and I'm screaming for Guy because Emma's lips are blue. Her heart is beating, but she's gasping for breath like she's drowning. And Guy just makes it to the top of the stairs when she stops.

She stops gasping, she stops moving, she stops breathing. She just…stops.

There are moments in your life when time slows down to the point where you feel frozen in place. Even though you're moving, you're frozen. Even though you're calling 911 and being told an ambulance is coming, you're frozen. Even though you're doing mouth-to-mouth resuscitation on someone you love more than life itself, forcing air into her little lungs, somehow, you're frozen.

The EMTs get there right before your baby's heart stops, and in between chest compressions, the defibrillator shock makes her body jerk. It takes three shocks to start your baby's heart again. Even as they rush her outside toward where the Life Rescue helicopter just landed in the driveway, and you trip over your feet as you follow them down the stairs, you're frozen. Barley won't stop barking, a loud staccato relentlessly contrasting with my breath choking in my throat, and I'm frozen even as I force him away by his collar when he tries to stop the paramedics from taking her.

As the helicopter lifts into the air without us in there with her, I wonder if I'll ever unfreeze from this moment again.

Guy has the truck keys, and between one blink and the next, I'm no longer in Emma's room, begging her to stay with us. We're driving down the highway to the hospital in Idaho Falls, but I don't remember getting into the truck. She'll get there before us because they're taking her by air. I cry as we drive, even though part of my brain tells me to stop. Get up. Be stronger. Guy's having to hold it together because I'm not. He's crying too, but somehow, he manages to drive and hold on to the back of my neck, because I'm still sobbing into my knees.

"She's okay," he keeps saying over and over, but there's no way to know. Our little girl is in a helicopter above us somewhere, and we just *don't know.* "Breathe, baby, breathe."

I want to be better than this for them, but I think something inside me broke when I realized *she* wasn't breathing. I'll never catch my breath again. Frozen. I'm frozen.

"She'll be okay," Guy whispers, steering with his elbow so he can wipe the tears from his eyes without letting go of me. It's the dangerousness of his action that finally forces me to sit back in my seat and inhale shakily. Emma needs her daddy, and he can't get in a car wreck today.

"She'll be okay," I agree, my lower jaw trembling but my spine straight.

The two-hour drive to Idaho Falls is horrifically long.

Acute CHF exacerbation, they tell us at the hospital. Emma's in heart failure. It's why she's been getting paler and why her blood pressure is so low. She's struggling to breathe because her lungs are filling with fluid. They have her stabilized, but she's being bumped to the top of the donor list. The only thing we can do now is wait and pray.

The top of the donor list. The person with the greatest need for a kidney. The sickest of all the little girls out there who are sick.

They take us to the intensive care unit, past a different row of holiday decorations, and into a darkened room. ICU rooms are never bright, as if everyone's so sick, even too much light is enough for them to slip out of our hands. The beeping is loud, and the scent of astringent is acrid in my nostrils. Emma's got wires connected to her little body, running to machines that seem too inadequate for what we need. We *need* her to be okay.

Only a couple of hours ago, I was in bed, curled up in his arms, feeling safe and warm and happy. My fingers are like ice, and I wonder if I'll ever feel safe again. I look over at my husband, and my heart crushes in on itself from hurting so much for him. Guy's been here all these years, dreading this day, alone and fighting to stay strong. And now the worst is happening. The top of the donor list. Which means we're nearing the end.

"I keep thinking if I'd just kept her at the hospital last night..." Guy says raggedly.

I know. I've second-guessed myself over and over again, but only when he vocalizes it do I find what to say, to him and to myself.

"She was happy last night," I whisper. "When she was in the hospital, she was so upset that this could have triggered sooner. We don't know. All we know is when she was home, she was happy."

"Yeah." Guy closes his eyes. "But I still keep thinking it anyway."

"Me too."

I love him. When he sits at Emma's side and takes her tiny hand in his, what was left of the doubt in my mind is gone. The worst is happening, but he's not in this alone. I move to stand beside Guy, staying on my feet and holding him while he holds on to his little girl.

"It's Christmas Eve," I whisper to my husband. "Miracles happen on Christmas Eve."

So we wait. And we pray.

Chapter 25

In all the movies and all the television shows, they never tell you how bad it hurts having chest compressions. How rare it is CPR works, how many bones it can break, or how much getting shocked hurts.

Emma's in a lot of discomfort, and they can only give her so much pain medicine because of how low her blood pressure is right now. Nephrology and cardiology are trying to figure out what symptom to treat, because the medicines to help her kidneys are bad for her heart. She pants because it's hard to breathe with fluid-filled lungs, which scares her so much that I lie down on the bed next to her and hold her, murmuring soothingly. Guy's leaning over the other side of the bed, and his arm is around us both. The nurses and nursing assistants are kind enough to work around us when they come in to take Emma's vitals.

We don't tell her she's dying, but I think she knows.

I'm trying, but I don't know if I'm functioning properly. It takes me too long to understand what the doctors and nurses are telling us as they pass in and out of the room. My brain is utterly consumed by Emma, to the exclusion of even trying to process anything else. I feel like my skin is stretched too tightly over my face, and my jaw and head hurt from crying. Where Guy keeps refusing to look at the monitors surrounding Emma's bed, I can't stop staring at them, memorizing her blood pressure, her heart rate, and her oxygen percentage. Each time an alarm goes off because she's too high or too low, ice refills my veins, washing through me. Guy has warned me from the day we met, but I'm not ready for this. I'm not ready to lose Emma yet.

I can't tell if Guy is simply stronger than me or if he's numb. Maybe he's just on his last leg and giving every last bit of what he has to his daughter. He's been talking to her in low, steady, comforting words for the brief moments she wakes. And when she cries, he hushes his baby, promising her that she didn't miss Christmas. Barley is okay, and he misses her. Santa knows where she is and won't forget about her.

I don't know what to do, and I don't know how to help them. My brain is screaming at me to save my family, but there's no truck to stand in front of, no hit to take. All I can do is hold them both, watching every rapid, shallow breath Emma takes as her lungs fill with even more fluid.

I have two kidneys, and she only needs one. Irrational anger at my body overwhelms me because I wasn't a match. That I failed in some fundamental way to be what Emma needs, just in existing as I am.

This is happening. We're sitting our baby's deathwatch, and there's nothing I can do about it.

My brain eventually registers that Guy should have something to drink with how much he's talking, and I could use something with sugar and caffeine for my headache. I find a vending machine but forget mid-task what I'm doing. I end up sitting on the bench outside her room, two cold soda cans in my hands, watching Guy sit in the chair, head bent, mouth still moving.

Every time she passes out, he starts praying. He only stops when she wakes up. *Just in case God changes His mind.* Fingers numb from the drinks, I close my eyes and silently beg for better than this for them. For Emma to have a lifetime of horses and dogs and snowflakes. For Guy not to have to walk out of this hospital with nothing but me and a shattered heart.

"Sienna?"

At the sound of my name, I look up and see Micah standing there a few feet away, his hat in his hands. It's only been two weeks since our divorce, but it feels like a lifetime ago. Another world maybe. He looks like a stranger, just another person in the hall.

I stare at him, utterly confused. "What are you doing here?" My words come out raspy, as if my voice is almost gone, and all I can process is Micah shouldn't be in the hospital. This is a family moment, a horrible family moment, and he shouldn't be there. It's not okay.

"Sienna, is your husband here?" Micah asks, which feels strange. Micah hates Guy. He's made it very clear from the start.

"He's with Emma," I say, unable to muster the energy to react to the question.

"You might want to go get him, honey. I've got some news I need to tell you."

My brain resists the suggestion, and I'm shaking my head before he finishes his sentence, stumbling up to my feet. "What? No, Guy needs to stay with Emma."

"I'm here, Sienna."

I look over my shoulder and see Guy in the doorway of Emma's room. He must have noticed us, or maybe he just heard Micah's voice. Guy's always stood at my side or at my back. He's never stepped between me and anything, not until he steps between me and Micah right now. I can't even see my ex from around Guy's shoulders, he's blocked me so completely.

"Whatever it is, today's *not* the day." Guy's voice is roughened too, but with a much harder edge to it than mine. "My daughter is very sick, and Sienna's in shock."

I'm in shock? I guess it makes sense. Half of my brain hasn't figured out I'm not still in Emma's bedroom. Maybe it's why Guy is between us, because he understands after finding her like I did, something broke inside me. The part of me that never understood what true fear was. The part of me that only *thought* I knew what all this would feel like going through.

"I'm sorry to bother you both, but something happened she should know about." For once, Micah sounds quiet, almost passive even. As if acknowledging Guy's not above dragging him out of there if need be. He has bad news, and I don't know what could be happening that matters right now. Not when Emma's on the top of the transplant list. Then Guy shifts sideways and angles his body a little so I'm not being fully blocked from my ex anymore.

I don't think I've ever seen Micah look so truly sad. A glance passes between him and Guy that I don't understand, then Micah adds even more softly, "She's going to need to sit down for this."

"Sienna, let me talk to Micah," Guy encourages me. "You can go back in with Emma."

"I'm fine," I insist, a feeling of dread filling me. "Just tell me what's going on."

Guy's arm wraps around my waist, and I'm unable to resist the gentle tug to sit down on the bench outside Emma's room. He's close enough to me our legs are pressed together from my knee to our hips. "Do this right, man. She's *not* okay right now," Guy adds in a tight voice as he holds me closer.

When Micah doesn't get mad and instead crouches down so we're at eye level, I think maybe I don't want to hear what he has to say.

"Sen, I got a call today from your father's facility," he says quietly. "They were trying to reach you, but your phone kept going to voicemail. They still had me down as an emergency contact, so they called me."

"My dad… Is he…"

"He took a turn for the worse, honey. He had a pretty bad stroke. I called Jess and just about everyone else in town trying to find you, and then I heard from the police station Emma was flown out here. So I went to the hospital, and I sat with him."

"They didn't bring him here?"

Micah shakes his head. "No, his medical directives said to treat him at Caney Falls. I think he wants to be where your momma was when she passed."

"Did he…" I don't know what I'm trying to say, but my voice is oddly level. "Is he…"

"They think he doesn't have a lot more time left. Maybe a few weeks, maybe more. The stroke was a hard hit, honey. He can't talk much, but he woke up once and asked for you. I told him you were taking care of your little girl, his granddaughter. He said that was good." A brief, pained smile crosses his face. "He was real hard to understand, but I'm pretty sure he cussed me out before he fell back asleep."

I can't help but exhale a laugh. I don't feel like I'm crying, but it's hard to see, and I keep blinking water out of my eyes. "He never liked you, but he always loved you."

"I always loved him too, even though the old codger and I never got along." Micah's hands squeeze his hat. "I'm so sorry, Sen."

It's too much. Today's been too much. I think my mind shuts off for a while, because when I check back in, my forehead is resting against the edge of Guy's chest, my nose almost in his armpit, with the weight of his arm a shield around my shoulders as I sob.

Micah looks lost, but I can kind of understand. I never cried in front of him. Not once, not during our whole marriage. It was never safe to cry in front of Micah. Guy is different. What we have together is a safe place, and that has changed so many things.

"Thank you for being there for him," I whisper, meaning it.

Micah looks like he wants to say something, then changes his mind. Instead, he says, "I've got Dominic out there feeding everyone for you.

He knows to follow your chalkboard, and I showed him how to take care of things. I tried to get Barley, but the old fluff ball won't move off the guest bed. Emma's room now, I guess. So Dominic's going to take care of him too. Jess is going to bring you both some clothes, 'cause it didn't feel right for me to go through you two's stuff." Micah looks at Guy as he stands up and takes a respectful step back. "I don't like you, and I probably never will. But I wouldn't wish what you are going through on my worst enemy. I really hope your little girl pulls through. You too, Sienna."

"Thank you," Guy says quietly, and if Micah expects more, he isn't going to get it. Guy's attention is on me, and he's going to keep shielding me from Micah until he leaves.

Boot steps take him away, finally leaving us alone. Only then do I hide my face completely away in Guy's chest.

"I'm so sorry, baby. I'm so sorry," Guy tells me, his voice raw with pain as he rests his chin on top of my head, hand stroking my hair. "If you weren't here with us… I'm *so* sorry."

"I'm exactly where I need to be." I wipe my eyes and pull back to look up at him. "Dad always put family first, and he would be the first to tell me I was a fool if I left you and Emma to go sit beside a dying old man who has better places to be."

Guy exhales a small breath of a laugh. "Tough old man. Must have got it from someone I know."

"I think it was the other way around. But you never met my mother. She was tougher than all of us put together." I wipe my eyes again, then whisper, "Emma's even tougher than Mom."

"Sienna, if you need to go see him right now, it's okay. Or if you just need to step away, I won't be angry. Don't push yourself too far."

He's holding me the way he holds Emma, those muscled arms wrapped around me as if to protect me from any more bad things by sheer physical presence. He's the kind of man who will take the hit over and over again, if he can, to protect the ones he loves. I understand, because that's me. That was my father. That was my mother. My parents would never walk away if there was anything left to fight for.

I shake my head, and then I unsteadily stand. I'm not ashamed I need Guy's arm around me as we head back inside the room. I'm not afraid to lean on him for support, because I know he'll lean on me too. Emma's starting to stir, and this time, I sit down on the chair next to her bed, and I'm the one holding our baby's hand.

"No," I whisper. "I'm exactly where I want to be."

———

I'm holding Emma close to my chest, cuddling her as best as the wires and machines will let me, and telling her about Barley's first Christmas as a puppy when a soft knock comes at the door. It's Emma's nephrologist, Dr. Sanghvi. She gives us a shadow of a smile, which feels wildly inappropriate.

"We have a kidney."

Guy's hand squeezes the bed rail so hard the plastic creaks. "I'm sorry, what was that again?" The expression on his face says he can't believe what he just heard.

Dr. Sanghvi moves to Emma's side, gazing down at her. "A donor kidney that's a match has come through. The kidney is en route, and their flight should land in the next hour. We need to take her back to get prepped for the surgery."

My lip trembles so hard, my teeth chatter. "She's going to be okay?" I whisper.

"Emma's a very sick child, and there are risks during any procedure. Her heart's weakened, so we need to do the surgery as soon as possible."

We both hear what isn't said. The surgery needs to happen before her heart gives out completely.

"But Em's getting a kidney?" Guy's lips are white from clamping them together so tight, and when his voice breaks, I begin to cry again. Relief and fear twist into some unrecognizable creation inside me.

"She's getting a kidney in"—Dr. Sanghvi checks her phone—"fifty-eight minutes."

"Oh God." With a low cry, Guy sinks to his knees, and I don't know if he's praying or puking or maybe both. I hear him whispering "thank you" though. I grip his shoulder, the only part of him I can reach, because Emma's stirring now, awakened by the noises.

The doctor gives Emma a smile. "Emma, before we take you to get your new kidney, there's something you should see first. It seems like you're a very loved little girl."

The nursing staff have a million things to unhook and rehook her to for them to be able to wheel Emma's bed out of the room. Guy staggers to his feet as I get out of Emma's bed, giving them room to work. As we cling to each other, following as they take Emma down the hallway, I realize for our miracle to happen, someone else's life was just destroyed. Someone's baby lost their life on Christmas Eve.

I don't even know who I'm crying for anymore: Emma, that child, their parents, Guy... Maybe I'm crying for all of us.

As we pass down a hallway of windows, Emma's nurse gives us a smile as he points to the nearest pane. "Emma? There's something you should see, sweetie."

Despite being nearly ten at night on Christmas Eve, it feels like half the town of Caney Falls is clustered on the snow-covered lawn below the hallway window, wrapped in heavy winter coats and warm blankets. They're all holding electronic candles, and in the front and center are Sanai, Jess, and Charley, standing next to where candles on the lawn spell out "We Love You Emma."

Even through the glass and the sounds of the hospital around us, we can hear everyone singing Christmas carols.

It's not easy to get Emma closer to the window, not with so many machines hooked up to her, but the hospital staff manage it. She's too sick for us to pick up, but they raise her bed high enough so she can peer over the windowsill. Emma leans her head against Guy's shoulder and watches them sing with the most beautiful smile on her face as "O Holy Night" fills the night.

"Do you see, baby?" he tells her. "That's your name. They wrote out they love you."

"I love you," I mouth to Jess and Sanai and Charley through the window. They give me their best and brightest smiles, and I can swear I hear my friends' voices better than all the others. The hospital staff are sneaking peeks around us, because big, fat snowflakes are swirling down from the sky, and I start to laugh softly, even as more tears well up in my eyes. For the first time, I can feel Christmas, the way I used to as a child.

A voice clears behind us almost apologetically. It's Dr. Sanghvi. "Mr. and Mrs. Maple? The transplant team will land in a few minutes. It's time."

Time to prep Emma for surgery.

With all the hope in the world and all the fear I never knew I could have, I nod. Then I take Guy's hand.

———

They let us stay with Emma up to the last set of doors, where we have to say goodbye. I kiss Emma's forehead, then I whisper I love her. I remind her that she's strong and tell her I'll see her when she wakes up. Then I step back and let Guy have a moment alone with her, as alone as they can get.

Emma starts to cry when she sees the people milling around, and Guy holds her because she's scared. She seems to understand this surgery is a good thing, but Emma wants her bed and her dog and Legs. She wants her daddy, and she wants to go home. I don't know what he says, but her little chin nods, and she says she loves him.

"I love you too, Mommy," Emma adds as they take her away.

Oh, sweet child. You have every last inch of my heart.

We're warned it will be at least two hours for Emma's surgery but maybe longer. For some reason, I'd thought they would make us go to a waiting room during the surgery, and I'm deeply grateful the staff says we can stay in Emma's room. The room feels far too big and empty without her bed in it, and even though a second chair is next to the one we've been using, I stand there, unsure of what to do.

For a moment, I desperately wish my mom and dad were here. I wish there was an adult to protect us from this, even though Guy and I *are* the adults in this room. I wish I could hold my father's hand, but I know I'm needed here more. I'm a parent now, and there's a hand that needs mine to hold.

"Should I go downstairs?" I ask Guy. "To thank everyone?"

"No, stay here with me." His arm curls around my waist, and he tugs me down to rest on his leg. "They'll understand if we send a text message. They'll understand even if we don't."

He's right, but they came a long way, so instead I send out a group message to all the faces I remember. Then I turn off my phone and slip it back in the bag. Some people stare at their phones, playing games or thumbing through social media when they are worried. For me, it just feels like too much noise, too much for my brain to have to deal with. Instead, I let Guy hold me, the way I held Emma.

"Sienna, try to sleep if you can." I look over at him and see my exhaustion mirrored in his eyes. The fear too, but Guy's voice is soothing when he speaks. "Even if you can't sleep, just close your eyes. Try to give your mind a break."

"What about you?" I ask him, even as I let him draw me deeper into his arms.

"I'll try to do the same."

Yeah right. I wrinkle my nose at him. "Don't lie to me on Christmas Eve, Mr. Maple."

"Never." Guy dips his face and rests his chin on my shoulder. "Sienna, I don't know what's going to happen in a few minutes or a few hours. I don't know if it's going to be wonderful or horrible, so I need to tell you something now. I know it's too soon for you, but you need to know."

"Guy…" I start to hush him, to tell him anything can wait, but he shakes his head and presses a soft kiss to my shoulder.

"The day we met," he says quietly, "I told you I couldn't promise I would fall in love with you. I could only promise I'd be a good husband to you, and I would always have your back."

"You have," I reassure him. "You have, every step of the way. You've been perfect."

Guy smiles slightly. "Not perfect, but I was trying. What I never told you is the day we got married, when you looked at Emma and asked her what name she wanted to have… That was the moment I fell in love with you. And I've held my breath ever since, because it seemed like too much to hope you could feel the same.

"Every morning, I woke up and I looked at you, and I made you a silent promise in my head. No matter what happens, for the rest of my life, I'm going to love you. I will keep showing up, no matter how hard life gets, no matter what road we take. You get all of me." He takes a slow, ragged breath. "Just maybe…be ready…because if I lose her, I might not have a whole lot of me left."

"You're enough," I promise him softly. "Who you are, it'll always be enough." I close my eyes. "But if Emma doesn't…" I can't even say it. "I think there might not be much of me left either."

We're both silent beneath the awfulness of the thought. Then Guy takes my hand, running his thumb over my ring finger. "I bought you a ring for Christmas. I was going to propose for real. On my knee with a dopey grin and everything."

"Yes. If you're asking me, my answer is yes. And if you aren't, the answer is still yes. I'm in love with you too."

When he looks up at me, the too-thin man in the coffee shop with the blue eyes, I know he's the love of my life.

"Yeah?" Guy asks softly, as if he can't quite believe this either.

"For better or worse. Nothing, not even this, do we part." I kiss him, and when he presses his forehead to my breast, I hold him for the first time of the rest of my life. "I love you so much, Guy. I'm yours, as long as you want me."

He sighs quietly, tightens his arms around me, and then he whispers against my skin, "Forever. Absolutely, one hundred percent, forever."

———

The air smells like Christmas. I don't know why, but as I wake up blurrily, I swear I can almost taste it.

Nope, it's not Christmas. It's the smell of a stale hospital candy cane being munched on above my head. Guy's foot is propped up on the second chair, and there's no way he could possibly be comfortable. I'm draped across his body like an exhausted pillow, my elbow in his stomach and my feet wedged against his knee to keep me in the confined space. My neck is already protesting sleeping in such an awkward position.

Instead of grumbling, the man is eating a candy cane.

The ICU is still dim, but the clock says it's already two fifteen in the morning. Emma went into surgery over four hours ago.

"I fell asleep? Oh no, it's been *hours*. Why isn't Emma back yet?" Panic hits me hard, then I realize Guy is grinning at me from around his candy cane. "Is she…"

I can't say it. The hope has lodged in my throat, and I can't even swallow around it.

"Emma's okay," Guy says. "A stranger gave her something wonderful, and it's working. They're going to continue monitoring her to make sure she stays stable, then they're going to bring her back pretty soon."

"Emma's okay?" I ask again, because even though I believe him, I'm probably going to keep asking it for the next twenty years. Or possibly the rest of her long, happy life.

"According to Dr. Sanghvi, everything went perfectly. We're going to spend Christmas in the hospital, but as long as there are no complications, the doctor thinks she should be home by New Year's."

New Year's at home with my new family. Nothing has ever sounded so good.

"What happens now? Emma's presents are at the house. So are yours. I can't let her have another Christmas in the hospital without making it special somehow." I'm a planner, and there are a lot of things to plan. I bite my lower lip, thinking. "I can make a few calls and—"

"Hey, Sienna?" Blue eyes sparkle as he catches my gaze, winking.

"Yeah?"

My brand-new, gorgeous, absolutely perfect husband gives me the best, most pepperminty kiss of my life, followed by a knee-melting grin. "This is our happily ever after. All we have to do now is live it."

Epilogue

VISITING MY DAD IS EASIER THAN IT USED TO BE.

True to his nature, he held on a full month, twice as long as anyone expected. Then, in a room right next to the one where my mother passed away, my daddy finally got to go home.

Losing him breaks my heart, but I have a good man who holds me every night and a little girl who lets me hug her when I miss my father too much during the day. Between the two of them and their love, I know I'll one day be okay.

We waited to bury Dad's ashes until after the spring thaw, with the hard rushing of the Salmon River the perfect song as we laid him to rest next to my mom on the property. There are several generations of the Naples family buried here, but he's going to be the last one. This is the Maple Ranch now, and a new wooden sign above the entry reflects the change to any of the infrequent visitors we have.

I still miss him every single day.

Emma likes to come and talk to him, her grandfather she only really met once. I like to listen to the water and my daughter and the wind playing through the trees. As we ride back and forth, Emma and I talk about how this is Nez Perce/Nimiipuu land and what it means. How just for now, we're caretakers of this beautiful place, but it doesn't belong to us. This land isn't something we own or something we should split and sell away like it's cash just waiting to be in our pockets. It's something we should care about. Something to be loved, like a spouse or a child or a little brother.

She's young, but my instinct tells me she understands. I think she particularly likes the little brother part.

So far, we've managed to keep it a secret, because things have a way of getting around small towns, and Guy and I have only started to relax now that I'm in my second trimester. But Guy's hauling the grain on Tuesdays while I lean against the truck and enjoy watching him work, like the voyeur I've always been when it comes to him. And when we go to the Daily Grind, I've been ordering my latte decaf. Sanai's got a knowing smile on her face again, and it's not because Guy and I sneak a breakfast biscuit together while Emma's in preschool.

I still haven't gotten used to the delicate white-gold band on my finger. Guy wants to switch it out with a diamond later, but he's going to have to pry this off my hand over my cold, dead body.

I know what I have. I don't need sparkling things to remind me.

I've spent the morning in town, talking to my ob-gyn in the same medical building where Emma used to get her dialysis. I don't miss those days, and I know she and Guy are delighted to be done with them too. It's why I went to the appointment alone, even though Guy's been there for most of them. He's started fixating on the baby's health in a way I think isn't good for him. I do it too, because after Emma, how could we not? But I can tell Guy is scared, no matter how hard he tries not to let me know.

Our family has some triggers, and sometimes, love is keeping someone from walking into a building that causes them stress. Besides, I've already sent the man about twenty annoyed GIFs today regarding my current mood.

When I pull up to the ranch, a little girl is riding on the front lawn. Emma's hair has grown longer beneath the riding helmet she hates wearing. She and Legs have formed the kind of bond only a passive-aggressive draft mule and a small child can have together. I swear the child was born with glue on the seat of her pants, and I know what it's like to be in love with these animals. I'm teaching her how to ride because I know it won't be long before our rules get broken, and she's taking off all over these mountains. If there's ever been a natural horsewoman, it's my daughter. She can ride him without being on a lead line if they stay in front of the house or close to the barn, because Legs won't let her fall. Grumpy or not, he's really good at this kind of thing.

I don't mind switching to the broad, stocky Appaloosa gelding I bought so Emma can have Legs. Guy and Lulu have hit it off, and this way, the whole family can ride together, motley crew that we are, with Guy's head about at Emma's shoulder as she perches on the tall mule and me on my tank of a gelding in between. I don't mind the incessant lowing of our new bull (he *never* shuts up) or how Barley is refusing to teach the two new puppies anything cattle-dog related in retribution for all the times they've chewed on his tail. I don't even mind Dad's truck breaking down again or how Guy spends a solid hour a day in the garage, clanking around and happily swearing at the thing when Emma's out of earshot. What *does* bother me is that as of this morning's ob-gyn appointment, I've officially been benched from riding. I thought I'd have a couple more weeks, but nope.

I swear I could hear Legs laughing at me the entire drive home.

Guy's waiting for me when I get back from the appointment, watching Emma from the porch with a sandwich cut into cute little shapes on a plate in his lap. I shudder when the smell of peanut butter and banana hits me, although it used to be my favorite comfort sandwich. He must have noticed me turning green because he gives me a sympathetic look.

"Is peanut butter on the list?" he asks, and I nod apologetically.

"Yep. As of yesterday."

"Sorry, I thought it might help after the ixnay on the iding-ray."

When I narrow my eyes at his cheerful tone, Guy is smart enough not to laugh. "Hey, I didn't say anything."

"Good, because I'm still considering getting a second opinion." Nothing makes a girl crabby like being cut off from her horses. Emma would understand. Unlike Guy, who is happy to have me benched, even if it triples his own work all over again.

He makes short work of the sandwich cutouts, then takes my hand. "Come on. I'll get you something else to eat."

"Good luck," I say grumpily.

Morning sickness has been a beast, despite doing my best not to let Guy know how awful I feel some days. Lucky me, I didn't get to phase out of this particularly fun stage at the end of the first trimester like some women. Throwing up is a particularly bad trigger for him after Emma's illness, and Guy's had the honor of listening to me hurl every morning and late afternoon like clockwork.

I keep telling him I don't need him to hold my hair or stay with me on the bathroom floor, but he's not the type of person who can listen to someone he loves being miserable and walk away. I've considered locking the bathroom door so he doesn't have to deal with it too, because I love the man more than I ever thought possible. Knowing him, he'd just sit on the other side of the door. He's a good man determined to take care of us, and I'm determined to take care of them. So we go round and round until we sneak off to bed and find more ways to show each other how much we love each other. Vomiting aside, I've never been this happy in my entire life.

He and Emma are everything to me. Seriously. *Everything.*

Guy probably knows, because he gives me a sexy smile as he moves about the kitchen, pulling out my favorite mug and a fresh jug of milk. We keep an eye on Emma through the kitchen windows as he pours me a drink.

"Just in case today was rough, Em and I picked up something in town while you were gone." He nudges something on a plate toward me. What I see must be a mirage, a pregnancy-induced hallucination. They only exist during Christmas, yet somehow a peppermint-dusted, three-inch-thick, triple-chunk brownie appears next to my milk.

"Is this for me?" I ask, cautiously hopeful as I sink into a stool next to the stack of mail.

"Do you think I'd talk the bakery into making a pan of these for my wife and not give her one?" He presses a kiss to my temple before bending over to sneak a quick kiss to my thickening waist. "Be nice to your momma, okay? She's having a tough day."

"Her day just got a lot better." A purring noise escapes my throat, and I give him a look I normally save for my favorite treats. "Want to chase me around for the second half of this later?"

Guy's already heading back outside to stay with Emma, but at the question, my tall, beautiful Montana boy looks over his shoulder and winks at me. "That's what the second brownie is for. By the way, Jess left something for you in the mail."

I knew I married this man for a reason.

Mid bite of the best thing ever, I pause and look at the sticky note attached to a newspaper, resting on top of the pile of mail.

"Thought you might want to see this," I read Jess's note aloud before I page through their newest handiwork. There it is, right on the front page of the classifieds. I'm not sure whether to groan or laugh. After all, the last time, this worked out for me pretty darn well.

WANTED: BABYSITTER FOR HIRE

Anyone less awesome than *Jess* need not apply.

Acknowledgments

The last time I wrote a book, my life was very different.

Less than three months after *Enjoy the View* was published, my husband was killed in a motorcycle accident. He was—and is still—my best friend. His was the hand I reached for when I was happy or sad or lonely. His was the hug I wanted to feel, the laughter I wanted to hear, the quick text in the afternoon I wanted to read and the tired yawns at night I wanted to fall asleep against. He was the man I wanted to spend every moment of the rest of my happily ever after with.

Life…doesn't always go the way you want it to go.

The best way I can describe his loss is a locomotive slamming through tissue paper. Losing my husband absolutely decimated me. All that was left were little paper bits floating in the wind. But with time, patience, and so much love, God gathered those little bits and knitted me back together again.

I'm not sure if any of us—myself included—knew if I'd be able to write another story. There was a lot of pain, a lot of prayer, a lot of therapy, and a whole lot of love from some very important people. It's been a long, hard road, but in the end, I finally put my fingers back to the page. *The Christmas You Found Me* is the result. It's a story about hurting, about loss, and about fear. But it's also a story about hope and faith and love. And really, I think that's what life—and marriage—is: hope and faith and love.

So, my first thank you is to God. Thank you for showing me your love, each and every day. For being the rock that I stand on, no matter what else is happening around me, and giving me a reason to hope. Thank you for proving you are faithful to all your promises.

To my parents and my brother. You are my favorite people in the world. I love you.

To my stepchildren and grandchildren. You are more precious to me than you'll ever know, and the greatest gift Kenney ever gave me. I love you all so very much.

To my Kronkbears, Jen Ludwig, Kim Lyon, Catherine Mantooth, Ashlee Sisson, and Lacey Wilcoxon. For giving me a safe place to laugh, to cry, and to climb mountains. I love you and I like you.

To Coach Larry Scott. You strapped a pair of boxing gloves on a broken woman and showed her how to be strong again. Thank you from the bottom of my heart.

To Chloe Nelligan. For your friendship, your enthusiasm, and always being up for the next new adventure. I'm so glad I met you.

To my Golden Heart sisters, the Rebelles. You have been a shield, holding me up on all sides when I couldn't stand on my own, and protecting me from a world that was harsher than I knew how to bear. I love you all.

To Violet Marsh. For not just being a great critique partner but for being a great friend. Thank you for holding my hand through the best and the worst.

To Sara Megibow. For not just being my agent, but for being my friend. I couldn't imagine navigating any of this without your wisdom, guidance, and support.

To my publisher Sourcebooks Casablanca, my editor Susie Benton, LaShaunda Parker at Tessera Editorial, and all the incredible and hardworking people at Sourcebooks. Thank you so much for waiting for me to heal enough to write again. Thank you for supporting the project of my heart.

To Lacey Wilcoxon and Leigh Stephens for vetting the medical info in this novel. Your experience and wisdom brought this story to life. Any and all mistakes are mine.

To my readers. You not only make this dream of being a writer possible, but you also make it so much more fun than I ever expected. Thank you for every time you pick up one of my books, even if to just squish a spider.

And lastly, to my husband Kenney and my son Kyle. Until we see each other again, I'll make sure your love and laughter live on through the words I put on pages. I love you and miss you both so very much. And I will carry you forever in my heart, no matter the unexpected paths this life takes.

"God grant me the serenity to accept the things I cannot change, the courage to change the things I can, and the wisdom to know the difference."

—REINHOLD NIEBUHR,

"THE SERENITY PRAYER"

About the Author

Sarah Morgenthaler is a romance writer, geologist, chocolate chip cookie lover, and bestselling author of the Moose Springs, Alaska series. She is currently out writing something, hiking something, or climbing something.

Website: sarahmorgenthaler.com